Chasm

Other Frankie MacFarlane Mysteries

Chasm

Susan Cummins Miller

Texas Tech University Press

This book is typeset in Sabon. The paper used in this book
meets the minimum requirements of ANSI/NISO Z39.48-1992
(R1997). ∞

Cover photograph/illustration by Ryan J. Miller

Library of Congress Cataloging-in-Publication Data
Miller, Susan Cummins, 1949-
  Chasm / Susan Cummins Miller.
    pages ; cm. — (Frankie MacFarlane mysteries ; 6)
    Summary: "While teaching on a trip to the Grand Canyon,
Frankie MacFarlane is attacked and tries to escape the canyons,
eventually up again ecoterrorist wannabes trying to destroy one
of the exits"— Provided by publisher.
    ISBN 978-0-89672-914-8 (hardcover : acid-free paper) —
ISBN 978-0-89672-915-5 (softcover : acid-free paper) — ISBN
978-0-89672-916-2 (ebook) 1. MacFarlane, Frankie (Fictitious
character)—Fiction. 2. Women geologists—Fiction. 3. Grand
Canyon (Ariz.)—Fiction. I. Title.
    PS3613.I555C48 2015
    813'.6—dc23   2014036334

15 16 17 18 19 20 21 22 23 / 9 8 7 6 5 4 3 2 1

Texas Tech University Press
Box 41037 | Lubbock, Texas 79409-1037 USA
800.832.4042 | ttup@ttu.edu | www.ttupress.org

For Tom and Mary Ryan and Judith Keeling,
without whom Frankie would be homeless,

and in memory of Dick Ryan, Jacob Anderson,
and Molly Cummins—

who left the world and its vibrant canyons too soon

Chasm: [geology] (a) A deep breach, cleft, or opening in the Earth's surface, such as a yawning fissure or narrow gorge . . . (b) A deep, wide elongated gap in the floor of a cave.
–Klaus K. E. Neuendorf, James P. Mehl, Jr., and Julia A. Jackson, eds., *Glossary of Geology*, fifth edition, 2005

Chasm: n. 1. a yawning fissure or deep cleft in the earth's surface . . . 3. a marked interruption of continuity; gap: *a chasm in time.* 4. a sundering breach in relations, as a divergence of opinions, beliefs, etc., between persons or groups.
–*Webster's Encyclopedic Unabridged Dictionary of the English Language,* Random House, 1996

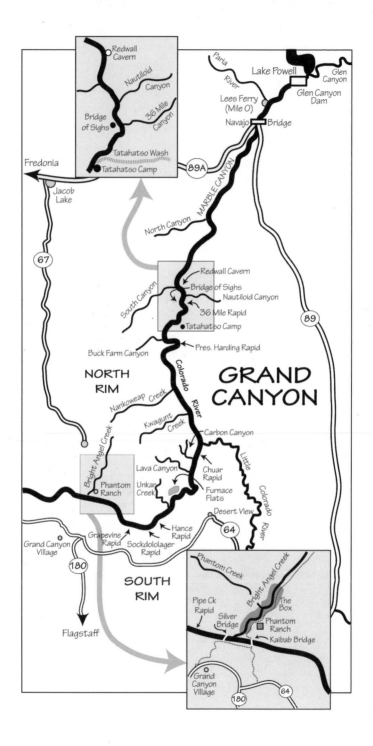

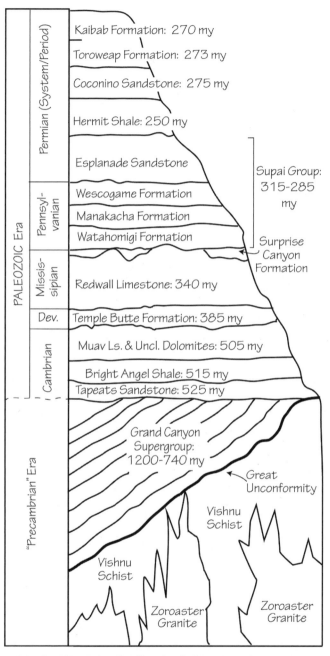

GRAND CANYON ROCK SEQUENCE

Part I

In the World above the Rim

Mr. Sherlock Holmes to John H. Watson, M.D.:
"'There's the scarlet thread of murder running through the colourless skein of life, and our duty is to unravel it, and isolate it, and expose every inch of it. . . .

'Now this was a case in which you were given the result and had to find everything else for yourself. Now let me endeavour to show you the different steps in my reasoning. To begin at the beginning. I approached the house, as you know, on foot, and with my mind entirely free from all impressions. . . .'"

—A. Conan Doyle, *A Study in Scarlet*, 1887

1

Naomi Sprague dawdled over the finishing
stitches on the doll's quilt. The other women and girls
had returned to the rented cabin to finish preparing supper. Naomi so rarely had a moment to herself that she
reveled in the quiet.

Her booth was near the door of the Coconino County
fairgrounds building. Soft light caressed the displays of
rag dolls and quilts, antique clothes and reproductions,
spinning wheels, skeins of yarn, and woven goods. By
the end of the weekend antiques-and-collectibles fair,
most goods would be sold. But if her plan worked, she
wouldn't be around to take inventory.

Just outside the sliding doors of the building, Naomi's
father's voice shouted orders to her brothers and cousins. She heard the thud of an anvil being set up in their
forge. Tomorrow the men would give demonstrations of
woodworking and metalworking, using old hand tools.
Naomi's specialty was doll clothes and quilts made from
bits and pieces of leftover fabric and lace. She'd been
sewing since she was four. She helped out with the period costumes and larger quilts when one of her sisters or
aunts was sick or in labor, but yard for yard, her small
pieces brought in so much money that her family pretty
much left her to her own work.

Naomi had always looked forward to the summer fairs. The Family made the circuit every year, earning enough to replenish supplies and stock food for the snowbound winter months back in the canyon compound. But this year was different. She would turn sixteen on Saturday. Her sealing ceremony was scheduled for Sunday evening, after the fair closed. Unless she escaped first, Naomi would spend that night in Ben Gruber's bed.

Only one girl had ever avoided the ceremony. Six weeks ago Carrie did it by climbing over the railing at Navajo Bridge and falling 470 feet to the green Colorado River below. The adults, including Naomi's mother, had rushed the children back into the vehicles before the rangers could get there. Naomi didn't know if her half-sister's body had been recovered. Carrie would have turned sixteen and married Ben that night.

"If you're not finished, it can wait till morning." Uncle Azer stood in the doorway. "Supper's nearly on."

Naomi made a knot and cut the crimson thread. Standing, she passed him the quilt. He held it close to his eyes, examining the stitches on the tiny Tumbling Blocks pattern. Nodding, he said, "This should fetch a good price," and handed it back.

She folded the quilt over a display rack, careful not to smile or look pleased with his comment. Demonstrations of pride, even pride of craftsmanship, weren't tolerated.

"You'll make Ben a good wife," Azer said as he led her outside.

Again she was silent. Naomi had learned early that she couldn't put her foot wrong if she didn't speak. She placed her needle and thread in a canvas bag she always carried with her. If it bulged a little more than usual, her uncle wouldn't notice. And the women would be too busy to miss the shirt until Sunday.

She entered the rented cabin through the kitchen

door, washed up, and helped set the tables for dinner. Each year at the Fort Tuthill fair, the Family rented the two-story house to serve as a hub for cooking, bathing, and laundering. It slept only a fraction of the Family and was reserved for the council elders, older wives, and those with babies. The others were in tents and RVs in the campground. Naomi shared a tent with three of her twenty-nine sisters. It was the most freedom they had all year.

But even the freedom of camping out had limits. At least two men patrolled the campground at night, escorting the girls and young boys to the toilets—and safely back to their tents. This kept the boys and girls from mingling, either with members of their own family or with members of other believing families traveling the same circuit. Part of the business of the fair was finding wives for the men. Ben Gruber had negotiated for Naomi a week ago, at the Aspen fair. She'd found out only after the fact. But she had no say. Ben felt he was owed a substitute third wife after Carrie's abandonment. The fact that he was thirty years older didn't enter into the negotiations.

After dinner, Naomi's mother whisked her upstairs for a fitting. The dress was the same one Carrie would have worn for her ceremony. Naomi was much smaller. Her mother would do the alterations tomorrow morning, before the festival crowds arrived.

Naomi slipped the inside-out white muslin dress over her head and stood quietly while her mother pinned the hem, sleeves, and darts. The mirrors were covered in all the rooms and bathrooms. Mirrors led to prideful behavior. But when she had a bathroom to herself, Naomi always lifted the cloth to study her changing body. And sometimes she sneaked a look at her reflection in a night-dark window. That was how she knew her face had lost its soft, childish edges. But the only way she'd know how she looked in this wedding dress was if she saw her wedding picture. And she didn't plan to wait around for the ceremony.

"Stop fidgeting, Child," her mother said, the words garbled by the straight pins held between her lips.

"I'm sorry, Mother. A pin pricked me. I'll try to do better."

Her mother took the pins from her mouth and studied her daughter for a long moment. Then she smiled. "I won't be calling you 'child' much longer. By Sunday night you'll be sealed to Brother Ben—in this life and for all eternity."

Naomi nodded, her eyes downcast. Her mother sounded pleased with the forthcoming marriage. But then, her mother followed the Family's way of life without question and ensured that her children did the same, no matter what it took.

"I'll miss your help with the little ones," her mother said. "But soon you'll have children of your own, God willing. Maybe by this time next year."

Naomi fought to control a shudder. Her mother noticed and said, "Brother Ben is a good provider, Child. He has assured your father and the other elders that he will control"—she stopped, cleared her throat—"that he won't use his fists or the rod if you displease him. Though of course it's within his rights to do so." Her voice trailed off, as if she were picturing the bruised cheek of Ben's second wife. He'd caught her reading a local newspaper last night, after the children were bathed and put to bed. Newspapers carried stories about the outside world. They were tools of the Devil.

"There. All finished." Naomi's mother closed the pin box with a snap and struggled to her feet. She was six months pregnant with her eleventh child. Hair turning coarse and gray. Face lined with fatigue. Youthful grace a distant memory. The privilege and status of being the Prophet's seventh wife had not protected her from aging quickly. But Brother Ben's wives, though younger, looked even older. Living in fear meant having no life at all.

Her mother seemed to sense Naomi's thoughts. " 'Whatever you do, work heartily, as for the Lord and not for men, knowing that from the Lord you will receive the inheritance as your reward.' . . . Do you understand what I'm saying, Child?"

Naomi's bleak future stared out of her mother's eyes. "I understand, Mother."

2

Philo Dain parked his Sierra on the gravel circle three feet from the rickety fence surrounding my property. He turned off the dome light, leaned over to unlock the glove box, removed something heavy and dark, then snapped the box shut.

By the glow of the carport light, I watched him check the magazine of his GLOCK 27.

"What is it?" I said.

"Something moved out front. Probably nothing."

"But—"

Philo touched my cheek. "Wait here, Frankie. The Beretta's under the seat if you need it."

He took a flashlight from the console between us, eased open the door, and slipped out. I unclicked my seatbelt and felt around under the seat. Found a holster and pulled it out. Contemplated following him. It was my house, after all. But I had no desire to be caught in the middle of a firefight—or to distract a private investigator when he sensed trouble. I settled for holding the Beretta in my right hand, my iPhone in my left, thumb ready to punch the last digit of 911.

Waiting had always been tough for me. I stared at the faded-red pickets illumined by the back-porch light. The fence didn't shout "Southwest." Nor did the California modern one-story house and guesthouse inside the perimeter. The place reminded me of an Eichler home I'd rented in Palo Alto when I was at Stanford. Floor-to-ceiling glass in the back of the house overlooked everything important—small pool, flagstone courtyard, native trees shading a patio and fountain. My oasis.

What was taking Philo so long?

I checked the views out the side and back windows. The wind made the shadows dance among the cholla, saguaro, ocotillo, and prickly pear. My maternal grandmother had left me the property when she died a couple of years ago. Since then I'd refurbished the main house, leaving the fence until I'd saved enough money for Phase II. That might take a while. Young community college instructors, even heads of departments, didn't make enough money to handle nonessential repairs on two-and-a-half-acre suburban ranchettes.

A small animal squealed, a mix of pain and fear. The cry broke off. I gripped the Beretta more tightly. A shadow moved on the far side of the ocotillo hedge abutting the guesthouse. A coyote eased around the guesthouse wall and trotted down the driveway, a rabbit dangling from his mouth.

I relaxed and flexed my fingers. *Any time, Philo.*

Lights went on in the center hall of the house, then, a minute later, proceeded in orderly fashion through the tiny living room, office, kitchen, and family room extension. That first minute had taken care of the two bedrooms and bath in the far wing. Philo was checking the house for unwanted visitors and booby traps and whatever else security professionals look for.

He stood in the doorway, backlit by the family room. Stepping out, he circled around my Toyota Tacoma, parked under the carport. "Front door was closed, but not locked," he said, opening my door.

I holstered the Beretta and slid it back under the seat. "I'm sure I locked it."

"He went out that way, but he went in through the patio."

"Someone was in my house?"

"Picked the lock on the French doors. Wasn't much of a challenge. Tommy could have done it."

Tommy is the precocious six-year-old son of E. J. Killeen, Philo's business partner at Dain Investigations.

"I'll call a locksmith in the morning." I headed for the back door. Stopped when I spotted a dark lump on the doormat. Backing up a step, I crouched down. The remains of a field mouse.

"A warning?" Philo said, looking over my shoulder. His breath tickled my ear.

"Doubt it. A feral cat visits every so often." I picked up the mat, carried it across the driveway, and tossed the remains of the mouse into a patch of cholla.

"Think he's still out there?" My voice couldn't have been heard more than a meter away.

"The cat?" Philo said, just as softly.

"The intruder."

"Wouldn't bet against it. Killeen's coming around to sweep the place, see if your two-legged visitor left any presents."

"Can't Killeen send someone else? Cinna or Griff?" Business was so brisk at Dain Investigations that previous part-time employees now worked full-time.

"They're on assignment. So are all the consultants. And Killeen . . ." Philo paused.

"He's fixed everything that needed fixing in their new home, and he's raring to get back to work?"

Killeen had been on paternity leave since the birth of his daughter a month ago. No one was sleeping through the night yet, except maybe Tommy. He'd stayed with me for a few days after the birth. I could testify that the noise of jackhammers, buzz saws, nail guns, and drills hadn't awakened him. The next-door neighbors were renovating their house.

Philo's grin showed white in the darkness. "Let's just say Killeen's grateful Sylvie didn't have twins."

"I'll bet."

I started back to the house. Hosed off the mat into a nearby desert willow. The monsoons had started four days ago, and already fragrant blooms were popping open, scenting the air. One of the many reasons I loved summer in Tucson. Propping the mat against the wall to dry, I followed Philo into the family room.

"You been smoking?" he said in my ear.

I smelled it, too—the faint, acrid aroma of marijuana. I sniffed my way through the kitchen to the pint-size living room.

Philo opened the French doors. Humid night air rushed through the screens. The air conditioner kicked on, and I shut it off before joining Philo. I whispered, "I'm staying at your place tonight. Just give me a minute to grab some clean clothes."

I headed down the hall to the master bedroom, which was marginally larger than the second bedroom. The odor of fresh paint lingered, though I'd finished my own renovations weeks ago. Philo watched while I grabbed a daypack from the closet and stuffed a change of clothes inside. I nodded that I was done. I'd been spending three nights each week at Philo's anyway and kept part of my wardrobe there.

He went outside with his flashlight and GLOCK again, returning just long enough to hand me a pair of latex gloves. My hands trembled as I tugged on the gloves. Delayed shock. Someone had violated my inner sanctum.

I started coffee for Killeen, then returned to my bedroom, looking for anything out of place, anything missing. The accrued layers of dust on the furniture helped. I'm not a perfect housekeeper. I'm a geologist with a penchant for rocks, fossils, and dirt. Even dust has a story to tell. My excuse for putting life ahead of housework is that I teach college all day, and each night prepare for the next day's class. I can't afford a house cleaner, so dusting must await either the impending visit of a guest or the end of a term. Coincidentally, the first summer session had finished two days before, and I wasn't teaching the second. I'd planned to throw myself into a belated spring cleaning tomorrow.

The coffee finished dripping as Killeen's truck circled the front acre. He and Philo came in together, wiping their shoes on the mat outside the door. It had been reasonably clean, I noticed, wondering if the intruder had waited out the rainstorm in the house.

I hugged Killeen and kissed his scarred, mud-brown cheek. Taking each man by a hand, I led them a little way down the short hall. The front windows were high. Underneath was a built-in cabinet for efficient use of space. On top, I displayed rocks, minerals, fossils, photographs, and my grandmother's collection of Pueblo pottery, worth thousands. The pots hadn't been touched.

The same wasn't true for the photographs. Marks in the dust showed they'd all been moved, and the intruder hadn't bothered to be careful. It was as if he wanted me to know he'd been there.

One of the photographs was missing. I picked up a tablet from beside the hall phone and wrote, *A family photo of my brothers and me, taken at Jamie's wedding.*

Both Killeen and Philo had attended my younger brother's marriage to Teresa Black on Memorial Day weekend. Philo had taken the digital image.

He put his arms around me. For a moment I relaxed against him. The trembling in my hands dissipated.

While Philo donned gloves and dusted the other picture frames for fingerprints, Killeen poured himself a mug of coffee. Setting a gym bag on the coffee table, he extracted a black scanner. The device looked like a small, boxy remote control with an antenna. He turned in a circle, but he'd taken no more than two sips of coffee and completed no more than 150 degrees of arc when the device lit up.

He set the mug down beside the bag, stuck hands the size of catcher's mitts into latex gloves, and used the control to zero in on the source. From under the lip of the kitchen counter, dead center in the living area of the house, he pulled an object that was roughly the shape of a nine-volt battery.

I looked from the object to Killeen's protuberant olive-black eyes. "Is—"

He held a finger to his lips. Philo dusted the unit for prints, lifting one beauty. Killeen dropped the unit into a glass of water I'd left sitting on the sink. His smile tugged at the scar that began at his right ear and wrapped around the side of his neck. Made his face look scarier to most folks. But we'd saved each other's lives more than once. I trusted him as much as I trusted Philo and my family.

Philo extracted a second scanner from the bag. It took them only a few minutes to sweep the rest of the house, the patio, the carport, the guesthouse, and Philo's and my trucks. I followed, turning off lights as they finished each room. They found no more bugs.

We reconvened outside around the wrought-iron table. The waxing moon and solar ground lights bathed the patio in a warm glow. I dried off the chairs and handed Killeen a fresh mug of coffee. Philo held a Negra Modelo. I drank water.

A breeze rustled the thin leaves of the old mesquites beyond the fence. The hairs on my neck stood up. A shiver traveled down to my toes. "I feel like he's out there in the dark, watching us."

Philo took my hand. "We checked for cameras, too, Frankie. It's clean."

I picked up my cell phone from the table. Pressed 6 for one of my brothers. "Luke? What are you doing tonight?" A minute later I ended the call and said, "He'll be over in an hour to hold the fort while I'm at your place. Just wants to check on the horses first." I looked at Philo, then Killeen. "You think he'll be safe guarding this place on his own? Maybe I should call Matt, too." I picked up the phone again.

"Why don't we leave that up to Luke?" Philo said.

Killeen agreed. "Your intruder broke in when you weren't here. Putting a bug in the house means he—"

"Or she." I grinned.

"Point taken. Anyway, your intruder wants to monitor your activity from a safe distance. I'd say there's only a slim chance he or she will try to enter an occupied home."

"Okay," I said, feeling reassured.

We sipped our drinks in silence. Mourning doves announced their third nests of the year. A Western screech owl called from a nearby saguaro. Something skittered on the roof. Perhaps the feral cat. The air smelled of creosote, damp earth, desert willow, and salvia.

"If Philo hadn't been here, I would have called the police," I said. "Should I do that now?"

"They won't be able to respond for a while," Killeen said. "A 911 caller reported a man with a rifle on the UA campus. It's all hands on deck tonight. But don't worry. I'll write up something, have you sign it in the morning, and turn it in so there's a record of the break-in. We can take a few pictures, let them know what he took."

"I'll print out a copy of the family photo to go along with the report. What else do you need?"

"Nothing," Philo said. "If we're lucky, Killeen will be able to trace the serial number on the bug."

"Even if the guy bought it online?"

"The manufacturer can give me a name and the shipping address," Killeen said.

"They tell you stuff, just like that?"

He shrugged. "It's all in the approach."

"Ah, quid pro quo."

"Everybody wants or needs something," Philo said. "It's a matter of figuring out what that something is."

"I wonder what our visitor wanted," I said. "Besides the photo."

"Tough to say. I found only a few partials on the other photos. Killeen will have to rule out your prints, mine, and Tommy's, of course. Has anyone else been around?"

I had to think for a minute. "Not since Teresa's bachelorette party. Twenty women were here that night. And the caterers. But they cleaned pretty thoroughly afterwards."

"No visitors since?"

"Just Tommy."

I drained my water glass. Went in the house and filled it again. I turned on the hall light and walked toward the bathroom, averting my eyes from the photo display. The window above the cabinet reflected a tall, slender, black-haired woman in a white tank top. Tense gray eyes. High, prominent cheekbones.

Was my intruder outside, looking in, feeling gratified that he'd rattled me?

3

Philo was standing by the bathroom door when I came out. "You okay?"

"I was thinking it might have been a student, trying to scare me—maybe someone I'd given a bad grade."

"Except that wouldn't explain the bugging device."

"Right." Back in the kitchen, I picked up my water glass and the coffee pot and carried them out to the patio. "Can you tell how long the bug's been in place?" I said to Killeen.

"Not long, I should think. A few days at most. Any longer and your neighbors would have noticed someone sitting in a car."

"Not necessarily," Philo said. "I followed his tracks back to that Mexican bird-of-paradise near the street. Found the impression of a box, probably a recording system he rigged up. Dirt was dry."

"So it was put there before the monsoon started on the third," I said. "Or maybe a day and a half ago, after we dried out from that first storm."

"Was the picture gone before tonight?" Philo said.

I thought back. I have one of those memories that forgets little. It can be both a blessing and a curse. "No. I'd have noticed."

"What about smelling grass?"

Killeen frowned. "As in marijuana?"

Philo nodded. "We opened the doors before you got here to air the place out."

"I caught a whiff of something Tuesday, when I stopped by to check the mail," I said. "I was on the patio. Thought it was coming from the workers next door."

"But not before that?" Philo said.

I shook my head.

"I bet that's when he went in," Killeen said to Philo. "He's probably been watching her for a while, checking out her schedule."

I picked up Philo's beer. He'd added lime juice. It tasted wonderful. I finished it off.

Philo grinned, pushed back his chair, and went into the house.

"I spent the last few nights at Philo's place," I said to Killeen. "Yesterday was the first time I was around much. Did laundry, filed my class notes, paid bills. Today I was up at the school, straightening up my office, getting ready for fall term. I drove home long enough to shower and change, then went to dinner with Philo."

"Just routine stuff," Killeen said.

"I hope I bored the hell out of whoever's been listening in."

Philo came back with two more beers and a plate of lime slices. Handing me a frosty bottle, he said, "Did you have phone conversations with anyone today or yesterday, anything that could have been recorded?"

I squeezed a lime wedge into the bottle. Took a healthy swig. "I talked to Matt about staying here while I was away."

Matt and Luke, my twin brothers, were three years older. They lived in the bunkhouse at our parents' place when they weren't outfitting and guiding wilderness tours and climbing trips around the globe.

"Talk to anybody else?" Killeen said.

"Philo. And Dora Simpson, of course."

"The Dora I met in the Mojave? The student who got kidnapped?"

"The same. But she's at UT-Austin now."

"How's she doing?"

"Fine, I guess. We didn't talk long. She asked me to fill in for a geology professor on a raft trip through the Grand Canyon. Dora thought I could teach, and Philo could come along for the ride."

"When?"

"This weekend."

"Kind of sudden."

"Dora's group was more than halfway from UT-Austin to Arizona when the prof broke his ankle. Something about a rabbit hole in the dark. They were camping."

"Lousy luck," Killeen said, and looked at Philo. "You going?"

"Nope. I was about to call you when we discovered the break-in. I head to D.C. in the morning."

"For how long?"

"Two days, two weeks, who knows? Can you manage?"

Killeen grinned. "No problem." Turning his big head, he squinted at me. "So who's taking Philo's spot?"

"Luke. He could use a break."

Killeen nodded. Lately my brothers had been moody. When I'd asked if anything was wrong, they'd both said no. Matt's new girlfriend had helped distract him. He'd be okay. But Luke, unattached and more introverted than his twin, seemed quiet and depressed. He needed something to take his mind off his troubles.

"Luke needs a girl," Killeen said. "What happened to Mindy?"

"She wanted to settle down. He wasn't ready yet." I wondered if Luke would ever be ready.

"While we're gone," Philo said to me, "I'd like Killeen to arrange for a mason to build a perimeter wall. This place is porous."

Killeen had his notebook out. "Can I put in a state-of-the-art security system?"

"Best you can find," Philo said.

I set down my empty beer bottle with unintended force, rattling the wrought-iron table. "Sorry," I said, as the men steadied their drinks. "But Philo, I don't have the money."

"I've got more money than I can spend—"

"In one lifetime. I know. And you give away more than I'll ever earn. But that's not the point. This is *my* home, *my* responsibility."

He picked up my left hand, kissed the garnet-and-gold ring. "Consider it an engagement present."

I tugged my hand away and crossed my arms. Philo settled back in his chair, rocking patiently, prepared to wait me out.

Killeen broke the impasse. "Philo's right. Someone's been in your home, bugged your conversations."

"But I don't—"

He held up a hand. "I'll draw up a loan agreement in the morning. You can pay Philo back on whatever schedule you want. Just let me know your terms so I can put them in writing."

I nodded, clearly outgunned.

"When do you leave?" he said.

"We meet in Marble Canyon on Saturday night. We'll be home on the eighteenth."

"That should give me enough time. I know just the guys to do the job. They owe me." Killeen's smile caught the moonlight.

"Thanks." Philo touched my shoulder, acknowledging how difficult it was for me to accept help.

I leaned over, kissed Killeen's cheek, and whispered in his ear, "I won't forget this. Quid pro quo."

"Counting on it," he said.

"One last thing, Frankie," Philo said. "Those phone conversations—were they cell or landline?"

"You and Matt were cell . . . and I called Luke on the

cell to ask if he could take your spot on the raft. But Dora called the landline."

"Did you put any of them on speaker?" Killeen asked.

I thought back. Remembered folding laundry during one call and needing my hands free. "Only Dora."

We looked at each other in silence. The intruder had heard both sides of that conversation.

"The good news is he didn't get much," Killeen said. "And you'll have Luke with you in the canyon."

"I can handle myself in the field."

"We know," Philo said. "But I'll feel better if someone's watching your back."

"And the bad news?" I said to Killeen.

"There's no cell reception in the Grand Canyon."

I laughed. "That's a plus, Killeen. It's one reason Philo and I keep trying to get away to—" I stopped.

Philo's dark blond hair, touched by gray at the sides, glowed gold in the light coming through the glass. His craggy face was as weathered at thirty-six as my father's had been at fifty. Half of it was in shadow as he turned to me. We'd spent exponentially more time apart than together in the last two and a half years.

"What?" he said.

"Just a thought."

"Your inspirations usually require physical exertion on my part."

"Yes, but you're trained for desert warfare. This'll be a cakewalk."

"You want me to meet you at the river."

My cell chirped. A text from Dora. I responded, remembering to ask how many students we'd be teaching. Waited a minute for her reply . . . She said she and Professor McKuen had received small grants from two oil companies for geoscience outreach. A targeted program, aimed at the neediest—those with an aptitude but without family support. Only enough funding for five prospective students. With the prof's daughter, that made six. . . . I acknowledged, signed off, and pressed a few buttons. Philo's iPhone beeped.

"I'm forwarding the trip itinerary," I said. "If all goes according to plan, we'll be putting in at Phantom Ranch on Wednesday afternoon."

"So if I finish in D.C. by Monday—"

"I know. Wishful thinking." I sighed and stood up. "It's impossible to get last-minute reservations at Phantom, so you'd have to hike down from the rim Wednesday morning. And you're right—a fast nine-mile hike might be pushing it for an old man with a gimpy leg."

"Them's fightin' words," said Killeen, who'd become a father in his mid-forties.

Philo caught my hand. "May I point out that you're only five years younger?"

"Five years, seven and a half months."

"Not that anyone's counting." He kissed my palm and released it. "If I can make it happen, I will. But don't get your hopes up."

I smiled. "Pack a night bag anyway. I'll take it along. Who knows? We might just get lucky."

All three of us stood up and knocked for luck on the wooden door frame. The hollow sound followed us into the house.

4

**Friday, July 8, Fort Tuthill County Park
near Flagstaff, Arizona**
10:15 p.m.

Naomi lay motionless on her air mattress in the
tent she shared with her sisters. She heard Uncle Azer
pass by on his rounds. He wouldn't be back for another
thirty minutes unless she signaled with her flashlight for
company to the toilets.

Swallowing her fear, Naomi crawled out from under
the thin sheet that lay atop her open sleeping bag and
grabbed the canvas satchel she'd used for a pillow. The
mattress rustled as she inched her way to the end. She
waited to see if anyone noticed. Her sisters' breathing
remained even, regular.

Taking off her nightgown, Naomi slid her arms into
the boy's shirt she'd brought from the booth, fumbling
with the metal buttons. She pulled on the worn pair of
Levi's she'd offered to mend for a younger cousin. The
pants were a bit loose at the waist, but her hips held
them up. She rolled the cuffs so they wouldn't show,
then donned her voluminous nightgown again. The
navy blue cotton wouldn't stand out in the dark.

She pulled on dark socks and her soft-soled shoes,
careful to make no sound. The shoes weren't cushioned
for running. Only young children were allowed to run
or play tag. Her father, the Prophet, permitted soft-soled

shoes because they cut down on noise. Silence was golden in all things, including housework.

Naomi waited another minute, listening to the campground noises and her sisters' breathing. Sarah snored, a sweet, chuffing sound. Naomi would miss it.

The Family shared the campground with other, non-Family campers. Someone strummed a guitar and sang a song about the city of New Orleans. New Orleans was in Louisiana. A hurricane had hit there one summer while the Family was on the circuit. She'd seen the headlines on a discarded newspaper. But when she'd asked about the hurricane, her mother had said, "What happens in the outside world is no concern of yours, Child. The Devil lives there, and we must be constantly vigilant lest he find a way into our midst."

Naomi wasn't sure she believed in the Devil. She believed in things she could see and touch, taste and feel. She'd felt evil's touch—in the days of bread and water and isolation when she asked the wrong questions. She'd seen evil in the bruises on Ben Gruber's wives and children. But she no longer spoke up. Her downcast eyes, fine needlework, and silence were rewarded by a bit more freedom than the other girls enjoyed.

Link by link, she unzipped the tent flap. She was slight, but it seemed to take forever to make a space large enough to squeeze through. Moving to the far side of the tent, the side away from the patrolled path, she got her bearings and stole into the woods. Tree by tree, she ghosted toward the trailhead. She'd found it several years ago, when she was watching the young ones play hide-and-seek. One of her sisters had gotten turned around and had run too far from camp. Naomi had gone to bring her back and discovered her standing on a wide trail. A scantily clad woman was running toward them.

Naomi had picked up her sister and asked the woman where the trail led. All the way to Flagstaff, to the university, the woman said. So last year Naomi had slipped away from the booth long enough to explore as far as she dared. Which wasn't far. The trail emerged from the county park and passed a housing development. Naomi noted the street names and drew a map in her head of what she'd seen.

Tonight, even by starlight, the track was plain. The trees stood well back from a passage wide enough for both a horse trail and a footpath. Naomi watched the track for a minute or two. She was alone.

Removing her nightgown again, she stuffed it into the bag, then twisted her long hair up and tucked it under a cap. She'd made the cap herself, reproducing one she'd seen in a photograph in one of the other stalls. Her mother had thought it good enough to sell in their booth, so Naomi had made twenty more, all from scraps of wool left over from the sewing of winter clothes.

Slipping her arm through the handles of the bag, Naomi began to run.

What if he isn't there to meet me?

She answered her own question. *I'll run all the way to Flagstaff, to the university.*

She didn't know what a university was, but it must be large, with lots of people to hide among. Why else would they name it after the universe?

Part II

On the River
Grand Canyon National Park, Arizona

Monday, July 11

"We have an unknown distance yet to run; an unknown river yet to explore. What falls there are, we
know not; what rocks beset the channel, we know
not; what walls rise over the river, we know not. Ah,
well! we may conjecture many things. The men talk
as cheerfully as ever; jests are bandied about freely
this morning; but to me the cheer is somber and the
jests are ghastly."

—John Wesley Powell, *Exploration of the Colorado River of the West
and Its Tributaries,* 1875

"The supply of adult women was running short, and
polygamy without a female population on which to
draw was a barren doctrine indeed. . . . Fresh women
appeared in the harems of the Elders—women who
pined and wept, and bore upon their faces the traces
of an unextinguishable horror. Belated wanderers
upon the mountains spoke of gangs of armed men,
masked, stealthy, and noiseless, who flitted by them
in the darkness. . . . None knew who belonged to this
ruthless society. . . . The very friend to whom you
communicated your misgivings as to the Prophet
and his mission, might be one of those who would
come forth at night with fire and sword to exact a

terrible reparation. Hence every man feared his neighbour, and none spoke of the things which were nearest his heart."

–A. Conan Doyle, *A Study in Scarlet*, 1887

5

Mile 35, Nautiloid Canyon Tributary, Marble Canyon

2:10 p.m.

Nico, the stocky head river guide, aimed the thirty-five-foot raft toward river left and throttled back on the motor. As the bow rubbed against the debris fan of Nautiloid Canyon, another guide ran lightly up the right pontoon, hopped ashore, and caught the line Luke tossed him. Beside us, the second rubber raft nosed the beach and shut down. The canyon reverberated with the thunder of coursing water. And the wind. Always the wind.

Kneeling in a puddle on the starboard deck, I wrestled with my daypack. Day two of our eight-day whitewater trip through the Grand Canyon, and I was still trying to master the heavy carabiner my brother had loaned me. The lock secured my daypack to one of the straps crisscrossing the gray tarp in the center of the raft. The tarp hid a small mountain of tents, sleeping bags, chairs, and personal gear.

"Need a hand?" Luke called from shore. He'd helped the other rafters disembark. I was the only one still aboard.

"Almost there," I said.

He planted his foot on the steel links connecting the pontoon to the bow and vaulted onto the forward deck.

From the pocket of his swim shorts, he produced a light-weight clasp.

"S-biner," he said. "Much easier to use when you're hooking and unhooking things all day. I should have given you this in the first place."

"I have a couple in my footlocker."

He grinned. "The one you misplaced."

We'd been over this before. I'd stored the trunk in my parents' bunkhouse five years ago, after my last trip down the canyon. That was just before Matt and Luke moved back into their boyhood lair. They'd shunted the trunk into the family storage shed. Or so they said.

"I did look," Luke said.

"I know." I unzipped the daypack, took out a water-resistant sack of items I wouldn't need on the short hike, and reclipped the dry bag to a strap. It wasn't Luke's fault I refused to buy new gear. He was kind enough to loan me what I needed. I said, "Sorry I'm taking so long."

"Don't be so hard on yourself. It takes a couple of days to get into the rhythm of the river when you're leading the trip."

He didn't mention my knee, but I saw the swift, assessing glance. That morning, on a hike up North Canyon, I'd lost my footing as I helped an older rafter climb a boulder pile. No broken bones, but my knee had a grapefruit-size swelling.

Luke edged by me and headed to the stern. I unbuckled my PFD—personal flotation device—and tucked it under the dry bag. Slipped into my field vest and daypack. My shirt was soaked with perspiration. The temperature was well over a hundred, the silver tarp burned to the touch, and my knee hurt like hell. I was grouchy because I was angry with myself. And Luke knew it.

He handed me a couple of ibuprofen and two full mugs of Gatorade.

"You're a godsend." I drained them both and clipped

them to the straps. Turning, I found Luke blocking my path to shore.

"Why don't you let Dora fly solo on this?" He lifted his UA ball cap and resettled it on his short black curls. "If she needs backup, she's got Nico," he said. "And me. We've each been to the site at least fifty times. And it's not like we can miss the fossils—they're right in the middle of the streambed."

Dora had organized this lesson and was more than capable of delivering it. Besides, she was trying to pack in as much teaching experience as possible before she threw herself into her dissertation research. At the moment she was standing on a boulder, holding a large, butcher-paper drawing of nautiloid fossils for the students she'd brought from Texas—five young men and Molly McKuen, the daughter of the prof with the broken ankle. When he and his wife had flown home from Albuquerque, they'd given Molly the option of continuing with the trip. No contest.

The other rafters, members of a church-sponsored group from Bismarck, North Dakota, clustered around Dora to hear what she had to say. The crew could have delivered the basic information, but I'd noticed Dora had a natural way of engaging people.

The mollusk in Dora's drawing had a shell shaped like a windsock—or an uncoiled chambered nautilus, a cousin of the fossil. A cross-sectional view of the shell showed internal walls secreted by the squidlike animal during growth. Ingenious architecture for structural strength and buoyancy. The students would see that cross section in the eroded Redwall Limestone of the canyon.

I'd been six when I'd first come down the river with my family and visited this site. I still remembered the feeling of awe as I traced the outline of a two-footer.

Luke put a hand on my shoulder. "Take a break, rest your knee for the Nankoweap hike tomorrow."

"But I hate to miss the nautiloids. Who knows when I'll get back here?"

"If you follow the beds around the point," he gestured to the left, "you'll find more fossils just above river level."

"Really?"

"You bet."

"Sold."

Luke jumped ashore and lifted me onto the sand. "A little alone time on a raft trip can do wonders for the psyche." He glanced at Dora as he spoke.

Something was brewing there. Luke had always dated women his own age or younger. Dora was six years older. But whatever helped lift the cloud of depression he'd experienced lately was fine by me. Only two days into the canyon and he already looked better. I said as much.

"I think I just needed to leave civilization behind—get out here where I can think," he said. His eyes, brown-black as burned wood, shifted to take in Dora's students. "And I've always liked working with young folks, teaching them about the outdoors."

Finished with her lecture, Dora gave us a little wave and rolled up the paper drawing. The students gathered their clipboards, mechanical pencils, notebooks, and water bottles. I still had trouble pinning names to the young men. It should have helped that they were in alphabetic order, A to E, oldest to youngest. Unfortunately the first four (Adam, Bobby, Craig, and David) all had blond hair, eyes of various shades of blue, and similar broad-shouldered, slim-hipped builds. Maybe it was a Texas thing.

Bobby was the tallest, David the shortest, and Craig had the habit of clearing his throat each time he spoke. They ranged in age from eighteen to twenty, though Adam could have passed for twenty-five. Only Ethan—the youngest by a couple of months—had darker hair and eyes. Hence, after a day and a half on the river, I was batting only 70 percent in the naming game. But at least I confined my misnomers to the middle three boys, who laughed and corrected me gently each time I erred.

"How do you know these are Mississippian rocks?" asked the leader of the North Dakota contingent. He'd told me at lunch the first day that he had a master's in hydrology from an Ivy League university. It was his second trip down the Colorado. "Don't you find cephalopods in older rock units? Even the Cambrian?"

Just for a moment, Dora's forehead tightened in a frown. "You're right, Harvey. The earliest cephalopods—the class that includes squids, octopi, nautiloids, and ammonites—*are* found in rocks the same age as the Cambrian Bright Angel Shale, which we'll encounter around Mile—" She looked at me.

"Forty-seven," I said. "Twelve miles downstream."

She smiled her thanks, then turned back to Harvey. "Those earliest cephalopods were nautiloids, as it turns out, but smaller and more primitive than the ones we'll see today. And they were found in China, not here."

Dora unrolled her drawing again and pointed to a geologic section showing the rock units and ages. "After the end of the Cambrian Period, during the Ordovician, nautiloid species grew in number, complexity, and size—up to several meters in length. They became the predators of the oceans."

She handed the diagram to Molly and climbed down off the boulder. "But as you know, Harvey, in the Marble and Grand Canyon sections, a time gap of 120 million to 165 million years lies between the Cambrian units and the overlying strata. We can't say if sediments and nautiloid remains were deposited here during this interval, then eroded away, or if they were never deposited. But we do know that the nautiloids survived glacial episodes and competition elsewhere. And we find them here, above the time gap, in Mississippian-age rocks."

"But you didn't answer my first question," he said. "How do you know these rocks are *Mississippian*? Why can't they be only five thousand years old? Or two hundred?"

I didn't want the daylight hours to be hijacked again. Harvey had spent thirty minutes yesterday questioning the origin of reptile tracks in the Coconino Sandstone. This morning it was horn corals, brachiopods, and crinoids in the Redwall Limestone. That's why we were late getting to Nautiloid Canyon.

I stepped in. "Geologists and paleontologists assign a mid-Mississippian age to these rocks because similar fossil assemblages are found in Mississippian-age formations elsewhere in the world—strata that have a more complete rock sequence underlying and overlying them."

"She mentioned glacial episodes, which might have triggered floods—"

"Why don't we talk about it tonight, Harvey? Looks like it'll rain any minute."

Dora looked up at the clouds that had been building since noon. "Jeez, you're right. Let's go, guys."

"I'll put your diagram in the raft for you, Dora," I said.

Molly handed me the rolled poster and joined the group following Nico up the debris fan to the mouth of the canyon. Luke and Roxy, the guide of the second raft, brought up the rear. She stopped to wait for me, but I waved her on. Luke would explain. The third crew member, Doug, was already stretched out in a patch of shade on Roxy's raft, hat over his face, snoozing.

A short, energetic, redheaded man lagged behind the others. He was half turned away, watching his wife climb the fan. His name was Roy, and he owned a string of hardware stores in Bismarck. He'd made a point of listening in on my geology lectures, staying a few steps beyond the little bunch of students.

"You have a question, Roy?"

"More of a comment, I guess. About what you talked about this morning."

This morning we'd hiked through the Supai Group section in North Canyon. Harvey's rafters had rushed ahead to see the little lake and dry waterfall blocking the trail. Roy had stayed behind at the base of the Escalante Formation, where the lag gravels provided evidence of a break in the depositional record. He'd heard me talk about how barren the early planet was before life began, and how rich and diverse life in the oceans became. About how life had spread onto land, leaving traces of plants in old wetlands and reptile footprints in fossilized dunes. We'd discussed the length of time it took for the rocks of the canyon to be laid down, buried, uplifted, and eroded, how the ocean swept over this area again and again, only to recede again and again. I stressed that each rock layer told a story. Put those stories together and we have the history of this small part of the planet.

"You asked your students to forget about everything they'd been taught up till now and just pretend that they were the first people here and had to describe this place for the folks back home. You told 'em not to make any assumptions, but to pay attention to what they could see and touch and smell and taste. First principles, you called it. So I did that myself."

"Discover anything?"

He was silent for a moment, then shot a look at Harvey, who was standing at the top of the trail, waiting. Roy said softly, "My father manufactured particleboard. I learned all about treating wood chips with heat, pressure, and resins until they formed a layer." He bent down, picked up a handful of sand, let the grains trickle through his fingers. "The time, heat, and pressure it must have taken to turn *this* into a rock layer, and then to pile up more than a mile of layers above it . . . Shoot, looks like I'll be going home with a lot more questions than I arrived with."

"Nothing wrong with that," I said. "We humans are

curious by nature. Problems crop up when we stop asking questions because we're afraid of the answers."

"You coming?" Harvey shouted.

Roy grimaced, then looked up at the red walls that dwarfed us. I saw that in only two days the canyon had changed him. But all he said was, "Next time, I'm traveling solo."

He gave a little wave and trotted up the slope. I stowed the diagram in its plastic tube, tossed it on the raft, and set off along the water's edge. Circling the first debris lobe, I crossed the dry creek bed as the rafters disappeared into the canyon. I was alone as I headed around the second lobe to a cliff of iron-stained limestone, eroded at the base by the river.

I navigated the rock ledges, looking for fossils. Cloud-diffused light reflected off barbell-shaped nodules of chert. Nearby were conical cross-sections of nautiloids, worn by wave and current action. I ran my fingers over the chamber walls, secreted 340 million years ago, frozen in time and space. Magic.

Pulling my camera from my vest pocket, I snapped photo after photo of fossils as I traced the bed upstream, lost in the story unfolding in the rocks, envisioning the shallow tropical seabed as it must have looked—

My peripheral vision spotted the tip of a reddish-orange kayak. A huge boulder obscured the rest of the craft. I was heading toward it when I sensed, more than heard, someone move. I stopped abruptly, my river shoes skidding on the rocky ledge. A man stepped from the deep shadow thrown by the boulder.

He was taller than I by several inches, lean, well-muscled, with face and hands burnished by the elements to a golden brown. He wore a military shirt, plain khaki in the torso, faded camo on the sleeves. A darker oblong marked where a name tag had been sewn. By contrast, his damp, dun-colored swim shorts looked new. He was barefoot. No hat. A piece of string caught sun-streaked brown hair at the nape of his neck. The end dangled over his left shoulder.

I'm good with faces. I'd noticed him twice—just downstream from the Lee's Ferry launch yesterday, and as he paddled past our North Canyon campsite at dusk. He seemed to be traveling solo. We'd waved in the way strangers do on the river.

"You didn't look as tall from the river," he said, walking toward me. His eyes reflected the glittering green water. "Take off your hat."

"Excuse me?" I said, wondering if fossil hunting had led me through a portal into a bizarre parallel universe.

He hesitated, as if unsure of his footing. "You're Frankie, right?"

Alarm bells clanged in my brain. How had he learned my name?

"Who wants to know?" I glanced around. A red PFD lay across over the stern of the boat. Next to the bow was a small pack. And leaning against it was an assault rifle. I didn't know enough about guns to tell what kind. Firearms were now legal in the park, but on the river?

"You can call me Jacob—like the lake."

He took a step, muscles tensed. His right hand moved to the sheath on his webbed belt. Light glinted on a heavy gold band. And on a blade. He was fast. Very fast.

I searched for an escape route. Came up empty. Backed up one pace, another, gathering myself for a sprint.

"Don't bother. You won't make it five feet."

He stood between me and the narrow path back to the rafts. To my left, an unbroken rock wall jutted into the river. I opened my mouth—

"Go ahead, scream. The river noise'll cover it."

"Why?" I'd backed up as far as I could. The river lapped at my heels.

Jacob smiled. Beautiful, shiny, straight white teeth. He took another step and his hand tightened on the hunting knife, honed sharp enough to take my head off with one swipe. Or gut me.

Given a choice between a knife and a rushing river, I'll take the river every time—even the frigid Colorado.

I threw my camera at his head and launched my body back and out over the water, twisting in the air to land in a racing dive.

"No—" I heard him yell before, eyes closed, I sank below the surface and let the current claim me.

6

Mile 35.1, Colorado River, Marble Canyon
2:25 p.m.

I held my breath, fighting panic and the urge to surface. If I could stay submerged until the river swept around Nautiloid delta, I'd be beyond the range of knives. And bullets.

The current pulled me out and away from shore and funneled me into a rapid. The turbulent water flung me against a boulder, knocking the air from my lungs. I opened my eyes and lunged for the strip of light above. My left arm wouldn't work. I pulled with my right. *One . . . two . . . three . . .* My head broke the surface.

Gulping air, I saw another boulder ahead. I turned in time to take the blow on my daypack. The contact sent me spinning off down a narrow chute. I searched for a handhold, a foothold, anything to slow my descent. At the bottom I could be trapped in a whirlpool and shunted along the bottom. My body might not surface for days.

My feet hit a ledge. I bent my knees, shoved off with my feet, and flung myself in an arc over the churning water. Landed with feet slapping the water in a flutter kick. The vortex tried to suck me back, but I fought it as I'd fight a riptide, by tucking my head in the water and pulling across the current. When I felt the suction ease a bit, I lifted my head.

My chest constricted. I couldn't take a deep breath.

I was long and lean and carried no extraneous fat to buffer me from the cold. In a few minutes, hypothermia would begin to set in. I needed to get out of the river.

Sheer cliffs rose on both sides. I was in the heart of Marble Canyon, on the right side of the river, in forty-eight-degree water. Ledges of pale dolomite swept by me as the river cut deep into the geologic section, transporting me back in time. I'd crossed over the unconformity between the Redwall and the underlying Cambrian strata. The Redwall caves and undercuts, previously at river level, now were well above the waterline. A small beach came into view. River left. With only one good arm, I couldn't reach it in time. My only option was to keep angling toward the right until I could latch onto a clump of vegetation.

Easier said than done. And once I achieved that impossible goal, could I leave the river unseen?

I knew Jacob wouldn't give up. I sensed he was hunting me already. At a calmer stretch of water, I twisted around so that I could check upstream. No kayak. I'd even lost sight of the rafts. What was keeping him? Or was I just being paranoid?

A minute later, he paddled around a slight bend in the river. He was looking down, tracking something in the water. I inhaled and let myself sink. Counted to thirty. Surfacing, I saw him nose his craft into the small debris fan I'd passed. He snagged something from the water and tossed it onshore before unsnapping the spray skirt and climbing out. He pulled the kayak well up from the waterline and went back to fetch the object he'd thrown. An orange PFD.

Damn. The bastard must have snuck up to the rafts and stolen a vest from right under Doug's nose. Jacob was trying to track me over water, hoping the current would carry the vest down the same path I'd taken.

It was the luck of the draw that I'd worked to hug the opposite shore. But when he didn't find a trace of me on that spit he was searching, he'd throw the vest back in and try again.

The rocks seemed to sweep by me as the current picked up speed. I turned my back on Jacob and searched for a way out. The river was running higher and faster than it had in thirty years. Fifty miles upstream, Glen Canyon dam was releasing twenty-seven thousand cubic feet per second of frigid water from the depths of Lake Powell. Around me, the water roared like a train in a tunnel. Up ahead was 36 Mile Rapid, a drop of four feet. Without a PFD, even a small rapid could drown me. If I didn't freeze first.

I rounded another small point and lost sight of Jacob—which meant he couldn't see me. But for how long?

My legs moved sluggishly, as if weighted down by lead cuffs. The frigid river sapped my strength. A riffle took me under, and I swallowed water. I struggled to the surface, knowing the next wave might be one too many.

In the cliffs ahead, a line of narrow, vertical caves, like wide arrow-slits in a castle wall, marked joints in the Redwall Limestone. Midway along the rock face should be a gully spanned by the Bridge of Sighs. If I passed that natural arch, I'd be in whitewater again at 36 Mile Rapid.

Dolomite beds, more than six feet high, flanked the river at the base of the cliffs. No handholds. But I spotted a break ahead, if I could just reach the shore in time.

My good arm pulled me slowly toward the right. The current fought me like a living thing. I wasn't going to make it. . . .

My knees scraped a submerged bar, a sandy mound of gravel and boulders at the foot of a small gully. I jammed my shoes into clefts between rocks and began inching my upper body toward a thicket of tamarisk protected by eroded wings of dolomite. Every time I released one toehold to find another, the current tried to reclaim me. I was so cold I could barely feel my fingers.

I reached the water's edge and tried to pull myself erect by the nearest bush. The first branch broke. So did the second. Above me, the Bridge of Sighs was a black shadow against pewter clouds. I smelled rain.

A squall engulfed me. Fat drops hammered my head and neck. The wind bit through my clothes. I swore at the tamarisks, the river, and the rocks, as the last strength ebbed from my legs.

Now or never.

I lunged again, this time throwing my arm around a slim bole and pulling my body up with grunts and another string of curses. The tamarisk—that introduced, invasive bane of the canyon—withstood the abuse. Dragging myself from bush to bush, I climbed the little beach and collapsed on a patch of sand. A green screen hid me from the river.

Chills raked my body. I clenched my teeth to keep from biting my tongue. Rain punished my upturned face. I didn't care. The sand and Redwall cliffs released waves of welcoming warmth. . . .

I must have passed out. When I came to, the wind had died, and the rain fell softly. My brain, shocked into incoherence by the narrow escape, finally clicked on. I wanted to lie there until the shivers eased, but I was too exposed. Jacob should be back on the water by now, following the vest.

I looked around for a better place to hide. Perhaps twenty feet above me, near the base of the Redwall, a wide slit showed black against the rusty rocks. I prayed it was large enough to hide me.

Pushing myself up to a sitting position, I felt my left shoulder and arm. I was able to make a weak fist. No broken bones, but I'd stung a nerve. Given time, I should have full use of the limb. But how much time? And could I make the climb using one good arm and one good knee?

Luke's voice answered, as if he were standing in front

of me. *John Wesley Powell climbed routes far rougher than this puny gully, and he had only one arm. Don't be such a lightweight.*

Another bone-rattling shiver took me. I looked at my knee. A wonderful shade of puce, but no more swollen than before, despite the brutal treatment. The impromptu ice bath had helped. The question was, would it bear my weight?

I levered myself upright, putting weight on both legs. I could manage. Just. The ibuprofen I'd swallowed back on the raft took the edge off the pain.

I crept back and tore off the branches I'd broken as I dragged myself from the water. Using the crude broom in one hand, I swept the sand where I'd lain, then tucked the broom under the straps of my daypack. The rain should take care of the rest.

Stepping from rock to rock to avoid leaving footprints, I climbed the shallow gully, keeping low, trying to stay hidden. Reaching the mouth of the cave, I peered inside. Beyond the lip, the limestone floor ramped down, creating a space that was larger than I expected, but not high enough for me to stand erect. A few bats, but no rattlesnakes. At least that I could see. Or hear. But I'd have to contend with red ants till evening, still hours away. And nightfall was when the scorpions emerged from their rocky homes.

Yet I saw nowhere else to hide. I crawled over the lip and into the cave. Turned around. The opening provided a limited view upriver. Jacob's red helmet and PFD sat on the bow of his kayak. The orange vest he'd stolen was out of sight. So was the hunter.

Rain pattered softly on the red-stained rocks, the only comforting thing in my narrow, steamy universe of river, cliff, cave, and sky. My brain told me I should think about collecting fresh water for later, but I didn't move. I couldn't move until I knew where Jacob was and if he'd spotted me leaving the water.

Come on, Jacob. Show yourself. The faintest hint of movement, that's all I need to start planning my escape. . . .

I waited. Jacob didn't cooperate.

And then, for the flimsiest of reasons, I smiled.

I'm not cooperating with you either, you bastard. I'm still alive.

7

Eldon Sprague parked his Dodge Ram in the turnaround above 27 Mile Rapid. "You coming?" he said to the man riding shotgun.

Benjamin Gruber disconnected a cell phone from the charger plugged into the dashboard. "In a minute. Want to see if I can get a signal. If not, I'll try the sat phone."

Sprague climbed stiffly to the ground. Slamming the door, he caught his reflection in the outside mirror and took a step back. An old man's face looked back at him. His father's face. Same high, broad forehead, widow's peak, receding hairline, and mane of wavy white hair. Same piercing blue eyes. Uncompromising eyes. When had he become his father?

He stretched the kinks out of his back and legs. Arthritis made his joints ache. The years had been hard on his body. Too many sleepless nights, worrying about the Family. Little things, like which sons to send away, which daughters were ready for sealing ceremonies, and which wife was fertile and waiting for his visit. Big things, too, of course—like overseeing the Family corporation, building new houses and warehouses, ferreting out who was plotting against him *this* month, and making sure all the welfare paperwork had been filed for newly eligible offspring.

In that last department it had been a good six months.

Nine new children, most of them girls. Only two things had marred the relative serenity of the community's life—neither of Ben's promised wives had stayed put long enough for a ceremony. After the wedding it would be Ben's job to see that his new wife honored the Principle, as he did with his other wives. But for Ben's family circle to increase, vows must first be taken.

From where Eldon stood at the edge of Marble Canyon, he couldn't see Navajo Bridge. But he turned and let his eyes follow the Vermilion Cliffs eastward to where they stopped abruptly not far from where the bridge crossed the canyon. Carrie, the first promised wife, had died there. By her own hand. Eldon had not seen her jump from the bridge. But he grieved her loss—the Family's loss.

Still, Carrie's rejection of the Family rankled. She'd been a loving child, seemingly content with their life. Of his fifty-three children, she'd been a favorite. Why had *she* chosen to break Celestial Law and damn herself for all eternity, rather than marry Ben?

Eldon Sprague, Prophet and Interpreter of the Truth, was determined that the same fate wouldn't befall Naomi. He would move heaven and earth till he found her and brought her home.

All around him, storm cells trailed wispy gray veils over the North Rim and the Navajo Nation across the river. The only sounds were the wind and occasional distant rumbles of thunder—and Ben, who had found a signal for his satellite phone. A shower had passed through this spot not long ago, and the gray rock and sand glistened as if millions of diamonds had been scattered across the surface. The scents of sagebrush, saltbush, and grass infused the humid air.

This is the day the Lord has made; let us rejoice and be glad in it.

The Prophet saw himself as a new Moses, leading his tribe out of the wilderness and establishing a homeland.

North of where he stood was the earthly paradise God had given his chosen people. A harsh land, but one that bore fruit when tended with care and discipline. All the Family wanted was to be left alone to follow their covenant in peace.

The chasm below was the dividing line between their land of milk and honey and the corrupting world to the south, west, and east—the twenty-first-century equivalent of Sodom and Gomorrah. The Family entered it only to sell their merchandise or buy goods they couldn't make themselves. At this distance Eldon could not hear the Colorado River. He never had. He'd never ventured down to river level, had never taken his children to play in the water, even when it was confined to Lake Mead or Lake Powell. He didn't swim.

Eldon put powerful binoculars to his eyes and scanned miles of the river, a narrow green line snaking between the roan, gray, and dun cliffs of Marble Canyon. He shivered, thinking about Carrie sinking into that cold green water.

He examined each raft, looking for a slim figure with long, reddish hair. She wouldn't be wearing the nightdress in which she'd left camp. He looked for the clothes his fourth wife found missing from their booth. He took his time but saw no likely candidates.

He wasn't even sure Naomi was on the river. He'd sent the rest of the family ahead to set up at the next fair in Salt Lake City. They'd put out the word that he was searching, and family members had asked questions where they could. Someone remembered seeing a long-haired girl, about the right age, stop at Cliff Dwellers Lodge with a group of rafters. It was a long shot, but worth checking out.

Naomi had been a dutiful daughter—obedient, quiet, productive, and God-fearing—right up until the day she left. Eldon believed at first that she'd been taken against her will, and they'd combed the park for her. He didn't inform the local police, but he alerted the sheriff back home, a member of the Family. And then the women discovered the shirt and hat missing from stock, things Naomi had designed and sewn.

Ben slammed the truck door and stumped over to stand beside Eldon. The Prophet saw so much of his younger self in Ben. At forty-five, Ben's thick hair was just beginning to show strands of silver. Another ten years, and it would be as thick and white as Eldon's. But in physique and temperament, they were worlds apart. Ben had short legs, a barrel chest, and massive shoulders and arms. His hands were clenched now, his dark eyes stormy.

Eldon's lieutenant had given vent to his anger a time or two, but his fits of temper were rare. And what counted most to the Prophet was Ben's quiet authority. He was Eldon's rod when faith and self-discipline weren't enough to keep a Family member in line.

"No leads," Ben said. "Any sign of her?"

Eldon shook his head and opened the truck door. "I suspect the group we're looking for is farther downriver. We'll drive to South Canyon, see what we see, and then go on to the point. Camp there."

"And if we spot them? You got a plan?"

"Working on it."

The skin tightened over Ben's jaw. Eldon put a hand on his shoulder.

"Trust in God, Ben. If he blesses your sealing, he'll lead us to her."

8

Mile 36, Bridge of Sighs, Marble Canyon
3:20 p.m.

I scanned the beaches and cliffs for Jacob, taking my time. My brain was stuck in a loop of questions for which I had no answers. *Who are you, Jacob? Why do you want to kill me? How did you learn my name? Did you overhear it as you followed us downstream? Did you bug my house in Tucson?* . . .

When I finally saw movement, it was much higher than I'd expected, and only for a moment. From his perch on the knob Jacob could survey a mile of the canyon—and keep an eye on the search-and-rescue operation that Nico would trigger as soon as he took a head count.

The storm and steep cliffs precluded any helicopter involvement for the moment. That meant two hours, maybe three, from the time my group returned to the raft from their hike. But when would that be?

The fossil beds were only a short distance up Nautiloid Canyon. Say thirty minutes for the group to reach the site, have a short geo-lecture from Dora, take photos, hike back, and climb into their vests. My watch said 3:26 p.m. I'd been gone for just over an hour. The team should be on its way. All I had to do was stay safely hidden until the cavalry arrived.

Unless Jacob finds me first.

He'd swarmed up that cliff in record time. He was

as good as Luke and Matt. Maybe better. One on one, I'd be no match for him, not with a bum shoulder and knee. I wouldn't be able to outrun or outclimb him. I'd have to outthink him. But my brain was as sluggish as a hibernating newt.

For a moment I'd forgotten about the rifle. Jacob was holding a handful of aces. I had a fistful of low cards and no chance at a straight or flush.

I sat still, trying to warm up. Dry clothes would help. But not yet. I needed a contingency plan.

To Jacob, the obvious places for me to hide were on the opposite side of the river, where the small beaches were. Another side canyon and debris fan lay directly across from my hiding place. Sure as the Redwall made caves, he'd scour every nook and cranny over there. Maybe a rattler would strike him. I should be so lucky.

I couldn't see him up on the knob, but the kayak hadn't moved. I was safe. For now.

With stiff, awkward movements, I shed my day-pack, field vest, shirt, and shorts. Underneath I wore a jungle-green tankini. I pulled that off, too, and draped everything over boulders to dry. I looked again at those boulders. They'd fallen from the ceiling.

Scrutinizing the uneven rock above me, I couldn't see any loose areas. But I knew that changes in temperature, an earthquake shock wave, or the pounding of a nearby flash flood could dislodge a chunk big enough to crush my head. For that matter, if it rained so heavily that my little gully became a stream, then I'd be dealing with different flood problems. But at the moment, I was more worried about Jacob and his rifle.

A tumble of boulders formed a crude barrier across the right side of the cave mouth. I hunkered down behind the wall's protective bulk. From this angle I had no view of the river, only of the Redwall cliffs and a sliver of sky. A shaft of sunlight pierced the clouds and painted a double rainbow on the fast-moving rain cell. Below it the limestone walls glowed crimson and gold.

I picked out a platform running from a point a few hundred feet above Jacob's vantage point to the tributary canyon across from me. Would Jacob climb farther up and follow the platform south until he could look across the river to the caves and the Bridge of Sighs?

I hadn't a clue what the maniac would do. My best option was to hide and watch. Let Jacob make the first move.

I tossed a few rocks out of my sandy nest, checked for dislodged scorpions, found none, and wiggled down into a more comfortable position. What was Philo doing right now? We hadn't spoken since I'd left Tucson on Saturday. Two and a half days. It seemed like a month.

I brushed an ant from my leg with naked fingers. Though I'd only worn my engagement ring for two months, I'd become used to the gold-and-garnet heaviness. But I'd left the family heirloom in Philo's office safe, unwilling to chance losing it. The soft waters of the Little Colorado River could slide a ring right off your finger.

I smiled. My cheeks, stiff and dry, felt as if they were cracking. If Philo were with me, this would be a lark. . . . Well, maybe not. Couldn't forget that rifle. But while we waited for rescue, Philo and I would have come up with a plan to outfox Jacob. . . .

Restless, I left the protective wall and eased into a position where I could see the river. The roar of water pulsated in the cave. I'd tuned it out, but now the river demanded attention, pounding in my head like the finale of the *1812 Overture*. Bass drums, brass band, cymbals, and cannon fire. The turbulent flow was shoving, dragging, carrying rocks and sand toward the Sea of Cortez, scouring the bed of the canyon. I put my hands over my ears, hoping to hear the steady rhythm of my heartbeat, but the waves of sound invaded my brain, my cells. I closed my eyes, took down my hands, and pressed two fingers over my carotid artery. Felt the pulse of circulating blood, the comforting surround sound a fetus hears and feels when it's in the womb . . . and overlying it, just for a moment, I thought I heard the *putt-putt* of a motor.

Couldn't be.

I opened my eyes and crab walked to a position with a better view. Hugging the protective shadows, I leaned right, then left, checking the river. The swift green water flowed almost due south in this part of the canyon. Ahead the course of the river became more sinuous, though not as contorted as the Goosenecks of the San Juan or the meandering Mississippi. A raft was just approaching the gentle bend that signaled 36 Mile Rapid.

One of ours?

I craned my neck. Same size and color. Same company. Someone small and slightly built at the helm— Roxy. And near her, hands on hips, scrutinizing river and shore, stood a compact shape. Luke. Even through the haze of rain, I recognized my brother and his red UA baseball cap.

Is that the first raft to pass or the second? Did I miss one?

The only reason both rafts would have proceeded downstream was if Doug, the third crew member, hadn't counted heads. I couldn't believe that had happened. But without being able to see Nautiloid Canyon from my cave, I couldn't know for sure.

What now? Climbing out wasn't an option. The ancient ones had found a way up through the sheer Redwall cliffs, but even if I located the route, Jacob would see me searching and climbing. There wasn't enough cover, and I'd have to move slowly on my gimpy knee. He'd be able to pick me off easily.

No, my way out was the river. Even injured, I should be able to move fast enough to hail the searchers.

Ay, there's the rub. No matter how careful I was, there'd be a lag time between when I signaled a boat and when that craft reached me. I'd be standing in the open, a cliff at my back, the river in front, a target painted on my chest.

Would Jacob risk shooting with the searchers around? If he did, there was no escape for him, not with so many witnesses clustered at the kill site and no practical way out but the river. Unless he had that covered, somehow . . .

Of course. All he had to do was take out the search-and-rescue team after he shot me. Two boats, max. Two searchers per boat. Sitting ducks on the water, if he were a decent shot. And if his military garb was a clue to his background, and not something picked up at an army surplus store, Jacob had experience with that rifle. He wanted to kill me. Would he stop at killing others?

Shit. That scenario applied to the people in our second raft, too—if they hadn't already passed by. A couple of well-placed bullets would capsize the boat. Passengers and crew would be in the water. At least one of the rafters wasn't a good swimmer. He'd panic. And even wearing life vests, how many would find their way to a safe harbor?

Showing myself could trigger a massacre. *Scratch that option.*

Only one avenue remained. I had to stay hidden till Jacob chose to leave. Or darkness fell. Or I dreamed up another way out of this mess.

Three dories passed by. Then a couple of rafts. I watched, helpless and pissed. In another couple of hours they'd be tying up at favorite camping spots. My party was heading for Nankoweap delta, seventeen miles downstream. If I'd been wrong, if they hadn't yet missed me, how long would it take them to reach camp? And when would they notice my absence?

I pictured last night's camp—storming the beach, dropping PFDs at tent sites, forming a human chain to unload the rafts, setting up tents. Washing bodies, hair, and clothes in the river. Communing at happy hour.

If both rafts had indeed continued on, then in the end-of-day hubbub Dora and Luke might not miss me till dinner. Dora would want to seek me out to discuss tomorrow's schedule while we ate. I was due to lead a hike up to the Anasazi granary and to the ancient ruins on the delta.

And when Dora didn't find me?

Luke and the guides would scour the camp. Only then would the skipper haul out the satellite phone and raise the alarm. But it would be dark. Search and rescue wouldn't begin looking till tomorrow morning.

Meanwhile, I'd be alone in this section of Marble Canyon with Jacob and his knife. And his goddamned rifle.

Who are *you, Jacob? How do you know my name? Why do you want to kill me?*

9

Mile 36.2, Marble Canyon
3:30 p.m.

Luke MacFarlane's raft entered the bend in the river at 36 Mile Rapid. He gave a last glance back toward the Bridge of Sighs, half hidden behind a veil of rain. Nautiloid Canyon, where Dora waited with the first raft, was already out of sight.

As a rule, rafting parties stick together. But they'd had no choice. The narrow canyon and inclement weather had prevented access to passing satellites. Every moment counted when someone was lost on the river.

Roxy had offered to take her raft, half the passengers, and Luke—a former guide—to 36 Mile Camp. The crew had selected that spot because it was only a mile or so from where Frankie had gone missing, and because the receding cliffs above offered a better chance of satellite reception. If that plan failed, they'd move on to Tatahatso Wash, which had a campsite large enough to accommodate twenty-six people. They'd all meet there tonight, once the search was launched—provided Roxy and Luke reached dispatch by sat phone.

The rain shower softened. The drops barely pocked the water surface as they landed. But the clouds wheeled above, and Luke could see another cell approaching. Roxy leaned to one side, then the other, easing the raft through choppy water, her eyes searching the east bank.

Where the hell did you get to, Sis?

For a moment, the guard he'd placed on his memories relaxed, the river and cliffs receded, and Luke was calling, calling, as he fought his way through walls of damp brush, branches snapping underfoot. A frigid wind moaned—

He shook it off. *Focus, Luke. Focus. . . .* Frankie had disappeared without a trace. No, that wasn't quite true. He'd found her camera on the outcrop. Had she accidently backed up too far when snapping a picture and tumbled into the river? Wouldn't be the first time. She'd fallen into more than one river, lake, and pool during their childhood years. But she was such a strong swimmer she'd never come to harm.

This was different. She'd left her PFD behind when she went for a walk. Surely Doug would have heard a cry for help. . . . But he hadn't. And if she'd climbed far enough onto the other raft to grab the missing vest, why hadn't she just stayed there?

Her camera images offered no clues. The last shot had been a close-up of a nautiloid, a mechanical pencil for scale. He'd located the fossil, twenty feet from the river's edge. She'd picked up the pencil. Dead end.

You'd better not be dead, Frankie. Shit, what would I tell Mom and Dad?

Luke stopped himself from going down that path, only to have one fear replaced by another. The muscles of his forehead and neck tightened. He felt as if he were caught in the crosshairs of a telescopic sight.

He tried to use logic to explain away the feeling. . . . Few hikers wanted the extra weight firearms and ammunition added to their loads. Water and food were more important. And no other crafts were in sight. The raft had passed a kayak, beached half a mile back, the owner presumably huddled under cover till the squall passed. But why would a boater carry a weapon when he couldn't hunt in the park?

Yet the feeling persisted. He remembered a hunting

trip when he'd accidentally entered the crosshairs of a novice hunter. Luckily, that man had been a bad shot.

Luke had felt a similar tightening when he and Matt were being stalked—once by a mountain lion, once by a bear. But there were no bears in the canyon. Mountain lions, sure, but downstream, after the river entered the Grand Canyon. Not here. The walls were too steep for anything but bighorn sheep and rock climbers. And the ghosts of the ancient ones.

Somewhere on river right was an Ancestral Puebloan ruin. If Frankie had gone into the river and floated this far, it was possible she'd climbed up there to recover.

He scanned the Redwall cliffs, buttressed against the cloudy sky. The ruin would be on top, with an unobstructed view up, down, and across the river. Perhaps that was where his hunted feeling originated—an energy left behind when the Anasazi abandoned the canyon more than eight hundred years ago.

Roxy waved to get his attention. He nodded and braced himself for the landing. She nosed the raft into the north side of the beach, river left, just shy of the rapids. He ran along a pontoon, grabbed the bowline, leaped off, and held the craft steady till Roxy cut the motor. Together they tied the line to a stake he pounded into the gravelly beach, then offered steadying hands to the passengers as they went ashore.

These rafters weren't part of Frankie's class, but they'd already formed a friendship of sorts with his sister, who tolerated their kibitzing on her geology lectures. Though they were, to a person, either staunch Creationists or leaning in that direction, they listened patiently and, except for one man, saved their questions for after-dinner discussions.

Tonight's discussion will have to be postponed, Luke thought. He refused to believe Frankie was on the bottom of the river, that there would be no more discussions, ever.

*I'd know if she were gone. I'd feel it. All I feel is . . .
frustration. And fear. But am I feeling* her *frustration
and fear, or my own?*

"Luke?" Roxy, standing a little ways away, had been
trying the sat phone. The rain dripped from the brim of
her Australian hat. She didn't seem to notice.

He walked to her side. "Any luck?"

She shook her head. Raindrops flew from her hat,
splashing his face.

Time for Plan B.

Turning as one, they studied the cliffs. A narrow cleft,
cut by runoff over untold millennia, provided the only
access through the Redwall Limestone. A thin stream
plowed its way down the bottom and across the alluvial
cone to the river. Higher up, the cliffs had been eroded
back to form a rough amphitheater. That was his goal.

"Nobody but a fool enters a narrow canyon when
there are storms on the rim," Roxy said.

"I know. But it's the only way. And if the stream does
flood, I'll be able to see it coming from above."

"Do you have the climbing skills for that?" Roxy lifted her chin toward the route to the top of the cliff. The
bottom of the cleft was lined with boulders. The first
part would be a scramble. The last part would require
a rope.

"Don't worry, I do this for a living. I brought my
gear." Luke traveled so light he had plenty of room for
ropes and a small selection of hardware.

"You lead climbing trips?"

"Used to." A bleak tide swept over him. He turned
away so that she couldn't see it on his face. "Will you
belay me?"

By the time Luke grabbed his gear off the raft, the squall
had passed. The rafters, huddled in the shelter of the
cliff, came out, knelt in a circle, and began praying. He
heard Harvey say Frankie's name. And his.

I'll take any help I can get.

Luke looked back to make sure Roxy was behind him before entering the cleft. The creek hadn't swollen, at least not much. "If I say run—"

"I'll run. Don't worry," she said.

He moved quickly, sliding around and over boulders, until he came to a giant chockstone blocking the canyon. No way around.

"Plan C?" Roxy said.

Plan C was Tatahatso Canyon.

"Not yet."

Luke jumped and grabbed a handhold. The limestone was rough as sharkskin, hot as asphalt fresh from the cooker. He dropped to the ground, stripped off his shirt, stuffed it into his daypack, and slipped on his climbing gloves. Now that the rain had stopped, the canyon was a sweatbox. He took a couple of swigs of water, then jumped for the handhold again. The climbing was a lot easier than El Capitan. Handholds everywhere.

In seconds, he was atop the chockstone, with a view up the tributary canyon. They'd lose valuable minutes going that route.

"You part mountain goat?" Roxy's voice echoed from the walls.

"Lipan Apache, three generations back." He looked down. Her tanned face was flushed. She fanned herself with her hat, dug a water bottle out of her pack, and half-drained it.

"I don't see or hear any flashfloods." He scuffed the chockstone with his right shoe. "But there are more of these ahead, blocking the trail. I'm going to free climb from here."

A frown pinched her forehead.

"Just toss me the phone." He caught it, tucked it in his pack, and said, "I'll be back in thirty minutes or less." He could tell by the look on her face that she didn't believe him, but that she desperately wanted to. "Go ahead, time me."

She smiled. "A beer says you can't make it in thirty."

"You're on."

"I'll wait up there on that ledge." She pointed to a shelf of rock thirty feet off the canyon floor. "Should be plenty high enough, even if a flood does come."

Luke nodded, then turned toward the opposite canyon wall. The boulder leaned toward canyon right. The route up the Redwall seemed easy enough. No need for a rope, except on the way down.

"Clock's ticking," she called.

Luke scaled the wall, which slanted slightly back and away. At one point he dangled by three fingers as his foot slipped on the rain-slick rocks. He used muscles he hadn't tapped in months. God, it felt good.

He levered his body over the Redwall lip. The limestone and siltstone of the overlying Watahomigi Formation weathered into a ledgy slope. The unit eroded more easily than did the Redwall cliffs, resulting in a natural trail that the Anasazi and earlier peoples used to traverse the canyon. He paused for a moment to try the phone. No signal. The canyon walls were still too close.

He didn't look at his watch, didn't want to know how quickly the time was passing. Starting out at a trot, he headed south on the trail. The sun broke through. Humidity soared. Light glared off the rock. The heat was a living thing. Well over a hundred degrees in the shade. But there was no shade. His stride lengthened into a ground-eating lope. He never took his eyes from the trail. One misstep would send him sliding into the canyon. He'd be no good to Frankie then. Or Dora.

Dora. She puzzled him. Intrigued him. Smart, competent, organized, focused, direct, caring. No nonsense, but very protective of her young students. She seemed comfortable in her skin, but wary—as if she didn't trust her innate appeal to the opposite sex. He wondered what event early in her life had caused her to wall off a part of herself. Maybe he'd find out before the trip was over. All Frankie had told him was how she and Dora had met in the middle of the Mojave Desert, after a madman had held Dora captive. Maybe that was the triggering event, though it was only nineteen months ago. She was thirty-nine now—

Rounding a corner, Luke skidded to a stop, nearly falling on his butt. A fresh rockslide covered the trail. He could see the headwall above, coinciding with the leading edge of the amphitheater. He didn't want to cross that slide. No margin for error. No backup.

He pulled out the satellite phone. Got through to park service dispatch on the first try. The connection was clear in the narrow canyon, but lasted just long enough for him to state the problem and relay his and Nico's positions. No time to ask them to alert the family or Killeen in Tucson. But they said they'd try to raise the first raft, waiting back at Nautiloid.

Luke's hands were shaking as he stowed the phone. He sank onto the path, drank water, and munched a handful of trail mix, legs dangling over the Redwall cliff, the Colorado River rushing by below. He considered the questions that had been hovering at the back of his mind for the last hour. Why would Frankie have left her camera on the outcrop before returning to the raft? And why would she take someone else's PFD, and not her own?

Rock walls gave no answer. Shouldering into his pack, he began running back along the rim trail, thinking about that missing PFD. No, his little sister didn't just fall off the raft. Something unexpected happened back there at Nautiloid.

Luke's gut twisted as a thought struck him. All the rest of the rafting party was accounted for, but had they all gone up the canyon to the fossil site? Someone might have stayed behind, might have heard or seen something. He'd check it out as soon as he hit the beach.

He slowed as he approached the tributary canyon. Roxy was sitting on her shelf, reading a book and eating an apple. She looked very small and far away.

"Well?" he called, giving her a thumbs-up.

She checked her watch. "Twenty-eight minutes, ten seconds. But you're not down yet."

He tossed her one end of the rope, looped the other around a substantial boulder, and lowered himself to the ground.

"Now you're just showing off," she said, striving for a light tone.

"But you owe me a beer."

"I'm good for it. . . . So, what's the plan?"

"The park service is sending SAR with two Zodiacs. They'll be at Nautiloid in a couple of hours, maybe less. They'll get the full info from Nico and Dora, camp there for the night, and get an early start tomorrow. Might be enough daylight to search a few miles of shoreline today. No promises."

"Then we'd better hustle our buns down to Tatahat-so, before somebody else claims it," she said, as they left the dark canyon. "I don't suppose you and Nico cooked up a Plan D in case the campground's occupied?"

He stopped. "They'll just have to share." Worry and frustration roughened his tone. "Leave it to me, Roxy."

10

Mile 36, Bridge of Sighs, Marble Canyon
4:45 p.m.

I watched a rainbow fade as, above me, the sun moved behind the Bridge of Sighs, casting an arcing shadow on the canyon walls. The cliffs turned a deep desert rose streaked with charcoal. The air was heavy with moisture evaporating from the rocks. My little cave felt like a sauna. Despite the damp heat, I shivered again.

Where is Jacob now?

As if I'd called him to me, I saw the kayak set off from the beach upriver. So he hadn't hiked along the platform. Maybe he didn't want to trespass onto the Navajo Indian Reservation without a permit. Whatever his reason, he was now paddling downstream.

He wore a helmet, but from the movement of his head I could tell that his eyes were shifting from the water to the riverbanks. He maneuvered the craft effortlessly, turning in a circle, tacking, slowing down. . . .

The angle of his head meant his eyes had found something in the tamarisks below me. Had I left something behind? Did he see the broken branches?

His helmet tilted up, turned. I could see a white logo and a word on the side, near the back: *SWEET*. The irony wasn't lost on me.

I shrank back, pressing against the cave wall as Jacob circled again. He gave a little shake of his head, located and dragged the orange vest from the water, and made for the delta across from me. Beaching his craft on the downstream side of the debris fan, out of sight from approaching river traffic, he hid the orange vest under the spray skirt. That done, he looked back again at the cliffs opposite. From my vantage point, the area below me looked pristine, empty. God knows how it looked to him as he took his helmet off, unlatched the sight from his rifle, and used it to examine the gully, the cliffs, and the caves above me. He took his time. I held my breath.

He reattached the sight, turned his back, and took out a backpacking stove. He poured liquid from a canteen into the pot, added dehydrated whatever, and set the pot on the burner. While his dinner heated, he searched the fan and ledges for signs of me.

I knew why Jacob was eating now. He possessed information I didn't. He knew whether both rafts had passed by or not. His actions suggested they'd split up—why, I didn't know. But my absence must have been noted. So Jacob was taking advantage of the lull before SAR arrived. He didn't want to answer questions, didn't want to appear on anyone's radar. He needed to stow his gear and be ready to move out ahead of the searchers. Or hide from them. He'd reveal his plan soon enough.

Watching him wolf down his food thirty minutes later, I salivated. I'd eaten only a light lunch. My body craved sustenance.

He rinsed the pot in the river, put away his cooking gear, and replenished his water supplies, zapping them with an ultraviolet purifier.

Definitely not planning to spend the night.

I remembered that he'd paddled quietly by our North Canyon camp the previous evening, nodding to me as he passed. He'd camped somewhere nearby, because I saw him only a couple of miles downriver this morning. He must have caught up to us at Redwall Cavern when we stopped for lunch. I didn't notice. I'd been talking to the students about cavern erosion and the geology we'd be seeing downstream.

I was only half-watching Jacob finish his chores when, with a clean jerk, he lifted the inflatable kayak and carried it up the fan toward the canyon.

What the hell?

He set the kayak down at the base of the cliff, screened by a rockfall. He was there for a minute before returning to brush out his tracks. Standing on a rock, he shouldered into his backpack and rifle, picked up the paddle and orange vest, and took one last look at the cook site. Nodding, he turned and retraced his route, hopping from rock to rock. He was munching on an apple. A green apple, I was sure, tart and crisp. I could taste it.

He disappeared into the shadows of the tributary canyon. I pondered his choice. The broad shelf atop the Redwall offered an escape route, north or south, should he need it. . . . Or perhaps he'd climb to a vantage point as he had before—a better position from which to keep an eye on the action below, or to see into the caves above me.

My safe haven now felt like a trap. If he climbed to the top of the Redwall, my little hole would be below him, but he'd see me descending the gully to the river. Any moving around I did would have to be in the next, say, thirty minutes, while he was out of sight in the canyon and getting into position. If not now, then I'd have to wait until dark.

But two could play this game. Growing up with four brothers and the family of my Apache godfather had taught me valuable lessons. The most important were patience in adversity and the refusal to see myself as a victim. No matter the situation, I would concoct some way to turn the tables.

Survival first. Then action.

Survival meant food and water. I'd swallowed a ton of river water, but the hot air would dehydrate me if I weren't careful. My skin already felt dry and gritty with river silt. The scraped areas burned. I needed to wash off and then tend to the abrasions so they wouldn't fester.

My shoulder hurt, but I could use my arm. The buzz had faded to a dull throb. Not so my knee. The pain relievers had worn off, and the swelling size had gone from grapefruit to cantaloupe. Maybe an icy dip would help.

I stuck my sandy feet back into river shoes and edged out of the cave. Inky shadows cloaked the bottom of the canyon. My skin, tanned a dark bronze, would not stand out against that background. Even the tan lines would add protective coloration and pattern.

Keeping my eyes on the cliffs above, I climbed down, circumvented the tamarisk thicket, and inched into a small, sheltered, water-carved inlet. Gasping as the cold lapped my skin, I rinsed my hair and body, careful to not stir up finer particles. Standing, I stepped around the dolomite ledge and into the current, then drank until I was full. I had a water bottle in my daypack, but it would have to last till Jacob left.

I was turning to climb back up when I saw something blue floating in the river, trapped by the tamarisk branches. A life vest. Nico had lost his last night. He'd knocked it off the raft in the dark.

This couldn't have been what had captured Jacob's attention. If he'd seen it, he would have paddled over to check . . . unless he'd left it there as a decoy, something to draw me out if I were still alive and holed up on this stretch of shore.

A dilemma. If I took it, I might alert Jacob that I was here. If I didn't, I'd lose the option of a water escape. I grabbed the vest and climbed the slope, knee screaming at every step.

Back in the cave, I sank behind the rock wall. My Timex Expedition had taken a beating, but the hands still chugged around the dial. *Five-forty-seven.* The raft crew would be serving dinner in another hour or two. Pork chops, mashed potatoes, and gravy. I could almost smell it. . . .

Find something to eat before you start hallucinating. I could survive for days as long as I had water. But food would raise my spirits.

My shirt was dry—my body, too, except for my hair. I braided that, finishing it off with a rubber band from my field notebook. I spread the shirt on a patch of sand, sat, and began inventorying the pockets of my Filson vest. The vest had a few tears but was in decent shape, though now stiff with silt. The back pocket held my hat, a coral-colored bandana, and the leg pieces that zipped onto my shorts. I'd stowed them there this morning. I always kept them with me in case my legs started to sunburn. I unfolded the bandana and laid it, the hat, and the pant legs over a boulder to dry. In a front pocket I found a plastic bag with beef jerky and a Luna bar, left over from my last field trip. The rafting guides had advised us not to carry food in our packs. Food attracted mice, ravens, and ants. I was glad I hadn't bothered to check my pockets for stale rations. The salted jerky would help me stay hydrated. I set the Luna bar aside for later.

I had shelter and a little food. My health was reasonably good, for the moment. But drinking unboiled river water was ill-advised, and I might already have ingested parasites. I had a liter of water in my stainless-steel bottle. And I could use the bottle to boil river water—once Jacob was gone. Until then, I couldn't risk lighting a fire, even if I found wood. The smoke or glow would give away my location.

I chewed slowly on a piece of jerky while I examined the contents of the day pack. Lip balm. I used it. Sunscreen. Swiss Army knife. Sunglasses. Two mechanical pencils. A damp Rite-in-the-Rain field notebook. The Leatherman multitool Philo had given me before I left. Tiny first-aid kit in a plastic bag. Inside I found two little packets of aspirin. I opened one and washed down the pills with water. Then I spritzed my scraped shoulder with antibiotic ointment. It stung like hell.

I pulled out my old Brunton compass. Wet, but undamaged. I might need the mirror to signal a rescue craft. I opened it and set it on the sand to dry. Found chewing gum in the bottom of the pocket. Gum kept the saliva flowing on desert hikes. These sticks were gritty, but I kept them anyway.

Only one thing left to inspect. The PFD. I found Nico's name, address, and phone number written in bold felt pen inside the neckline. The vest was new, and he'd lamented losing it. Wouldn't *he* be surprised when I turned up wearing it.

Hold that thought, Frankie. Hold it tight.

I felt a lumpy area in back of the vest. Inside a zip pocket was a fifteen-liter dry bag. I unrolled the yellow sack to find a handful of Tootsie Roll Pops, an unopened pack of Marlboros, and a disposable lighter. Pity I didn't smoke, but the cigarettes would make perfect tinder, if I had anything else to burn.

And if Jacob would do me the huge favor of quitting this canyon.

I studied the dry bag, wondering what I could use it for. The top folded over itself and then locked with a plastic clasp. Closed, the loop worked as a handle. The sack was water-resistant, which meant it could also carry water, though I'd have to come up with a secondary closure to prevent leakage.

So what did I have now that I didn't have an hour ago? A PFD to help keep me from drowning if I reentered the river, some sugar for energy and to keep the saliva flowing, and a way to transport water. Two ways, I amended—the candy and beef jerky had been enclosed in a small plastic bag.

To leave, or not to leave, that is the question.

If I waited till morning, and Jacob stayed, he'd shoot me when I emerged from the cave to signal a passing craft. He might miss. He might also hit one or more of the passengers or rescuers.

If I left the cave tonight, and he had a night scope, there was a good chance he'd nail me. But at least I'd be moving, not pinned down.

But where would I go? I'd studied the river guide last night. The booklet showed topography, rapids, and elevation drop at each rapid. Just around the bend lay 36 Mile Rapid. Four-foot drop. Category 4. At night, even in a PFD, I might not survive the run. Depended entirely on whether I could avoid the pockets and whirlpools.

I'd never smoked, but God, was I temped to start.

And then I heard the *whuff*ing of a helicopter, flying low over the canyon. The search-and-rescue team. They'd be dropped off at a safe spot upriver, deploy their gear, then motor down to be briefed by Nico and Dora.

My spirits soared, then crashed. Jacob would have reached his rocky lookout by now. If I showed myself, I was dead. So were the SAR rangers. And the rafters who were waiting for them at Nautiloid Canyon.

11

Molly McKuen had watched Roxy for the past two days, fascinated by her skill at handling the raft in the rapids. Roxy had let her help in the kitchen, once Molly showed she was comfortable cooking for a large group. This morning, she'd learned how to make eggs to order, breaking the yolks upon request, cooking them over hard, or sunny-side up, or scrambled. She had to keep an eye on the bacon and sausages, toast and bagels, too. Molly had never seen such abundance.

"You'd make a good short-order cook," Roxy had said, taking over the spatula.

"Or a guide?"

Roxy looked her over and nodded. "I started swamping when I was sixteen. How old are you?"

Molly hesitated, unsure how to answer without revealing she was an imposter. The real Molly McKuen had left the trip in Albuquerque, when her dad broke his ankle. It was pure coincidence that Naomi had called Dora's cell number that same day, begging for help. Dora had come up with the plan to have Naomi take Molly's place. But the crew didn't know. And now Roxy was asking her age, and Naomi hadn't a clue when Molly's birthday was.

Molly decided it was safer to stick to the facts of her

life as Naomi Sprague. Then she couldn't be caught out in a lie.

"I'm sixteen," she said. "Just. My birthday was Friday."

"Sweet Sixteen! Then we'll need a cake tonight. I'll show you how to bake one in a Dutch oven."

With Frankie missing, Molly thought Roxy would forget her promise. But the guide seemed to understand that making comfort food was a good way to deal with tension and uncertainty. When the rafters had finished unloading the gear from the raft, Roxy told Molly to meet her back at the kitchen area in thirty minutes.

At Molly's campsite, the red ants still bustled about. She hoped they'd quiet down as soon as the sun set, like they had last night.

Molly thought about her future as she helped Dora set up the tent and lay out the sleeping mats. She had found Dora's name and phone number in Ethan's pocket, when she was doing the laundry a few months ago. She didn't tell anyone, just copied the number down before handing it back with his clean clothes. He'd been crying. His father, Elder Ben, was sending Ethan away in the morning. Adam's mother had given him the number. She made sure all the boys had it before they left.

Dora's daughter and son-in-law, Annie and Paul, had left their child with Paul's parents in Austin and flown to Flagstaff to meet Naomi Sprague. Rescuing her was that important to them. It was then she knew she'd made the right decision in calling Dora.

Naomi had expected to drive straight to Austin. But Dora, Annie, and Paul feared that the roads were being watched. They remembered what had happened when Carrie ran away. They wanted to wait until they'd transformed Naomi into Molly, someone unrecognizable to the Family. And until the hunt for her had cooled down. They argued that no one in the Family traveled on the river. They'd never look for her there. And so Molly had embarked on a whitewater adventure, and the transformation had begun.

"You can be anything and anyone you want to be," Dora had told her when they'd met at Cliff Dwellers Lodge in Marble Canyon. "For this trip, you're Molly McKuen. When we get home, you can call yourself whatever you like. A new name for a new life . . . What do you like to do?"

Molly hadn't been sure how to answer. A world crowded with possibilities was almost as frightening as one with none.

"I don't know what I like to do, besides making quilts and clothes. I'm told to cook and sew and take care of the young ones. In the Family, you do what you're told."

Dora's smile was part grimace. "I remember."

"But you got away."

"Not in the sense you mean."

"What?"

"I was fifteen and pregnant. I would have done almost anything to escape from the man who raped me and forced me to marry him."

Molly stared. "Raped you? A man from the Family?" She noted the warning look Dora gave Annie, who was unpacking the things she and Paul had bought at the Walmart in Page. This was a touchy subject.

"I'm sorry," Molly said. "It's none of my business."

"It *is* your business. I just wasn't prepared. The boys don't know I was born into the Family. They think I'm just a compassionate stranger who opened her house to them. Safer for Annie and me that way—and for the boys."

"This man who, um . . ." Her voice petered out.

"Ben Gruber." Dora said the name as if spitting a mouthful of dirt. "Father had one of his revelations, and I didn't have a say. I ran away, again and again. Ben kept finding me. I even ran away the night of the sealing ceremony. That was the last straw. Father decided I was incorrigible and abandoned me."

"You mean he just dropped you off somewhere?"

Dora nodded. "In the mountains. On the day after Thanksgiving. No coat. No food. It was snowing."

"Then how—"

"I stumbled on a hunters' camp—Bill and Dot Simpson. They wanted to take me to the authorities, but I wouldn't go. I was too afraid of being sent back to the compound. The local sheriff had ties to the Family."

"Still does," Molly said. "So the Simpsons took you home with them?"

"To Glenwood Springs. That's in western Colorado."

"They sound like good people."

"The best. They'd lost their daughter to leukemia the year before. She was about my age. After they did their own research into the Family, saw what I was up against, they more or less adopted me. Told friends I was their niece. They let me stay in their daughter's room, wear her clothes. I used her birth certificate to get a driver's license. They helped me get my GED and find a job."

"What's a GED?"

"General Equivalency Diploma. If you pass the test, you've graduated from high school. Anyway, I lived with them till Annie was two. An old friend of theirs offered me a job in his geophysical exploration company, so Annie and I moved to Austin. Dot Simpson gave me her car when we left." There were tears in Dora's eyes. She brushed them away.

"And after that, you really were on your own."

"I had Annie. And the Simpsons stay in touch. You'll find you make your own family."

Making a family. Molly hadn't thought that far ahead. She'd been more concerned with finding a safe haven.

Molly watched in the bathroom mirror as Annie, a

hairdresser, cut her long russet hair. First the heavy braid fell to the sheet covering the floor. Then Annie began to trim and shape the hair.

"From a distance, you'll pass as a boy," Dora said. "Safer that way."

Molly didn't want to think about Ben or the Prophet searching for her. She studied the stranger in the mirror, expecting at any moment to be reprimanded for paying attention to her looks. Annie worked black dye into the short hair. As they waited for the color to set, Annie set out stencils and a bottle of henna on top of the dresser. Temporary tattoos—all part of the Molly McKuen disguise.

"How did you become a geologist?" she asked Dora, who was watching the transformation from the doorway.

"I got interested while I was working for the exploration company. When Annie was in high school, I started taking night classes at the community college. By the time she graduated, I'd discovered I was good at geology and paleontology. One of the teachers helped me find a program that suited my interests. I finished my degree at UC Del Rio. That's where I met Frankie MacFarlane. She's filling in for Dr. McKuen. You'll meet her at dinner."

"I don't know what UC means."

"University of California."

"But you live in Texas now?"

"When Annie and Paul had the baby, I decided to go to graduate school in Austin so that I could be close to them."

That was something Molly understood. She loved her sisters and brothers, especially the little ones. "Were you making *your* family when you started taking in the boys?"

Dora smiled. "I hadn't thought of it that way, but you're right. When Adam was sent away, they left him at the Austin fairgrounds with the clothes on his back, twenty dollars in his pocket, and his older brother Julius's address. Julius and I belong to the same church in Austin."

"I liked Julius. He was nicer to me than some of the other boys. Do any of my brothers know you once belonged to the Family?"

Dora shook her head. "You're the first person I've shared it with, other than Annie, Paul, and the Simpsons. It's the only way we could be safe. And it wasn't hard to keep the secret. I lived under an assumed name. I was supposed to be dead."

"Father never mentioned you."

"Not surprising. I disappeared the year Julius was born, and he's the oldest of the boys who relocated in Austin. All he knew when we met at church was that I had a spare room. He explained the situation and asked if I could put Adam up for a while. That's pretty much how it started. Julius sent the cell number to his mother. Told her it was a rooming house. Which was the truth."

"It must have gotten crowded, once Bobby, Craig, and David showed up. And Ethan."

"It did." Dora laughed and tucked a strand of brown hair behind her ear. "So I bought a house with five bedrooms and a huge kitchen. Don't worry, there's space for you."

Molly relaxed. "The boys go to school?"

"I tutor them till they catch up with their current grade levels or pass their GEDs. And I help them get official government identifications. You can't work or go to school without them. It means getting copies of your birth certificate, getting a driving permit, learning to drive—"

"I'll get to drive?"

"Of course."

"Women in the Family—"

"Aren't allowed to drive. I know. They're afraid more of us might leave."

Annie rinsed Molly's hair and toweled it dry. The cut

made her look very young. A quick brushing revealed unknown cowlicks and natural waves.

"It suits your gamine face," Annie said.

Molly wasn't sure what that meant, but it sounded okay. She ran her hand over her head. She'd never realized how heavy long hair was.

Annie slipped a silver-colored ring over Molly's right nostril. The nose ring drew attention away from her eyes, making her feel safer. Annie held up the stencils for the henna tattoos. "Last decision for the night, except what you want to eat for dinner."

Molly chose a pattern of vines and flowers to run from the backs of her hands up to her elbows. Giggling, she held out her right arm. "No one will recognize me after this—not even my mother."

Annie smiled. "That's the point."

That had been two nights ago. Molly hadn't realized how much a person could change in two short days. When she'd put her braid in an envelope for a charity that made wigs for cancer patients, she felt that shy, submissive Naomi had been sealed in with the hair.

Now, with every mile down the river, Molly learned more about the girl who'd hidden her light under a bushel of long hair, long sleeves, and ankle-length skirts. She was coming to like that girl as much as she liked her borrowed name.

Molly. It suited her. She just might keep it when the trip was done.

Once she'd set up the sleeping area, Molly grabbed biodegradable soap and shampoo and ran down to the beach. The water was cold, but she loved the feeling of clean skin and hair. After changing into dry clothes in the tent, she spread her wet things over rocks that still held the heat of the day. When she reached the cooking area, Roxy was setting out a cake mix, eggs, oil, and water. Molly had only made cakes from scratch. This seemed a lot easier.

Molly finished stirring the cake batter and poured it into the cast-iron Dutch oven.

She smiled at Roxy. "Thank you for teaching me."

"You make it fun for me, too." Roxy set the pan on the stove to cook. "This'll take a while. You have time to catch up on your notes before dinner."

Molly collected her notebook and went to sit by the rushing water. Was Frankie sitting by the river, too, watching the flaming light on the cliff tops? Or had her life, like Carrie's, been claimed by the rushing river?

Molly missed Frankie. She answered any question about the rocks and fossils, no matter how basic or silly. Frankie, Luke, and Dora talked to Molly as an equal, an intelligent adult. Most remarkable of all, they and the rest of the group weren't being nice out of fear of the Prophet or his rod, but because they were generous of spirit. The outside world was not the den of iniquity and ugliness her parents and the elders said it would be.

She'd begun to question other things she'd been taught, too. Now that she'd walked up a few canyons and had seen fossils in the rocks, she sensed the time represented in the canyon walls. Frankie had shown her a drawing of this canyon from nearly a century and a half ago. It looked identical to a picture she'd taken yesterday on Dora's camera. That suggested that the Earth changed and rocks formed and weathered very slowly. Six thousand years just didn't seem like enough time for the carving of this canyon.

Molly shook her head, feeling sad and empty, as if her old world had been built on sand. One good earthquake and the walls had collapsed. It would take years to lay a new foundation. Maybe a lifetime.

12

Mile 36, Bridge of Sighs, Marble Canyon
6 p.m.

The two SAR searchers in the motorized Zodiac seemed close enough to touch as they checked the tamarisk thicket below my cave. Another team scouted the far shore. I felt an overwhelming urge to break cover and call to them.

And then what? If I moved, Jacob would shoot me and any witnesses. I couldn't risk it.

Time to play possum, Frankie. Philo's voice echoed in my head. I wondered if I'd see him again.

Forty minutes ago, I'd seen Nico guide our second raft safely downriver. Good. The whole party was beyond the range of Jacob's bullets.

I leaned my head against the warm sandstone wall, watching the searchers circle for another pass around the debris fan. For a moment I thought they'd spotted Jacob's kayak, secreted in a channel at the base of the cliff. I willed my heartbeat to slow, as if the thumping could be heard above the roar of the river. They didn't put in.

I breathed again as the boats passed slowly from sight around the curve of 36 Mile. Tomorrow a shore search would begin. Could I sit tight and wait till Jacob moved on? No. He wouldn't go without checking out the caves on this side of the river. He'd do it tonight, under cover of darkness. It's what I'd do.

Night was a couple of hours away, but twilight already touched the canyon depths. Like Jacob, I couldn't move until darkness hid me. In the time that remained, I began to write notes. If I died tonight, at least I might point Philo, Dora, Luke, and the rest of my family in the right direction.

I picked up my field notebook and pencil and began with Jacob's description. Then, skipping a line, I wrote, *1. Who is Jacob?*

He'd mentioned Jacob's Lake, a town at the juncture between Highway 89A and State Route 67, which led to the North Rim viewpoints. So he was familiar with the Arizona Strip, the remote area bounded by the Colorado River on the south and east, Utah on the north, and Nevada on the west. But was he a resident of the Strip? The region was home to polygamous Mormon sects, renegade break-off groups, and self-sufficient ranchers. It was like a separate country. I had no ties to it, no contacts there. But members of my family might. Or Philo . . .

2. Jacob wore a scruffy military shirt. Is he someone from Philo's past who wants to hurt him by hurting me? I couldn't rule it out. Philo must have alienated a host of people over the years during clandestine military operations and his P.I. work.

And Philo wasn't the only person in my life who had pissed people off. Killeen had worked in military intelligence. I had friends in law enforcement. At least one had been in the military police. And one of my brothers is a lawyer. Lawyers make enemies. The list was long, and I couldn't pursue the thread while I was sitting naked in a cave. I put a star next to that question and skipped another line.

3. How did Jacob know my name? Admittedly, he'd hesitated, framing it as a question. He'd mentioned that I looked taller in person than I'd looked from the river. So he'd been watching me. Or the group. Had he simply heard someone call my name as he paddled past our camp or one of our geology stops? Possibly. But that wouldn't explain why he decided to kill me—unless he was a nut job who didn't need a reason. But would a nut job be so persistent?

Maybe. If the motivation was strong enough. Or if someone had paid him to kill me.

The pieces fit. He'd shadowed our rafts down the river, as if waiting for an opportunity to strike. He'd asked me to take off my hat to confirm he had the right person.

But who had hired him? The person who'd bugged my house? Was he or she directing traffic from behind the scenes? Or was Jacob my intruder, the person who'd stolen the photograph?

I wrote, *4. Identify my intruder.* I put a star next to that question, too.

And then, *5. Did I—or Philo, Killeen, or one of my family members—provoke someone enough that he hired a killer to follow me into the Grand Canyon?*

However improbable and implausible the scenario, it was possible.

13

**Near South Canyon Point, North Rim,
above Marble Canyon**
6:15 p.m.

Eldon Sprague and Ben Gruber had driven deeper into House Rock Valley over kidney-jarring roads, stopping at two vantage points. They'd seen no one who looked like Naomi.

From the rim at Buck Farm Canyon they picked their way cross-country toward South Canyon Point. When they could drive no farther, they'd strapped on packs and split up. Ben had headed for a sheltered spot to set up camp and start a cook fire—illegal, but who was going to stop him?

Eldon cut over to the rim. A thumb of land jutted out to a magnificent overlook. Pulling a trail map from his pocket, he located himself by the tributary canyon across from him. Nautiloid Canyon. Camp gear formed a mound on the little beach, but no one was around. Eldon could see the insignia on one box. National Park Service. Search and Rescue. Maybe these same men had pulled Carrie from the river—if she'd ever surfaced.

He didn't want to dwell on Carrie, shut out of heaven and the opportunity to people a new kingdom in the stars with Ben and his other wives and children. Ben was late to the Family, not born to it, but he believed passionately in their way.

Eldon shook his head at the waste of it all, and

trudged on, thinking about the two searchers he'd sent to the South Rim to look for his daughter. Those men were just as committed as Ben to serving Eldon's ministry. He'd ordered them not to cross the Navajo Reservation because he didn't want them caught without the proper permits. Getting permits required identification. This search had to be carried out in secret. Publicity would not be good for the Family. They would have to curtail travel until the fuss died down. Or be more discreet.

Yet it was possible that one of them had disobeyed Eldon's orders. The Marble Canyon rim directly across from him was accessible by road. You could stand on the rim and look two thousand feet down to the river. If one of his men had shown initiative—or given in to the temptation to take the easier route across reservation land—Eldon hoped he'd used a fake I.D. All the elders had them. They made escaping from sticky situations easier.

Eldon had used his fake passport to enter Mexico on several occasions. He rather liked being "Joseph Green, El Paso, Texas." He did own houses there, and businesses—a Laundromat, a garage, an orchard, and a greenhouse. In that warmer climate, the Family grew fruit and vegetables year round, something Eldon hadn't been able to accomplish in their northern Arizona compound.

A movement below caught his attention. He scanned the river with the glasses, then the trail paralleling the river several hundred feet above the water. Nothing. But on a bit of beach, almost hidden at the base of a cliff, he saw a splotch of orangey-red. He traced the outlines. A long, slender kayak. And partway up the cliff, half-hidden by a thumb of rock, he spotted a man, lying prone. He was studying the cliffs across from him with a rifle sight. Eldon couldn't tell if it was one of his men, but if so, he seemed to be taking his duties seriously. Praise the Lord.

Eldon hiked on, stopping finally at the southernmost tip of the peninsula. He could see two rafts below him camped near Tatahatso Wash. Sunlight had left the canyon bottom, but Eldon could see well enough to pick out details. Two separate groups. One large, one small. The members of the larger group sat in a circle on green chairs. None wore hats. A few looked to be in their teens or twenties. Several were women. He studied the faces, the shapes of their heads, their clothes—shorts and T-shirts. Bare legs and arms.

How odd. None of them are laughing or smiling. They look as if there's been a death in the family . . . or as if the search team is looking for one of their group.

That had to be it. He said a quick prayer for the lost traveler, then checked again to make sure Naomi wasn't part of the circle.

Satisfied that she wasn't, he turned his attention to the smaller group. . . . He started, and almost slipped over the edge. Backing up, he lay down on his belly, inching forward until he could see over the brink. The sun was low behind him, but the rocks still radiated heat. Sweat dripped from his face and neck. He shook it out of his eyes and looked again at the small cluster of people.

Six young men had their backs to him. They wore khaki pants or shorts and long-sleeved shirts, the sleeves rolled up to their elbows. The four tallest had pale hair that seemed to glow in the shadows. The fifth had brown hair. The last wore a wide-brimmed hat with a back flap that covered his neck.

The first five boys—four of his sons, and one of Ben's—he'd sent away because they were competition for wives. He recognized the shape of their heads, the set of their shoulders. He'd heard through the grapevine that they'd gone to live in Texas. Fine. They could live and work anywhere they chose, as long as they didn't try to return to the compound. This must be a school or church outing of some sort. They wouldn't have the money to pay for it, so they must have accepted charity.

He couldn't identify the boy in the hat. Too scrawny to be one of his. And too young to have been sent away. The boy could be no more than eleven, twelve at the outside. Perhaps he was the son of the woman who faced them near the river's edge. Eldon could see her features clearly. Late thirties. Small-boned. Light brown hair caught back in a ponytail. Delicate features. Olive-skinned like his second wife, Linda, God rest her soul. She'd run away to Las Vegas with their daughter, Esther—had found a job as a hotel maid, where her Spanish helped. The job didn't pay enough to support her and a ten-year-old child, so she'd sold her body. Eldon's spies told him she'd turned to alcohol. When Eldon finally sent two men to fetch Esther, they reported that her mother was almost comatose, in no shape to fight them for her daughter.

He hadn't thought about Esther in ages. She would be thirty-eight now—no, thirty-nine. Her birthday was July 4, the same as his. She had been fifteen when he promised her to Ben Gruber as a first wife, soon after Ben joined the Family. Esther had pleaded with her father, saying she wasn't ready for marriage. She'd run away. Ben brought her back—but not until he'd anticipated the sealing ceremony.

Eldon had disciplined her and locked her in a room. Ben had joined her there. The words were spoken, though Esther had been mute. And on their wedding night, after Ben was asleep, she'd run away again. She didn't get far. But she swore it would happen again and again, until she was dead or free.

In theory, she was Ben's problem. But her continued mutiny affected the entire compound. Eldon had prayed to God for a solution. The answer came to him in a dream.

Like Abraham with Isaac, Eldon had bound Esther and taken her up into the mountains. He could still see her in the rearview mirror as the snow started to fall. No tears. No pleading. He'd consigned her to God's hands, and she'd welcomed her fate.

He took another look at the woman's face, so like his late wife's. . . . But if Esther hadn't died on the mountain, word would have leaked back to him from one of his contacts in the outside world. Unless someone had sheltered her, given her a new name.

Anger blinded him for a minute. He wasn't sure whether he was angry with God or with some anonymous person who might have interfered with his Prophet's plans. Eldon prayed, and felt a wave of calm wash over him.

He turned his thoughts again to the woman in the canyon. If that was Esther, she must feel secure in her assumed identity, sure that the Family had forgotten all about her. She'd been gone for nearly a quarter of a century. She would have protected herself by staying silent. Eldon would bet that his sons didn't know who she was or where she came from.

Standing, he took one last look at the rafts below. Memorized the numbers on their sides. He and Ben would track the group tomorrow. If Naomi was with them—

Another surge of anger. His head throbbed. If Naomi was on the river, he knew how and when to retrieve her.

But what should he do about Esther?

Eldon decided to say nothing to Ben until he was sure of Esther's identity. Old eyes played tricks. Tomorrow. Tomorrow was soon enough. He'd look for both girls in the morning.

14

Mile 36, Marble Canyon
6:25 p.m.

Jacob studied the cave-riddled cliffs opposite. They resembled a house with open windows. Good places to hide.

The picture blurred. His head hurt, and his eyes were playing tricks on him. Squinting to clear them didn't help. He saw his brother and sister, roped together, climbing the cliffs on the other side of the river. Jenny tugged on the rope, laughing as she looked up at Sean. He told her to quit playing around. They were climbing toward the Bridge of Sighs. Ironic. The original Bridge of Sighs, in Venice, Italy, had connected light and life with darkness, unbearable pain, and the welcome release of death. Jacob, too, inhabited a dark world. He'd lived there for months.

He lowered the sight he'd detached from Sean's AR15 and looked at his hands. They'd begun to tremble.

Strong, capable hands. Deft fingers, with the power to heal the body. But not the mind. And certainly not the soul.

Timing was everything. You had to reach casualties in time, or you didn't have a chance to heal them. And Jacob had been too late. When they'd needed him most, he'd been too far away, in every sense of the word.

He swallowed a couple of aspirin to ease the pain.

When he looked back at the cliffs, the vision was gone. He felt bereft.

He trained the scope on the river, looking for the patch of blue he'd spotted earlier, caught in the tamarisk and willow. Couldn't see it now. And the search boats hadn't stopped there to pick anything up. But their wakes might have dislodged it. Or maybe it, too, had been an illusion.

He hoped the woman had drowned. If so, he regretted only one thing in the way he'd handled today. He wished he'd told her why she had to die.

15

Mile 37.9, Tatahatso Campsite, Marble Canyon
6:40 p.m.

Luke left camp and hiked a short way up Tatahatso Wash, stopping at a boulder that looked like a
dozen giant tortoises stacked on top of each other. He
climbed to the top. The sky above had cleared tempo-
rarily, but it might be raining to the east. If the canyon
flooded, he'd wait it out from his perch.

To the west he could see a slice of the Colorado and
the Tatahatso debris fan. The river was an indigo snake
reflecting the deepening sky, its roar muffled by the
canyon walls. He was tempted to climb to the top of
the Redwall for a better view. He could follow the trail
north, back to 36 Mile, or even to Nautiloid Canyon if
he wanted. Do a little checking on his own. But by the
time he reached the trail, it would be pitch-black out.
Frustrating.

He could almost hear Frankie laughing and saying,
"Let it go, Luke," in her best Obi-Wan Kenobi imita-
tion.

Luke let it go. If she was alive, he couldn't do anything for her tonight. And if not . . . He slammed that
mental door, unwilling to contemplate a world without
his sister.

He refocused on the canyon. This was one of the two

times of day he liked best—first light, with all its potential energy and mystery, and last light, when alpenglow tinged the peaks and cliffs with red, mauve, and gold. In those rare times when he was alone at dusk, he loved to take stock of what he'd accomplished that day. And what he hadn't. Today had started with promise and laughter, ended with despair. He dreaded what tomorrow would bring, yet wished the next ten hours would fly by.

Ten hours. The past year had shown him how precious every moment was—how one could be alive, vibrant, and playful one instant, gone the next. He was terrified that had happened to Frankie.

Below him, Dora picked her way through the boulder-strewn canyon, heading for his chockstone. Scrambling up to sit beside him, she put her hand on his. Comfort. He turned his hand over and interlaced his fingers with hers. She didn't draw away.

Luke had once asked his older brother, Kit, how he'd known Lara was the right woman for him. Kit had said he'd known the first time they watched a sunset together. Lara didn't ruin it with talk. She just took his hand as if they'd known each other for years, instead of hours.

Dora didn't speak, but Luke sensed a tension hovering about her. Not sexual tension, though that might be part of it. This seemed more like the strain that precedes a difficult conversation. It couldn't be about Frankie. If they'd found her, he'd have heard the shouts.

"I need to tell you something," she said.

"Your students are all related?"

She laughed. Her shoulders relaxed. "How'd you know?"

"Four of the boys look enough alike to be brothers, and the youngest one slipped and called you 'Sister Dora.' Now, I know you're not a nun, so I'm guessing those kids are either LDS or a fundamentalist sect of some kind."

"I'd give you a B-minus, Sherlock. You missed a few clues." Dora looked up at the cliffs as she told him about her history with the Family. And about Molly. "Her real name is Naomi. Eldon Sprague fathered all of us except Ethan."

It explained a lot. Molly's near-silence and her wonder over every new experience, as if she'd just been hatched. Not at all like a professor's daughter who's been out in the world since day one. It explained the contrast between the white skin of Molly's arms, legs, and neck, and her tanned face. It explained Dora's protectiveness.

"Does Frankie know? And the crew?"

"No."

"What's Molly's natural hair color?"

"Russet."

"Whose idea was the Goth look?"

"My daughter Annie's. Naomi now looks a lot more like the real Molly McKuen. And the tattoos are temporary."

Luke smiled. "They've already begun to fade."

"I know. I'm going to touch them up tonight."

"But why escape by river? Wouldn't it have been easier and quicker to put Molly on a plane to Austin?"

"To fly, you have to have a picture ID. Or, if you're underage, a parent or guardian has to vouch for you. Molly doesn't have a driver's license or a copy of her birth certificate. Annie and Paul aren't old enough to be accepted as her parents, and they have no paperwork declaring them her legal guardians. Neither do I. Plus, I was already committed to this river trip."

"What about the bus or train, or having Annie and Paul rent a car and drive her home?"

"There are security systems in all those places. Molly's half-sister, Carrie, ran away from a fair in Aspen last month, to avoid marrying Ben Gruber. Their local sheriff put out an interstate be-on-the-lookout alert for her as an underage runaway. It went to all the bus and train stations, airlines, and law enforcement in the western states. And to all the shelters. They caught Carrie at the bus station in Amarillo. She'd gotten that far by hitchhiking. She pleaded with law enforcement to let her stay in Texas. But she was a minor. They gave her back to her parents. On the way home, she threw herself off Navajo Bridge."

"Jesus." They'd passed under Navajo Bridge the first morning. Luke had seen Molly look up and wipe moisture from her cheeks. He'd thought it was spray from the river. "So what's the plan?"

"You sure you want to know?"

"In for a penny . . ."

"Okay, but don't say I didn't warn you. Annie took a picture of Molly with her new haircut and color before we left. Annie and Paul have a friend in Flagstaff who can make a fake ID. It won't stand up to TSA scrutiny, but it should hold up long enough to get us home. She'll be traveling as Paul's sister Molly."

"Another layer of separation from her old life."

"Right. Paul will hike down to Phantom Ranch on Wednesday. He'll meet Molly and they'll climb out to the South Rim together. If necessary, he can carry enough water for both of them. By then, we hope, the initial furor will have died down, and the search will be focused farther afield. Even if it isn't, the Family will be expecting Molly to stick with the trip all the way to the end."

"Whitmore Wash. That would put her on the North Rim, with easier access for them."

"They'd love that," Dora said. "But when they don't find her with us, they should give up. It'll have been eleven days by then."

"What happens when she and Paul reach the South Rim?"

"We have friends in Flagstaff. The Merrills. That's

where Annie and Paul are right now. The Merrills will drive them to Grand Canyon Village, wait for Paul to collect Molly, and surround them when they reach the top. The Merrills will keep them undercover till the end of the raft trip. Then the boys and I will pick up Molly, Anne, and Paul, and drive home in the van. Molly won't stand out in such a big group."

"Sounds complicated."

"It's the best we could come up with on the fly. We only had a day or so to plan."

"And you're sure the Family won't think to look for her inside the park?"

"Unless he's received a report of a sighting, the Prophet will focus his search on the bus stations and highways. He won't want to draw attention to the Family, so he'll send just one or two men to quietly investigate the rim areas. And he only has a few men to choose from—the rest are on the summer fair circuit or aren't allowed to have solo contact with the outside world."

"For fear of moral contamination?"

She smiled. "Hikers wear skimpy clothes, drink alcohol, and sometimes take the Lord's name in vain—or worse. . . . But on the upside, Molly couldn't have picked a better time to escape. Most of the Family will be in Salt Lake City this week. I checked."

"So you and Molly's brothers feel you can protect her at the bottom of the canyon for a few days, especially with her disguise and different name."

"In a nutshell."

Luke was silent for a moment. Then he put his left hand over their clasped ones. "I think, to be on the safe side, you'd better alert the crew. I know you believe the Family won't think to look for her on the river, but if you're wrong, if Frankie ran into someone acting suspiciously around the rafts—"

In the distance a gong sounded, calling them to dinner.

"I'll tell the crew after dinner," she said. "You don't really think that Frankie. . . ."

Luke put his arm around her and gave her a quick hug. "If she's alive—and I feel in my bones that she is—then she'll find some way to make it to safety. Now, let's go stoke our furnaces."

When they were both on the sand and heading downhill, she said, "Did you know Frankie almost died trying to save my life before?"

"In the Mojave? She told me you rescued yourself. She was most impressed that at the end of that ordeal all you wanted to know was whether Annie had had the baby and whether Frankie'd already defended her dissertation. Apparently you didn't want to miss either event."

Dora laughed. "I missed the first, but not the second. It was a great defense—albeit three months late. She called it 'anticlimactic.'"

"That's my sister. When she summits a peak, she doesn't spend time patting herself on the back. Mentally, she's already moved on, eager to see what's over the next horizon."

"A MacFarlane trait?"

"For better or for worse."

"Luke." Dora stopped and reached for his arm.

They were fifty yards from camp. No one could overhear them. He looked down at her in the half-light. Her large, almond-shaped eyes were serious. "What is it?"

"I've a favor to ask."

"Name it."

"After we find Frankie—"

"Alive and well."

"Of course. But if something should happen to me, would you make sure Molly's rendezvous with Paul takes place? And that she and the boys get back to my house in Austin? They'll be safe there."

"As long as Ben doesn't find out about Annie."

"If my father and Ben Gruber thought for a moment that I hadn't died twenty-four years ago, they'd have come for us long before now."

"Then don't worry. Nothing's going to happen. But if by some crazy quirk it does, I'll see that the kids get home safely. And anonymously."

She reached up and kissed his cheek. "Thank you."

"We aim to please, ma'am."

As they turned toward camp, she said, so softly he barely heard it, "You please. You please just fine."

16

The spot Ben Gruber chose for their camp was no more than four hundred yards from where they'd parked the truck. He'd stumbled across the draw one year when he'd been hunting. Poaching, the law would call it, but Ben didn't split hairs. Deer were thick on the ground that late-spring weekend, and he had his bow in the old Suburban. Arrows are silent, but just as lethal as bullets. He liked that. He much preferred knives and arrows to firearms, though he'd mastered the use of each, as befitted the Prophet's right arm, the enforcer of the Law.

The draw drained the center of a broad, tilted depression. Ben walked the perimeter of the shallow pit, checking to make sure they'd have the place to themselves. He startled a young buck from its bed and followed the tracks of a hunting bobcat. But he found no trace of recent human activity.

Reassured, he dropped the two packs, then gathered deadfall brush and grasses. When he had enough fuel to last the night, he piled it at the foot of the draw. Selecting two long, forked branches, he grabbed his hatchet and walked up the draw to inspect the campsite for snakes.

Limestone ledges ran on either side. Lots of places for snakes to hide. The sandy floor was damp. He watched for snake sign. Saw only the tracks of birds and lizards.

The draw widened into a circular area with a waterfall at the far side. Earlier, runoff had coursed through the wash, leaving behind a small pool of clear water in the smooth rock at the base of the falls. But the little cave halfway up the wall, large enough for three sleeping mats, was dry. And occupied. A rattler coiled against the back wall. Ben fished out the snake with the forked sticks, pinned its head, and killed it with the axe.

Where there's one, look around for its mate. Ben could hear his father's voice. He'd taught Ben and his brother, Vern, lots of useful things in the old life, before Ben met Eldon Sprague.

Ben spotted a second snake slithering up a crack on the opposite cliff. Dispatched it quickly, then skinned and skewered them both. Appetizers. "Waste not, want not," his father always said.

Walking back to collect the gear and firewood, Ben thought about his father. Howard Gruber had been a simple, straightforward man who believed in only three things—hard work, God, and man's dominion over the things of this world, including women and children. He worked as a miner on the Arizona Strip and adjacent parts of Utah and New Mexico, moving from one uranium or copper mine to another as they played out.

Ben remembered the Hack Canyon mines the best. He'd been thirteen when his father started there, old enough to understand his father's talk of pipelike ore deposits of pitchblende and uraninite. *Collapse breccias*, his father had called them. A fancy name for a column filled with rubble, cemented together. The uranium ore was in the natural cement. The pipes formed, his father said, when water dissolved parts of the Redwall Limestone, and blocks of the overlying formations collapsed downward into the void. Howard believed that the process must have taken place many millions of years ago. The concept of an ancient Earth didn't trouble him. His wife disagreed, but only to Ben. She never crossed her husband in anything.

The Kaibab Plateau was dotted with hundreds of these pipelike deposits, some reaching the surface, some not. Some bearing uranium minerals, others barren. The depression cut by this draw might be the top of a pipe. He knew they occurred nearby. But the government had put a hold on uranium mining on the Strip. All those resources, all those jobs, going to waste. At least Ben's father hadn't lived long enough to see that happen. He'd died of lung cancer years ago.

His parents didn't follow the Law as taught by Eldon Sprague. They'd closed their ears and their hearts to Ben when he'd found the true path. He was sure they'd suffer for all eternity for abandoning him.

More rain was coming. Ben could smell it permeating the air. He stashed the sleeping gear in the cave before digging a fire pit up against the cliff wall. Overhanging rocks would diffuse the smoke and screen the firelight from anyone who might be camping nearby. Unlikely, but Ben had learned to be careful.

The men traveled light. No air mattresses or tents—just blankets, food, utensils, and a pot for boiled coffee. Eldon had told him that the ban against drinking caffeinated beverages had been lifted by Eldon's father forty years ago, while living at their *colonia* in Chihuahua. Eldon hadn't bothered to reinstate it after they moved to the compound on the Strip.

Another storm cell swept over the draw. Ben tossed the firewood into the cave, climbed in after it, and listened to the wind whistle down the draw, the sound of running and dripping water. The rain passed quickly. The air behind it was fresh and cool and smelled of sage and limestone. A slender thread of water slipped over the falls to plink into the pool, swelling its size. He climbed down and built the fire.

The venison steaks had been frozen when they left the compound that morning, half-thawed by the time he'd parked the truck. Ben threaded the chops on a sharpened branch and laid it and the spitted snakes across the flames. When they were sizzling nicely he heated refried beans in the can, directly on the coals. The column of beans rose like toothpaste from a tube as the trapped air expanded. He stirred the beans with a fork to let the steam escape, added some pepper flakes, and put a foil-wrapped package of tortillas to warm on a nearby rock.

Eldon arrived just as the venison and rattlesnake finished grilling. With a grunt of thanks, he dropped his daypack, dried off, said a quick prayer of thanksgiving, and dug in. Only after his belly was full did he tell Ben what he'd seen.

"If those *were* our boys down on the river, their sister might be close by," Ben said. "Why else would they be here right when Naomi takes off?"

"Coincidence? That raft trip must've been planned for months, maybe a year. But if we confirm Naomi's there in the morning, we have time to plan. The trip ends at Whitmore Wash six days from now. Helicopter drops 'em at Bar 10 Ranch. We can drive right in."

"Why wait that long?" Ben said. "If we know she's there, we can hike down to Phantom Ranch tomorrow night. The moon'll be full. Trail should be clear. We'll be in position and waiting when the rafts dock the next day."

"You sure they'll stop?"

"Can't imagine why they'd skip it. But just to make sure, I'll call the outfitters. You have the raft numbers?"

Eldon nodded and poked the fire with one of the skewer sticks. Watched the fatty residue blaze up. "If we hike down to the river, how do you plan on getting her back to the rim? We can't carry her that far, and someone would call the park police if we tried."

"There's one way."

"What's that?"

"Threaten to kill her brothers if she doesn't come quietly. I've used it a few times with my wives. Women are protective. They're just built that way."

Eldon's eyes shifted from the fire. Ben met his gaze. Felt his neck muscles tighten. Tension flowed down his body into his hands, legs, toes.

"Did Carrie know this?" Eldon said.

Ben gave a shrug. "Zilpha and Carrie worked together in the canning shed. You know how girls talk."

"And Naomi?"

"Probably. Carrie and her were close. "

Eldon stared out at the night, brow furrowed. "Is that why you sent Ethan away? To bring his mother into line?"

"You agreed, don't forget. He was of age."

Eldon was quiet for a long time. Ben sensed the Prophet was waffling about Naomi. Ben stood, took the empty bean can, and stomped it flat. The action cleared the mist of anger that blinded him. The rages came more frequently these days, leaving him with a dull headache after they were gone.

Ben stuck the can in his backpack and pulled out a plastic bag of coffee. "Want some?"

"No thanks. I'm going to turn in after we pray. Have to get an early start."

Ben dumped a handful of coffee into the pot of water. It boiled up and foamed. That's how he felt inside. "My revelation said Naomi and I would be sealed for all eternity. God expects us to abide by what he decides, whether it's easy or hard—and whether we like it or not. Isn't that what you've always preached, Prophet?"

Eldon turned his head. His pale eyes glittered like light on lake ice. "But humans are fallible, Brother Ben. I think sometimes they want something or someone so much that they convince themselves that God supports their desires."

"You're questioning your own revelations?"

"Not mine."

"Perhaps it's time we elected a new Prophet."

"*I'll* decide when it's time—and *I'll* choose my successor. That's the way it's always been. The elders can reject the Prophet's choice, of course, but they never have."

"You'll choose one of your sons, then." When Eldon didn't reply, Ben pressed him. "Which one?"

"God hasn't revealed his name to me. There's still plenty of time. And speaking of time, I've decided to wait and retrieve Naomi at the end of the trip—at the Bar 10. If she's on that raft, let her come to us. Easier all the way around."

Ben bowed his head. "It's your decision, Prophet."

"God may yet change my mind. Let's pray on it, Brother Ben."

With that, Eldon stood and retrieved a towel from his pack. When he'd finished washing in the rain pool, they knelt together by the fire. Eldon prayed for guidance and thanked God for the joys of the day. Then he got up, climbed into the cave, and rolled himself in his blanket.

Ben finished his coffee, set down the cup, and added sticks to the fire. Robust snores came from Eldon's bedroll. Ben's anger, banked while the Prophet was awake, burned like a forge fire. Ben fought to quench it and to stifle the hammering in his head so that he could hear God speak. But all he heard was the Prophet's voice: *There's still plenty of time. Plenty of time. Plenty of time.*

"Maybe," Ben Gruber said softly to the glowing coals. "Maybe not."

17

Mile 36, Bridge of Sighs, Marble Canyon
7:40 p.m.

I put the notebook away. Somewhere in the recesses of my mind lay the answer to who Jacob was and
why he'd attacked me. I just had to find it. But not now.

Movement on the river. The searchers, returning to
base camp. Even in the fading light, Jacob would be able
to see that my body wasn't in one of the Zodiacs. Soon
he'd come down. He might already be moving. I had to
figure out a way to escape—or find a safer hiding place.
The fact that he'd stuck around this late meant that he
wasn't going to leave till he checked the caves above me.

The easiest access to the caves was up the little gully.
He might not have noticed my hiding place yet, but he'd
explore it in passing.

No place to hide. Nowhere to run.

My biggest obstacle, at the moment, was his rifle. I
couldn't show myself too soon. He might risk a shot,
if he felt sure of killing me and getting away. But he
wouldn't risk discovery by shooting blindly into the
caves above me, hoping to flush me out. That would
alert the searchers, half a mile upstream. No, he'd prefer
to use a knife, and then hide my body.

I looked at the shadowed cliffs. How long would it
take him to climb down? Was there any way I could turn
the tables and isolate him before he crossed the river?

Take his boat. Philo's voice echoed in my head.

The kayak was unguarded. But not for long. I'd have to chance taking it before he reached the beach.

You waiting for an invitation?

"Shut up, Philo," I said aloud.

If she moves now, she'll be shot. Great. My godfather, Charley Black, had joined the conversation. *Fifteen more minutes, and it will be dark enough.*

Didn't the Apaches lose the wars?

"Stop squabbling," I said. And then, "When I tell this story to our grandchildren, Philo, I'm leaving out the voices."

I thought I heard laughter, but it was only the wind curling into the cave.

Fifteen minutes, Charley reiterated.

Swim the river in the dark? Are you crazy? She'll drown!

Better than being butchered or shot in a cave. Remember the Camp Grant Massacre?

"Okay, okay. I'm going." I pulled on my damp swimsuit and shoes, strapped on Nico's vest, then stuffed everything else, including my notebook, into the dry bag. Pressing out the air, I rolled the top and clipped it closed. What had I forgotten?

I might not be able to contact Search and Rescue directly, but I could leave evidence that I'd been alive and in this place—something to keep the family's, and Philo's, hopes up. . . .

The broom. Philo's voice.

Right. A good tracker would be able to discern when the tamarisk was broken off the bush.

I felt around the floor of the cave. Found the branches in the back where I'd tossed them. Setting the dry bag near the cave mouth, I swept blindly, back and forth, back to front. Then, in a patch of sand near the entrance, I made a footprint. Placed the branches beside it. Shades of Daniel Defoe and Robinson Crusoe.

"I could use a man Friday right about now," I said to Philo and Charley. They'd gone silent.

Kneeling just inside the cave opening, I zeroed in on the place Jacob had chosen, a knob a few hundred feet above me. Clouds now roofed the canyon. The gray gloom of evening was giving way to inky darkness. Jacob's roost was hard to pick out, which meant that he couldn't see into my slit in the rock. But he'd see movement as soon as I slipped out. If he were watching. And I had to assume he would be, unless he'd already started down.

I had to hurry. But I took one last moment to check the route and the goal. I couldn't see his kayak, but I knew where it lay. If I entered the water where I'd exited, the current would carry me too far downstream. My only chance was to make my way upriver far enough that I could half-swim, half-float across on the diagonal.

I looked upstream. The low ledges of dolomite that had kept me from leaving the river the first time were on my left. I could picture the rough, uneven surface. If I was careful and took my time, I could follow it for about a hundred yards. I hoped that would be far enough for my plan to work. But if I missed the debris fan across the river, Tatahatso was only two miles downstream. I could survive that long.

If you make it as far as the river. If he doesn't shoot you first.

Shut up, I said to the frightened child who'd added her voice to the chorus.

You know, talking to yourself is a bad sign. Charley again. There were altogether too many voices competing for attention.

I'm okay.

Define "okay."

I closed my mind, picked up the dry bag, and stepped out into the night.

Mounds of talus stabilized by bushes capped the resistant dolomite ledges. The bench formed a pale gray strip between the Redwall cliff and the water. A hot wind tipped the black waves with white brushstrokes.

I moved slowly, hoping the sounds of my passage couldn't be heard above the rushing river. Shifting from one deeper shadow and bush to the next, I tried to make my movements flow like tai chi. Nothing sudden. Nothing sharp. Planted one foot. Paused. Glided to the next spot. One more moving shadow in the night . . .

It took me perhaps thirty minutes to cover the distance. Along the way I sought a hiding place. Found nothing. Finally I reached a break in the ledge too broad for me to jump.

I looked across the river. Saw the glow of a headlamp below the knob where Jacob had been. He was climbing down. Whether he'd seen me and decided not to risk a shot, or was just following his own plan to cross and check out the caves, I didn't know. But it was a race, now, for the kayak.

The fan below Jacob's side canyon was a pale broad cone dotted with brush. I'd have to swim like hell to make that beach before he did.

Just do it.

I took off my shoes, added them to the dry bag, and clipped it to the belt on the back of the vest. I turned and felt my way down the ledges, into the cleft I couldn't cross. When I could go no farther, I grasped the rocks and lowered my legs into the water. Christ, it was cold. Worse, the current was pulling me under the ledge. This wouldn't work.

Shivering as much from fear as from cold, I climbed back to safety and considered my options. There were only three. One, find a safe place nearby and wait for Jacob to leave. Two, go back to my cave, which Jacob would certainly check on his way up the gully. Three, launch myself in a racing dive to get as far from shore as possible.

But I'd found no safe places nearby.

I assumed the diver's stance, chin down, left foot back, fingers and toes of my right foot curled over the edge of the ledge. My knee protested. I pushed the pain away. Pictured a warm turquoise pool as the referee in my head counted down. *Three, two, one.* Deep breath.

I launched my body, brought my arms up tight against my ears, arched my back, and sliced into the water. I surfaced, already churning toward the far shore. I'd swum competitively as a child. Most kids did in Tucson. Swimming lessons are included when you sign up for swim team, and parents want to ensure their offspring are water safe. But swimming in an eighty-degree pool is a lot different than swimming in what felt like glacial meltwater. I'd done that, too, a time or two, after a long day in the field. If I hadn't had the vest on, the cold would have squeezed my chest muscles until my lungs would no longer function. The brain would follow.

My arms and legs felt like lead. I kept pumping, but I could feel them slowing. I lifted my head and saw the beach parallel to me, across a short stretch of dark water. The current was carrying me past it. Too fast. Too fast.

Don't panic. Don't flail. Charley again. Then Philo: *Kick harder. Pull. Pull.*

I reached deep inside and put on another burst of speed. My right hand brushed rock. I grabbed for it. It came loose and rolled away. My left hand touched another rock. Slid across the smooth surface. My feet were being pulled downstream. I was swimming against the current. I kicked and kicked, pulled and pulled, until suddenly the current slackened.

I was in a small cove, protected by the bulk of the debris fan. For the second time that day, I used bushes and reeds to drag myself onto warm sand.

Thanks, guys.

Turning over, I lay staring at the sky until my breath returned to normal and the shivers slowed. My dry bag dug into my kidneys. I didn't care. How long did I lie there? Two minutes? Five? I didn't have the strength to lift my arm and check my watch. But as I warmed up, my mind activated. *Where was Jacob? Had he seen my crossing?*

If he found me like this, I'd die right here.

I smelled rain. The clouds seemed to capture and hold the moonlight, brightening the canyon. If I were going to steal Jacob's kayak, now was the time.

My fingers seemed to belong to someone else. It took me four tries to unclip my dry bag. But after wasting precious minutes, I had the sack open and my river shoes out. Putting them on was like watching a two-year-old struggle. Eventually, my shaking fingers tightened the elastic laces.

I stood and nearly collapsed. Part of that shaking, I realized, was due to hunger. I'd burned too many calories crossing the river. No reserves left.

I found the protein bar in the sack, tore the package open with my teeth, and took a hefty bite. Closing the bag again, I looped it over my shoulder.

The debris fan felt like a mountain. But the climb warmed my legs. I aimed for the blacker maw of the tributary canyon. The kayak lay against the base of the cliff, just to the right. Storm runoff had formed a rivulet in the fan. A small pool reflected moonlit clouds. Toads chirruped around the edges, plopping into the water as I passed. Ripples marred the reflection. The pool brightened for a moment as the moon found a hole in the clouds. Another time, this would be a magical place.

I listened for human sounds—cursing, scuffling, scraping—but heard nothing but the toads, wind, and river. I couldn't see the light from Jacob's headlamp. How close was he?

Feeling my way along the cliff, my bad knee connected with the tip of the kayak. I bit back a yelp of pain, then bent down, turned the kayak on its hull, and tested its weight. It was an inflatable, but too heavy. Or I was too weak.

I rummaged inside, under the spray skirt, and found a sack of what felt like canned goods and cooking gear. Pulled it out and set it aside. A second small sack seemed to hold clothes or rain gear. Not heavy enough to make a difference. I left it there. Wrapping my arms around the stern, I lifted the bow high enough that I could edge my back under the midsection. I bent my knees and straightened them. The kayak came off the ground smoothly, easily. I picked my way carefully down to the water's edge, set the boat down, then felt inside for the paddle.

No paddle. I went back to where I'd left the food sack. Did a quick search. Came up empty. He must have hidden it in case I tried something like this. Clever man.

What now?

I was up a literal creek without a paddle. I could lie on the kayak and paddle with my hands, like a surfboard. But I needed something substantial inside the hollow center to prop up my stomach. I picked up Jacob's food bag. In the canyon, I heard rocks shift and click. Jacob was coming.

I ran back to the kayak, tripping once, falling flat. I scrambled to my feet. Adrenaline poured through me. I loped the last few yards. Adding my dry bag to Jacob's bags, I dragged the kayak into the water, climbed awkwardly aboard, and pushed off. Just as I left the little cove, I heard a shout.

I didn't look back. Paddling as hard as I could, I steered into the swiftest part of the current. Expecting a gunshot, I tried to make myself as small a target as possible. Paddled harder. Felt the current roughen. The kayak was swept around the bend in the river and into 36 Mile Rapid.

I hung on for dear life. White water buffeted me. Pressing my stomach and abdomen into the spray skirt, I tried to prevent water from getting in and swamping the boat. Then we dropped into a hole.

My face was under water. I couldn't breathe. I struggled to lift my head.

Just as I ran out of air, the kayak popped out the far side of the hole. We were caught by an eddy and twirled around. When we stopped spinning, my feet were facing downstream. A Redwall cliff hid Jacob on his beach.

18

Below 36 Mile Rapid, Marble Canyon
8:50 p.m.

I was alive. The craft was sound. But I wanted no more rapids. I might not be so lucky next time.

I turned the craft around and faced downstream, picturing the river log. What lay ahead? Relatively smooth water for the next eight miles. But I didn't have eight miles in me. I was shivering again.

How far had the rafts gone before stopping for the night? Probably not far. They'd wait for the results of the shore search tomorrow morning. But they couldn't afford to wait long. They had a schedule to keep.

Tatahatso was the nearest campsite. Mile 37.9. Even if my own group wasn't camped there, I'd have to stop. I needed rest, warmth, food. And if my luck had turned, maybe I'd find someone with a satellite phone.

The Tatahatso Wash debris fan reached well out into the river. I shouldn't be able to miss it, even in the dark. The camp was on the downstream side of the fan. Only two river miles from where I'd left Jacob, but more than two miles by land. I'd feel a lot safer if it were twenty.

I could relax a bit now that I had a destination. The lack of a paddle would slow me down, but even so, I'd reach Tatahatso within thirty minutes. I pressed the glow light on my watch. I should be there well before ten. Maybe the crew would still be up, drinking and smoking and talking in the tearoom on one of the rafts.

My hands were freezing. My back hurt from being bowed. My knee was at an awkward angle. Careful not to rock the kayak, I turned over, let my butt sink into the center hole of the craft, and watched flashes of lightning illumine clouds and cliffs. I couldn't hear the thunder over the crashing, rumbling, rushing sounds of the river.

Drifting on the current was like lying on an air mattress in my pool. I hadn't realized how tired I was. I felt my eyelids droop. . . .

Starting awake, I almost capsized the boat. I wasn't sure where I was for a moment. Then the past hours flooded back like a tidal bore. How far had I come?

I looked at my watch. I'd been out for five minutes. The cliffs seemed to float by as if in a dream. I could hear my father's voice teaching me a mnemonic for remembering the canyon rock sequence. *Know The Canyon's History. See Rocks Made By Time Very Slowly.* I'd taught the ditty to my students the first day.

To keep myself awake, I recited the rock units, starting at the top and adding in the geological formations the mnemonic didn't cover: *Kaibab, Toroweap, Coconino, Hermit, Supai Group (Esplanade, Wescogame, Manakacha, Watahomigi), Surprise Canyon, Redwall, Temple Butte, Muav, Bright Angel, Tapeats, Sixtymile, Chuar Group (Kwagunt, Galeros), Nankoweap, Unkar Group (Cardenas, Dox, Shinumo, Hakatai, Bass), Zoroaster Granite, Vishnu Schist.* . . . I went through the whole list five times, the words like a sacred chant binding me to the night, the rocks, the restless river—to this place where time seemed to stand still.

The chanting wasn't enough. I felt myself drifting off again.

Turning over, I stuck my hands back in the water and started paddling. *Harder. Faster. Kick some oxygen back up to the brain. Only another mile.*

My brain cleared. I could see a bulwark of rock slowly approaching on the right. The bend in the river opposite Tatahatso Wash. As long as I beached some-where along that fan, I could walk the rest of the way. Either someone would be occupying the camp or they wouldn't.

I was a quarter mile above the delta when the storm descended. I steered closer to river left, trying to glimpse the shore. Blackout, above and below. Water, sky, cliffs, rain. Couldn't tell up from down. *Water, water, every-where.* And soon it would be roaring through the slot canyons, too. Maybe it would wash Jacob into the river.

The kayak hit something solid, tipping me off. I grabbed for the craft as the stern swung around. Lugged the boat ashore. Collapsed. I couldn't feel my fingers. I was so wet that it took me a moment to realize I was crying.

I struggled to stand. A thousand needles pricked my feet. I dragged the kayak into a patch of brush and tied the bowline to a boulder. My fingers fumbled with the line. I resorted to my teeth. Not the prettiest knot I'd ever tied, but it would do.

A flash of lightning revealed that I was on the up-stream side of the Tatahatso fan. The deeper darkness of the canyon was on my left. Water poured out of its mouth. I started walking downriver, wading through the rivulets that braided the face of the fan. Rain coursed over me, but it was warmer than the river. My shoes filled with sand. I stumbled over rocks. When I paused to catch my breath atop a little hillock, another flash of lightning showed two rafts. Our outfitters. And tents, strung out like mushrooms along the beach.

The rain cell had moved away by the time I reached the rafts. I found I didn't have enough voice to halloo the crew. I picked up a handful of pebbles and flung them at the closest raft.

"What the fuck?" Nico's voice.

"I'm returning your vest," I croaked, before I dissolved in a puddle on the beach.

19

**Mile 37.9, Tatahatso Campsite,
Marble Canyon**
9:45 p.m.

Luke and Nico linked hands and carried me,
wrapped in someone's sleeping bag, to my tent. Luke
had set it up. An act of faith. My eyes blurred with tears.

I tried to tell them about Jacob, but my teeth were
chattering so badly I could barely get words out.

"There's a man named Jacob, with a gun, and you
stole his kayak?" Luke said, catching the main points.

I nodded.

"Okay," Nico said. "We'll keep an eye out. The rest
can wait till you warm up."

"Do you need some help stripping off?" Dora said.

"I don't know. Let me try." That was a little clearer.

"Your night bag's inside." Luke's voice cracked on
the last word. He took a deep breath and knelt to unzip
the tent.

Standing up, he hugged me tightly, rocking from side
to side. I kissed his damp cheek. No need for words. He
understood. *Thanks for believing I was still alive and
that I'd need the tent. Thanks for not giving up on me.
Thanks for being my brother.*

He sniffed and grinned. "Mom and Dad wouldn't
have forgiven me if I'd lost my little sister. . . . And Philo, well, he and Charley would have skinned me alive."

I smiled back, feeling like my face was going to crack. Pointing to where I'd left the kayak, I asked Luke, in abbreviated language, to make sure it was secured, and to recover my dry bag full of odds and ends.

"Sure thing," he said, and loped off across the boulder-strewn dunes.

I threw off the sleeping bag, ducked inside the tent, and wrestled with my swimsuit. Like peeling a second skin. I sponged off my body with wet wipes. Torture. The alcohol found every nick and abrasion. In the dark, I couldn't see the bruises, but I felt them, especially when I pulled on shorts and a tank top. My silt-laden hair would have to wait till morning. I couldn't bear the thought of venturing back into the river to wash. I settled for twisting my hair up off my neck and securing it with a clip. Slipping my headlamp onto my forehead, I clicked the switch to the red-bulb setting. I could see well enough but wouldn't disturb anyone sleeping. I scrounged in my bag for painkillers. Swallowed them without water. I was ready to face the inquisition.

I'd been hearing rustling outside the tent. When I emerged Dora had laid out my plastic tarp, pad, sleeping bag, and sheet on a flat space. The sand was damp, but the tarp would keep my bag dry.

Dora pointed me in the direction of the closest portable toilet, and I trudged through the sand till I saw the boat pad the crew used as an Occupied/Vacant sign. Apparently the toilet wasn't in use. I followed a faint trail through the undergrowth, rounded a bend, and almost tripped over the ammo can with the seat cover, balanced precariously on some rocks. I didn't linger.

Back at my tent, I wrapped myself in my sleeping bag despite the hot, humid night. My core was heating up, but it would take a while to reach my extremities. Food would help.

"Roxy's bringing soup," Dora said softly. Most of the camp was asleep.

Molly materialized from the shadows and handed me a stainless-steel mug with a plastic lid. "It's yours," she whispered. "I kept track of it in case—" She stopped, cleared her throat. "It's coffee, with milk. Nico said he added 'a slug of boat gas,' whatever that means."

Nico had parted with some of his Wild Turkey. I laughed. A real laugh. Reassuring to know I still could.

"Ssh," somebody called from two tents over. This campsite was small, the tents close together.

"It's a slang term for a kind of bourbon," I whispered. "You know, whiskey. For medicinal purposes." When she smiled, my red light reflected off her teeth. The coffee sent a warm glow through my innards. I decided I might live after all.

Molly passed me a napkin with a mound of something dark in the middle. "I saved you a piece of my birthday cake. Roxy and I made it."

I took a bite, then inhaled the rest. "Manna from heaven," I said, washing it down with coffee.

She giggled. "I thought so, too."

Luke plopped Nico's dry bag in the sand next to my feet. His other hand held a mug of Top Ramen. Chicken. Reminded me of dorm life.

Two seconds later the guides—Nico, Roxy, and Doug—joined the little group. "I couldn't get through to dispatch," Nico said. "I'll try again after you tell us what happened, if you're up to it now."

I told them about Jacob and the Bridge of Sighs cave. I felt the adrenaline melt away as the whiskey and food did their jobs. The moon played peekaboo with the scudding clouds. The concerned looks on their faces gave way to frowns. I was hot now—and I wanted sleep more than I'd ever wanted anything in my life.

"This man, Jacob, had you seen him before?" Luke said.

"Last evening. On the river."

"And he called you by name?"

I nodded. "It was more of a question, as if . . . as if someone had sent him to look for me, and he wanted to make sure I really was Frankie."

The group was silent. I could sense the tension. Dora and Luke looked at each other, and then at Molly. She was stretched out on the tarp beside me, sound asleep, her head on Dora's knee. Something else was going on, something I knew nothing about.

"I think he'll come after his kayak, if he can," I said. "And he'll come after me."

"Do you want to move camp downriver?" Luke said to Nico. "Make it harder for him to get to us?"

"Not even a fool would attempt that trail in the dark," Nico said. "He sounds crazy, but not stupid. So I think we're safe enough. But I'll keep trying till I reach dispatch. They'll alert the search team. SAR can motor down and check out the place you left him." He got up to go back to his raft and satellite phone.

"I'll keep an eye on things tonight," Luke said to me. "I can sleep on the raft tomorrow."

"Me, too," said Doug. He wasn't in charge of operating either raft, but supported both. "I'll watch the water if you watch the cliff trail."

"Deal," Luke said.

"I've made up a thermos of coffee. It's on the table," said Roxy, taking the empty mugs from my hand. "And I'll bring back your mug after I've washed it, Frankie."

After the guides had gone, I turned to Luke and Dora. "Jacob was wearing a headlamp when he climbed down the cliff."

"Make it easier to spot him." Luke was staring up-river, where no lamplight bobbed above the sheer black Redwall cliffs. "Speaking of which, we should turn our own headlamps off except when absolutely necessary. If he should find a way to come hunting you tonight, he'll have a tough time picking you out of a bunch of shadowy shapes."

We all flicked off our lamps. I felt better, safer. I said,

"A few minutes ago, I sensed that you and Dora weren't telling me something, something about Molly. What's up?"

The waxing moon bathed their faces in light. Luke and Dora exchanged that look again. He put his hand over hers, linking fingers. "It's your story, Dora."

There are touches, and there are touches. This one wasn't platonic—or brotherly.

Dora frowned and thought for a moment, as if trying to find an entry into a structural geology problem. Finally she shrugged and told me about the family she, Molly, and the boys had been born into, and about the men Molly was trying to escape. Dora spoke quickly, sensing how tired I was.

I said, "Did the crew know you were borrowing Molly's identity for the trip?"

Dora hesitated again. "I told the crew tonight. Nico read me the riot act just before you arrived."

"You think Ben Gruber and Eldon Sprague might have figured out she's on the river with you?" I glanced at the slip of a girl lying next to me. Too young and innocent to be exposed to the Bens of this world.

"We were careful. But if by some miracle they do find out, I think they'll decide to intercept her at Whitmore Ranch. It's on the North Rim, and they can drive right to it. Which is why Molly will hike out with Paul from Phantom Ranch."

"But we have to at least consider that the Family sent Jacob—that someone may already be on the river," Luke said.

"So we'll keep up the pretense," Dora said.

"Right. She's Molly. No problem," I said. "But if Jacob or someone else manages to kidnap her in the canyon, how would he get her out? He couldn't carry her up a trail. And once you alerted law enforcement, they'd search all boats."

"I don't know, Frankie." She ran a hand over Molly's

hair, like a mother soothing a child. "They may not plan to reclaim her at all. They may just want to do to her what they tried to do to me."

"Abandon her without food or water?" Luke said. "They'd never get away with it."

"They have before. Their local law officers protect them. And the elders know how to disappear to Family property in Texas and Mexico. They all have false IDs."

"But where do *I* fit in?" I said. "It makes no sense. Why would Jacob try to kill *me*?"

We sat in silence. The sky had cleared. The moon transformed the canyon palette to black and white and shades of gray, like the earliest etchings of canyon country. Luke went down to the kitchen area, found two mugs, and filled them from the thermos of coffee Roxy had left.

"I did think of one possibility while I was holed up," I said when he returned.

He handed me a mug. "That Jacob's connected to your intruder?"

I shivered, despite the hot night. "Or *is* my intruder."

"What's this?" said Dora.

While Luke gave Dora the short version of the Tucson break-in, I sipped coffee. Luke had added more of Nico's Wild Turkey. The chills faded.

"So Jacob may have nothing at all to do with Molly," Dora said. "I don't know whether to be relieved or even more worried. Who was in the missing photo?"

"My four brothers and me," I said.

"Well two of you are here. That's 40 percent. Could someone have started a vendetta against your family?"

I shrugged and sipped more coffee. The night grew softer at the edges, more dreamlike.

"I suppose Kit could have pissed off a drug dealer," Luke said. "And there's no telling what Philo's been up to. It's all hush-hush."

Our older brother Kit practiced international law,

much of it related to Latin America. He was also Philo's best friend and legal counsel. They'd played baseball together from middle school through the University of Arizona. On occasion, Dain Investigations had done contract work for Kit's firm. Was that the link?

"We'll call them from Phantom Ranch," Luke said. "We just have to stay safe till then."

I emptied my mug. "Forty hours, give or take. Piece of cake."

20

Mile 37.9, Tatahatso Campsite,
Marble Canyon
10:30 p.m.

Molly, eyes closed, floated in a state somewhere between sleep and wakefulness. She heard someone crunching up the dunes. A stumble. Soft swearing. Nico. She smelled his cigarette smoke. Cloth rustled on sand as he crouched near her.

"Couldn't get through to dispatch," he whispered, his voice raspy. "I'll get some shut-eye and try again at four-thirty."

"You need to sleep, too, Frankie," Dora said, but no one moved.

"Every time I close my eyes I see Jacob," Frankie said.

Jacob sounded like a bogeyman, one of the lost souls that lived in the world outside the compound. Molly's mother and aunts told stories about them to scare the children into behaving properly.

How many Jacobs did Molly know? She reviewed all the men she'd met at family gatherings: six Jacobs. Frankie might be talking about any one of them.

She sat up and touched Frankie on the arm. "Could you describe this Jacob?"

"Maybe six-three, athletic build, muscular upper body. Military shirt, tan swim shorts. Sun-streaked brown hair that hadn't been cut in a while. He tied it back with a bootlace. . . . Green eyes—" Frankie stopped, as if she'd just now thought of something. "I need a piece of paper."

Dora pulled a field notebook and mechanical pencil from her pocket. Molly passed them to Frankie.

"Think it's safe to use a headlamp?" she asked Luke.

"If you're quick."

A single red beam shone down on the paper as Frankie drew a symbol that looked like a little spinning top turned upside down on a larger one. She followed it with the word *SWEET*.

"What is it, a tattoo?" Dora said.

"A logo." Nico sucked on his cigarette. The end glowed like a crimson eye. "On his helmet?"

"Yes—white on red."

"Not sure it'll help much," Nico said. "Those helmets are expensive, but I've seen plenty of them on the river this season."

Frankie's shoulders slumped. She handed the notebook and pencil back to Dora, then turned off her headlamp.

Nico took a last pull on the cigarette, stubbed it out on the side of his sandal, and tucked the butt in his pocket. "I'll see what I can do about putting the rafts in a more protected location."

"Jacob has a rifle," Frankie said as Nico turned toward the rafts. "He doesn't have to come close to cripple us."

"If he'd meant to damage the rafts, he'd have done it before now. He's had plenty of opportunities."

Molly watched him trudge down to the water. "I don't think Jacob's one of the Family," she said when he was out of earshot. "At least, he's no one I've ever met. Our men don't serve in the military. And they don't have the money to buy expensive helmets—or the time to kayak down the river. . . . Unless—" she looked at Dora, "unless he's one of the boys who were sent away by the Prophet before I was born."

"I don't recognize the name or description," Dora said. "But I've been gone a long time."

Molly studied the faces around her. Her new family. Unlike the one she was born into, this one would protect her. Or die trying.

"We know one thing," Frankie said. "Jacob will want his kayak back." She turned to Luke, shaking her head. "I should have asked you to deflate it."

"It's not too late." Luke put a hand on the knife at his belt. "You want me to trash it?"

Molly, facing upriver, saw a dark shape drifting toward them. A boat or raft without running lights. Moonlight reflected off numbers and an insignia. "What's that?"

Frankie turned. "Looks like one of the search rafts."

"But empty," Luke said. "I'll get Nico."

"The kayak—," Frankie began. But Luke was out of earshot. "Shit," she said, and took off at an awkward, hobbling jog.

"This way, Molly," Dora said. "Grab your stuff. I'll take Frankie's. I know just the place for you both to sleep tonight."

21

Mile 37.9, Tatahatso Campsite, Marble Canyon

10:45 p.m.

Luke saw a second Zodiac as he reached the shore. This one drifted sideways. It also appeared empty.

Roxy had fixed a spotlight on the first Zodiac, and Nico and Doug had set out in one of the big rafts. Luke watched them snag the SAR craft, then hustled over the fan to where he'd left the kayak. Frankie was there, studying two sets of drag marks. One coming, one going.

"He's a frigging *ninja*," she said.

"So, where is he now?"

She pointed to a shadow moving against the far wall of Marble Canyon, skirting the edge of the spotlit area. "I'll sleep better tonight knowing he's not up in the rocks."

"And tomorrow?"

"We'll think of something."

They joined Roxy and a few of the other rafters lined up along the shore, shining their flashlights and high-beam headlamps onto the river. Roxy had what looked like a Peacemaker in her hand. Luke was careful not to startle her as they joined the group.

"Kayak's gone," he said.

"What?" She was only half-listening. "*What?*"

"The Zodiacs were a diversion," Frankie said. "We're just lucky he decided not to shoot holes in our rafts."

"Maybe you should go back with the search team in the morning," said Dora. She was standing just behind Luke's left shoulder, staring downstream at the point the kayak had disappeared from sight. "I can handle it from here."

"I will, if that's what everyone wants," Frankie said. She looked at Roxy. "What do you think?"

"That he's on the run. Can you imagine how pissed off SAR will be when they discover he's stolen their Zodiacs?"

"You have to admit, it was a ballsy thing to do." Frankie smiled, but it seemed like an effort.

"Yeah, but it hasn't bought him much time," Roxy said. "If he travels on the river during the day, the helicopters will spot him. If he opts to hike out, the park service will have the trailheads and roads covered. His days as a free man are numbered."

"Then you don't think my presence on the trip will put anyone in danger?"

Roxy shook her head. "How could it? Jacob'll be too busy to come after you on the river. He'll wait till you're out of the canyon. So if you want to stay, I'm good with it."

"How about Nico and Doug?" Luke said.

"I'll sound them out tonight. But Frankie'd better canvass the other rafters in the morning. They might see it differently."

"Will do," Frankie said. "But when you or Nico call dispatch to let SAR know you've recovered their boats, will you ask them to have the park police do a computer search for anyone named Jacob, recently separated from the army?"

Roxy caught the bowline from one of the rescued Zodiacs. Luke fielded the second line and watched her tie her own special knots through the eye of a metal stake driven into the sand. Dusting off her hands, she said, "You can tell them yourself in the morning. You're the first person they'll want to talk to." She turned and headed over to Nico and Doug.

"I'm going to hit the hay," Dora said.

Frankie stretched and yawned. "I'm right behind you."

Luke looked up at the stars. "It's turning into a beautiful night. I think I'll stay up for a while."

"You don't trust the son of a bitch either?"

"Bingo."

22

Ben Gruber lay on the damp sand of the draw and watched the stars wheel overhead. An owl called from a nearby tree. He saw lightning a few miles off. Heard the faint rumble of thunder. Knew another storm cell was headed their way. Fast.

He prayed for guidance, prayed for direction. God refused to be rushed. But Ben was patient. Finally he received an answer.

Ben nodded, sat up, and piled more wood on the fire. Taking out his hunting knife, he climbed into the cave, stabbed Eldon Sprague once in the abdomen, sliding the knife up and under the ribcage, careful not to knick a bone. A second, shorter cut across the belly formed a cross.

Sprague woke with a scream. His voice started strongly, then tapered to a whisper. "Ben?" Question and accusation. He put his hands over his gaping belly.

"It's time for a new prophet. God spoke to me through Peter. He said, 'There will also be false teachers among you, who will secretly introduce destructive heresies, even denying the Master who bought them, bringing swift destruction upon themselves.'" Ben sat back on his heels. Drops of blood dripped from the end of the knife. "I'm sorry, Eldon, but God instructed me to sacrifice the false prophet and restore order to the lives of his chosen people."

But Eldon didn't hear him. He'd stopped breathing.

The voice in Ben's head said, *He must be left naked and available for the coyotes and buzzards and ants.*

Ben did as the voice commanded. He cut Eldon's clothes from his body and put them in the fire, along with the blood-soaked blanket. Then, after stripping off his own clothes, he wrapped Eldon's body in the ground cloth, picked it up, and started for the edge of the cliff, half a mile away. The load was heavy, but God made it seem light as thistledown, as if they were floating over the ground. Ben barely felt the rough limestone underfoot, the cactus spines that brushed his ankles. He was Moses, lifting up the bronze serpent in the wilderness. . . .

The moon came out just long enough to show Ben the way. But he could smell rain, see flashes of light on the horizon. At the rim he paused, unwrapped the tarp, took a deep breath, lifted the body high, and heaved it over the edge. He heard it hit, bounce, hit again and again, like a large, soft, skipping stone. And then silence.

There was no trail nearby. The body would be just bones by the time anyone found it. If they found it.

He considered that possibility. Suppose someone did stumble over the remains. What then? The authorities would have no way of identifying them. Ben's footprints would have been washed away. And the Family would not report a missing person.

Ben turned his back on the chasm. The moon went behind a cloud, but he knew the way. He draped the bloody ground cloth over his shoulders. As if responding to a signal, the heavens opened, washing the blood from his body and the tarp. God, showing his support.

Lightning struck three hundred yards from him, and Ben inhaled the smell of sulfur and scorched grass. The burning brush flared up, showing him the entrance to the draw just ahead. The campfire was out. Only a few bits of charred cloth and leather remained. He dug a hole and buried them, along with the ashes, as the rain moved away.

After washing himself and his knife in the rock pool, swollen now with runoff, he dressed in fresh clothes. He felt holy, cleansed, a vessel of light and power, a sword of truth.

He packed up the tarp with the rest of their gear, thinking about what he'd say to the Family when he returned home without Eldon. He prayed to God for inspiration. And God answered again. Ben should tell them that he had left Eldon at the rim while he, Ben, had continued the search for Naomi. It would be the truth after all. Eldon lay only a little way down from the rim edge, no more than two hundred feet. Below his final resting place was more than half a mile of rock.

And Naomi, when Ben retrieved her, would testify that her father had not been in the truck when they returned. His gear was there, packed and ready to go, but Eldon must have wandered off. Ben would say they waited and searched for hours before calling home for help. But they found no sign of Eldon Sprague.

As he picked up their packs to hike back to the truck, Ben heard coyotes baying in the distance. No doubt they smelled blood. If a game trail led down to the body, they'd find it. Or make one. The vultures and ants and ground squirrels didn't need a trail.

Two days and nights from now there'll be nothing left to show who Eldon was or how he died. Praise the Lord, he who rewards his faithful servants.

The lightning-struck brush still smoldered. Ben stopped in his tracks and watched it for a moment. The ground was too damp and the brush too sparse for the flames to spread. But that wouldn't be true farther west, where forests of evergreen and aspen covered the plateau.

If park service employees are fighting a fire, they won't be interested in Ben Gruber or Naomi Sprague.

But first Ben had to find her. Even if she wasn't with the boys on the raft trip, they might have an idea where she'd gone. And he had ways of making people cooperate.

23

**Mile 41.6, downstream from Buck Farm
Canyon, Marble Canyon**
11:30 p.m.

The man couldn't sleep. He didn't have many
nights left, and he didn't want to squander a perfect one,
especially in the most beautiful place on earth.

He sat on the sand, back against a boulder, headlamp
shining down on his open journal. He was searching for
the right words to describe his emotional attachment to
this place. Tomorrow it would be too late to capture
the feelings. Tomorrow, he'd meet up with the rest of
the crew. This would be his last night, ever, alone in the
canyon.

He'd been down the river with Ed Abbey a time or
three. And with others who could wrangle words at
least as well. They'd shared laughter, liquor, tobacco
and weed, songs, stories, and poetry back when the river hadn't yet been tamed and overrun. They'd shared
women, too. But it was the liquor and the cigarettes that
had nailed him. Cancerous tumors riddled his pancreas,
liver, lungs, and kidneys. Chemo had only delayed the
inevitable a few months—and made him wretchedly ill.
So he'd walked away from the cancer center, the doctors, the cures that felt worse than the illness.

This journey down the river was his final hurrah. All
the old guard were gone or had slipped behind the curtain of old age. Today was his sixty-sixth birthday. He'd

leave behind two ex-wives and no children—at least that he knew of. But there was one last thing he could do so that this country he worshipped would remember his name.

A coughing fit swept over him. When he could breathe again, he plucked the bottle of Jack Daniel's from the sand beside his thigh. Raising it to the fat moon, the turbulent river, his departed friends, and the rock walls holding the near-sentient essence of time, he said, "Happy birthday, you lucky bastard."

He drank deeply from the bottle, wiped his mouth, and picked up his pen again, writing, "I, Charles Augustus Rennie, being of sound mind and failing body, do hereby take full responsibility for the destruction of the two suspension bridges that cross the Colorado River at South Kaibab Trail and Bright Angel Trail, respectively. I acted alone, and with complete foreknowledge of the deleterious effects of my actions." He paused. Chuckled. Which brought on another spate of coughing.

He was tired. He needed rest. He'd hand off the materiel tomorrow, but he needed to be there when it was used. Otherwise, he couldn't claim credit for the act. From some deep reserves of strength or stubborn pride, he had to find the energy to paddle forty-six more miles down a whitewater river. It used to be so easy.

He touched pen to paper again. "I will have gotten three things old Abbey didn't—a few more years of life, the gift of death in the Mother Canyon, and the demolition of the only avenues for the hordes of hikers crossing this blessed river. It is a decent way to close out a life.

"My legal practice in Tempe and my clients will go to my partner, Cyrus Foxworth. He has my will, spelling out the disbursement of my possessions. If my body is retrieved from the Canyon, I wish it to be cremated and the ashes scattered here."

That's all she wrote, Chuck decided. *Except . . .* He skipped a couple of lines, then jotted a final note, unrelated to the formal statements. "I want to milk one final sunset from the sky after the riparian apocalypse. I want to witness one more dawn among the oldest rocks in the canyon. I want to write one final haiku—to touch those left behind and make them understand what a sacred trust this land is."

He signed his name and was closing the book when a figure emerged from the darkness. "Halloo the camp," a man called.

Chuck looked at his watch. Nearly midnight. Late for visiting, even in the relaxed atmosphere of the river.

"Welcome," Chuck said. "You're out late." He held up the bottle of Jack Daniel's. "I have sustenance, if you're thirsty. But you'll have to either drink from the bottle or bring your own cup."

The code in canyon country says that the person you meet is a fellow wayfarer. You share what you can spare. Swap stories and cigarettes (or joints), coffee, food, or alcohol, depending on your supplies.

A startled look crossed the man's face. Then he smiled and said, "Thank you kindly. Straight from the bottle will do." He took a package from the pocket of his shirt, tore the bag open with his teeth. "Peanuts?"

"A veritable feast." Chuck took a handful, popped them in his mouth, dusted off his hands, and held the right one out. "Chuck Rennie."

"Jacob Presley."

"Have a seat, stranger, and tell me what kept you on the river till the wee hours, and why you chose to stop at my humble campsite."

Jacob sat down, took a swig from the bottle, passed it back, and pulled a joint from his pocket. "Mind if I smoke? It's a long story."

"I only mind if you don't share the bounty."

Jacob grinned. "Not a problem."

Lighting the joint, he handed it to Chuck, who drew in a lungful, coughed, and handed it back, looking at Jacob expectantly.

Jacob checked his watch.

"You have somewhere to be?" Chuck said.

"Something to do within the next fifteen minutes."

"Ah, a sacred ritual as the clock strikes midnight."

"Precisely." He inhaled and passed Chuck the joint. As it went back and forth, the night and the moonlight and Chuck's mood all brightened immeasurably. Chuck waited patiently for the story that would be released by the smoke. He was no longer tired. He watched Jacob move the sand around with the toes of his river shoes, making little dunes like long-horned crescent moons.

"Two years ago," Jacob said, "I camped with my family at Phantom Ranch. It was the last vacation I spent with them. I headed overseas the next week. Afghanistan."

"Something happened while you were gone?" Chuck asked softly.

"My brother and sister died in an accident. My mother . . . died of grief, you might say." He was silent, looking out to where the moonlight cast a silver path across the water. "I've brought their ashes with me. They didn't leave last requests, but I think they'd have wanted to begin their final journey in this canyon. I'd planned to release them last night, but . . . I guess I wasn't quite ready."

"This is a good place," Chuck said. "Plenty of privacy."

He waited, expecting Jacob to ask why Chuck was here, traveling solo down the canyon. But Jacob must have been so lost in his own grief that he couldn't think of anyone else—or didn't care. So Chuck left it. Maybe in the morning, before they set off, there'd be time for him to share a final thought with the young man.

"Okay if I camp nearby?" Jacob said. "My stuff's over there." He nodded down the beach, where Chuck could see the black shape of a kayak.

"Mi playa es su playa."

"Gracias, mi amigo." Jacob took another pull of whiskey, then stood and brushed the sand from his shorts. The wind was picking up, changing direction. Clouds streamed in luminous waves across the black sky. Jacob shivered as if his clothes were damp. They probably were, Chuck thought.

"It's time," Jacob said. "Want to join me? I could use a bit of moral support."

"Be an honor, sir. Do you have a flashlight?"

"The batteries on my headlamp died last night. But I've got good night vision."

"Here, borrow mine. Don't want you tripping over a boulder in the darkness."

"Nice of you. Thanks." Jacob slipped the elastic band around his forehead and aimed the light at the sand. "Meet you at the water then."

He'd taken only a couple of steps when he stopped and turned. "Don't suppose you know the words to 'Shall We Gather at the River?'"

"Only the first verse and chorus. But we can sing them twice."

"That'll do."

The moon was sliding over the far cliffs when Jacob met him at the water's edge. Canyon moonset was near. Jacob set three metal urns down in the damp sand.

Picking up the first urn, he waded a couple of steps into the river. In a rich strong voice he began to sing. "'Shall we gather at the river, / Where bright angel feet have trod—'"

"'With its crystal tide forever / Flowing by the throne of God?'" Chuck joined in, thinking of the camp songs and spirituals they used to sing, long ago, on river trips and camping trips. God, how he ached for those days.

Jacob had emptied the first urn by the time they reached the chorus. He picked up the second urn and returned to the water. "'Yes, we'll gather at the river, / The beautiful, the beautiful river; / Gather with the saints at the river / That flows by the throne of God.'"

Chuck's voice was rusty, but he started the verse

again, wanting to celebrate this ceremony that transcended the ages. Jacob's face was wet with tears. He picked up the third urn, struggling with the tape that held it closed. He stumbled a bit, and Chuck put out a hand to support him. The wind gusted, catching the ashes, blowing a gray cloud back over Chuck.

The singing stopped abruptly. "I'm sorry," Jacob said, and quickly poured the rest of the ash into the water.

Chuck brushed the ash from his shirt, shorts, and legs. It was like a scene from a dark comedy. He wanted to laugh, as Abbey would have laughed. No, Abbey would have guffawed. But that wouldn't be seemly tonight.

And then Chuck couldn't help himself. Maybe it was the alcohol, lowering his inhibitions, but first a chuckle escaped. That turned into a chortle that triggered a coughing spasm. He bent over trying to catch his breath so that he could apologize. Pain exploded at the back of his head, driving him to his knees, blinding him. He grunted, brought his eyes into focus, tried to stand. Jacob's shadow arm, holding the urn, rose, then descended to the words, "You think death is funny, old man?"

Chuck felt the damp sand under his chest. He was deaf to anything but the thundering in his head. He felt Jacob's weight on his back, Jacob's hand pressing his face in the water.

Chuck didn't struggle as river silt clogged his nose and mouth. Thought only, *I'm dying, in the canyon. . . .*

Part III

On the River
Grand Canyon National Park, Arizona
Tuesday, July 12

"We are three-quarters of a mile in the depths of the earth, and the great river shrinks into insignificance, as it dashes its angry waves against the walls and cliffs, that rise to the world above; they are but puny ripples, and we but pigmies, running up and down the sands, or lost among the boulders. . . .
"With some eagerness, and some anxiety, and some misgiving, we enter the cañon below, and we are carried along by the swift water through walls which rise from its very edge. They have the same structure as we noticed yesterday—tiers of irregular shelves below, and above these, steep slopes to the foot of marble cliffs."

—John Wesley Powell, *Exploration of the Colorado River of the West and Its Tributaries,* 1875

"The finest workers in stone are not copper or steel tools, but the gentle touches of air and water working at their leisure with a liberal allowance of time."

—Henry David Thoreau, *A Week on the Concord and Merrimack Rivers,* 1849

24

**Mile 41.6, South of Lower Buck Farm
Campsite, Marble Canyon**
12:12 a.m.

Jacob held the man's face underwater for a full two minutes. It took that long for Jacob's anger to subside. He'd already distanced himself emotionally from the man whose life force and energy were dissipating and transmuting.

He looked up at the stars, heard his sister Jenny's voice saying, "We're all made of stardust," and his brother, Sean, replying, "Einstein?"

"No, dumbshit. Lawrence Krauss."

Now their ashes were being carried down the river, finding their way to what Jenny had called "the great soul-sea." Their mother's ashes, too. In a way, Jacob envied them their journey.

My turn will come soon enough.

He felt empty. "I'm sorry, old man," Jacob said, pulling the body from the water. He meant it. He'd planned to kill Rennie later, while he was sleeping. But Chuck had laughed.

As they'd passed the toke back and forth, Jacob had planned what he'd do with the body. It had to be hidden well enough that it wouldn't be found for days, if ever. Jacob would then have full use of Chuck's kayak, while leaving his own less sturdy vessel behind at the mouth of Buck Farm Canyon.

He picked up the body in a fireman's carry and trudged up the fan and into the blacker tributary canyon. He tipped his headlamp down, wary of rattlesnakes in the boulder-choked draw. When he'd gone perhaps a hundred feet, he set down the body and scanned the cliff faces for a likely receptacle. Just downstream, the cliffs weathered into stunning concave recesses called the Royal Arches. He remembered seeps, marked by black lines of discolored rock and green trails of vegetation, trickling down from their bases. He expected to find smaller-scale recesses here. . . . He glimpsed one, perhaps forty feet above his head.

Jacob scouted a route up the ledges of rock, one that zigzagged at low angles that he could ascend with a dead weight. Dropping back down, he toted the body awkwardly up to the cleft and crammed it into the narrow space. As an afterthought, he rooted through the pockets of Chuck's shorts. They yielded packets of ibuprofen, a clean handkerchief, a tube of lip balm and another of sunscreen, a small black notebook, a pen, and an obsidian arrowhead that looked as if it had been fashioned yesterday. He ran his finger lightly along the edge. Sharp as a scalpel. Jacob wondered where Chuck had picked it up, and what it had meant to him.

Should Jacob leave the arrowhead as a funerary offering with the corpse? He was burying the body as the Utes once did. It would be appropriate. On the other hand, the point might prove useful.

He stuffed the arrowhead in his pocket with the other things and set about collecting rocks, using his shirt as an improvised carryall for the smaller stones. He worked quickly, but it still took an hour. Climbing down the last time, he inventoried the site to see if he'd left anything behind. . . . *Disturbed sand. Crushed vegetation. Small holes where rocks had been. Footprints, already losing their shape . . .* He doubted anyone would notice those things.

He put on his shirt. The body would be found eventually, but not soon. It wouldn't start to smell till after law enforcement had searched this area for Jacob—if they bothered. A week from now, they'd have to identify Chuck by his dental records. It would slow them down. By then Jacob would be on the other side of the world.

He checked his watch. Oh-one-thirty. He needed to be out of here by oh-two-thirty, at the latest, just to be on the safe side. So much to do. So little time.

Jacob trotted down to the shore and washed his hands and face. The air was still warm, whipped by the wind. Sand peppered his bare legs. His heart felt light. He had a plan and the means of carrying it out.

He brought his kayak, still filled with gear, over to Chuck's campsite. Chuck hadn't bothered with a tent. His bedroll and tarp were laid out neatly next to a small bag of clothing and toiletries. Jacob went through them. Took an old waterproof jacket and a couple of changes of clothes, left the rest.

Chuck's kayak, a Pyranha Fusion hardshell in lime and dark green, was customized with splashes of tan and brown to create a camouflage pattern. When beached in a thicket, or with outlines disguised among rocks, it would be invisible from the air. Or the ground.

He lifted the bow. Heavier than his inflatable. Weight concentrated in the rear cargo area. It was made for whitewater kayaking. The waterproof nylon deck covering the cockpit was closed tight against the rain. He released the cords, reached inside the skirt, and flipped up the backrest. Opening a rear storage hatch, he discovered a waterproof bag, padlocked shut. He tugged on it. Heavy.

Jacob searched the new kayak for cooking gear and food. Found the bare minimum, a duplicate of his own stores, stowed just behind the seat. He left them there, adding some of his own MREs. Transferred a wet-sack with Chuck's clothes, some of his own, and a few necessities to the forward foot compartment. He kept it simple—a daypack with emergency medical kit, rain gear, water, purifying pen and tablets. A river map. Chuck's old rain jacket would have to go in the rear compartment.

Jacob didn't want Chuck's fingerprints found in the inflatable kayak. He piled the dead man's gear on the tarp, weighted it with stones, tied the corners into a bundle, and tossed it in the river. He traded his toiletry kit for Chuck's, making sure to remove a waterproof zippered pocket with the man's keys, ID, boating permit, wind-up razor, and money. Jacob put rocks into the kit, zipped it shut, and threw it, too, in the river.

Where had Chuck left his vehicle? Back near Lee's Ferry? Probably. Unless someone had dropped him off and driven his vehicle to the South Rim.

He wished he'd asked Chuck some questions about his journey. Too late. But maybe he'd be able to find Chuck's vehicle using the key. By the time Jacob left the canyon, the police might have identified him. In that case, an extra vehicle would be handy.

He checked his watch again. Oh-two-fifteen. No time to explore the padlocked sack. If it wasn't something useful, he could always chuck it later.

There wasn't enough room for both the jacket and the bottle of Jack Daniel's on top of the locked bag. The liquor had more uses. He closed the rear hatch, patted down the jacket to make sure the pockets were empty, then repacked the inflatable kayak. Looked at the rifle. He'd scratched out the serial number, so the AR-15 couldn't be traced back to Sean. Or their father. Sean had inherited the entire gun collection. Jacob hated to part with anything that had belonged to his brother, but nothing says, "I'm outta here," like leaving your weapon behind.

He broke it down and slid the parts into the waterproof stuff bag containing his extra magazines. He wasn't worried about leaving fingerprints behind. He'd painted his fingertips with Super Glue before shopping for the kayak and loading it with supplies, and he'd refreshed the coating a few times since. He wasn't going to give the police a quick and dirty way to ID him.

He dropped his helmet and vest on the seat. Closed down the spray skirt. *Ready as you'll ever be, Dr. Presley.*

He took off Chuck's headlamp. From here on out he'd work under blackout conditions. Slipping on Chuck's vest and helmet, Jacob tied the inflatable to the rear of the hardshell, launched both crafts, and started paddling upstream. Fighting the current was tiring, but he couldn't portage his kayak upriver along the rocky talus slope. And even if he could, he wouldn't want to try and tiptoe, vessel on head, through the sleeping campers he'd passed at Buck Farm.

He was going to miss the AdvancedFrame inflatable, though he'd been damn lucky to get this far with it. The craft was designed for flat water, not rapids— especially not Category 5 and greater rapids. He'd pushed that limit time and again during the last three days. Against all odds, and due more to luck than skill, the inflatable had held air and stayed upright in the whitewater.

But the inflatable was never meant to take him far downstream. It was no match for the big rapids lurking beyond Nankoweap. He'd expected to work quietly and quickly, scuttle the kayak, and hike out. But life hadn't cooperated.

Well, now he had a boat better suited to the conditions, and a world of new possibilities.

Twenty minutes later, without waking the crew on the rafts at Buck Farm, he reached the upstream edge of the fan. He shed the sweat-soaked clothes the woman could identify, rinsed his body again in the frigid water, and dried off with the clothes before tossing them away in the river. Chuck's clothes fit him loosely, but that was better than too snug. Jacob doubted anyone would notice.

He left a few obvious footprints in the wet sand, then walked up the debris fan till his footprints were lost in the soft dune sand. Walking backward the way he'd come, he climbed into the kayak and pushed off, holding the paddle flush against the outer hull with his left arm. He curved his right arm around his head, bending forward until he could see the shore through a slit under his armpit. Anyone turning a headlamp on him would see only the formless lump of Kokopelli, the Humpbacked Fluteplayer, floating by in a kayak.

A light moved down the dunes, weaving between the tents. A headlamp, beam pointed at the ground. Probably looking for snakes, or for rocks and cactus. The light changed direction, seeming to follow a path. Someone heading for the privy, Jacob decided.

He stayed motionless, drifting with the current till the camp was out of sight. Sitting up, he set off by the light of the stars. It would be dawn in a couple of hours.

He should be exhausted, but he felt buoyant, alive. Adrenaline coursed through his veins. Chuck's was the first life he'd ever taken. As an army surgeon he'd lost men and women, but he'd fought death with all his skills and intellect. He'd expected to feel diminished by the act of murder. He didn't. John Donne had lied. We're not all pieces of a continent. We're individuals, traveling solo through life. The pecking order and random events determine who lives and who dies.

Three months ago he wouldn't have thought he was capable of murder. How easily he'd switched roles from healer to life-taker.

The first kill is always the hardest, they say. Well, his first kill was in the bag. The hunted had again become the hunter.

25

The moon was long past its zenith, the blackness of the canyon intense. President Harding Rapid was less than three miles ahead. The new kayak maneuvered easily and tracked well, but Jacob decided not to risk a night run. Too much chance of losing everything he'd gained.

Before the rapid, on river left, were a series of campsites. He'd take the first small beach he came to that had a level place for him to stretch out.

A dry wind gusted down a side canyon, the smell and the feel of it reminding him of Afghanistan. He allowed his mind to drift back, just for a moment, lulled by the comforting rhythm of his paddle. Another desert night, felted black sky pierced by crystal shards of light. Brilliant flashes of ground fire. The Chinook crashing. Pilot, one arm and both legs shot to ribbons, barely alive when Jacob arrived to airlift him and his injured crew to safety.

"Take my legs," the pilot said. "Take my arm, if you have to. Just save enough of me so I can hold my daughter."

Jacob and his team had worked for a night and a day. Two of the men who'd kept their captain alive died on the operating table. Jacob had saved the captain's arm, but not his legs. Exhausted, Jacob had walked out of surgery to hear the news about Jenny and Sean. Two hours later he was on a military transport home. Ten days after that, he'd had a memorial service for his only siblings and his mother. Etta Presley's two younger children had come home in boxes, just like her husband had from Desert Storm. She'd collapsed and died of a heart attack before Jacob arrived.

Alone in the family home, his mood had alternated between despair and a tamped-down anger that threatened to explode. His mind turned to Revenge. Capital R.

He'd called a psychiatrist, one of his classmates from medical school, and asked her for a prescription for marijuana to calm the symptoms. Shaky hands. Violent dreams. Sensitivity to noise and flashing lights. Grass was better than pills, Jacob told her. Tough to OD on Mary Jane.

After a couple of marathon counseling sessions— marathon because his leave was almost up—he'd gotten the prescription . . . along with a laundry list of diagnoses, none of them serious enough to make him unfit for duty. But serious enough for her to extend his leave.

He hadn't told her about his plan to even the score with the MacFarlanes.

Now his leave was almost up. In a few days, he'd be back in Afghanistan. Or another conflict. They'd begun to meld together.

But for the moment he was here, on this river wending its thunderous way through a heart of stone. Today, for the first time, the world had color and texture. Even in the inky blackness, he could sense the color. The curtain had lifted. Remembering no longer made him want to walk to the edge of the rim and step out into space.

Jacob heard the roar of President Harding Rapid. Half a mile ahead, max. Category 4, four-foot drop, made treacherous by storm runoff. Adjacent to two big camping areas on river left. He had to assume they'd contain rafting parties. It was the height of the season.

He put his headlamp strap over his helmet, turned on the lamp, and steered toward the shore. Rocky shelves. Sparse brush. Vertical cliffs. A small beach should be coming up anytime now. . . .

The edges of his headlamp beam caught a pale hump rising from the river. Dead ahead, maybe twenty boat lengths. Approaching cautiously, he discovered an empty debris fan, a sloping boulder pile with pockets of sand and a few dense thickets. Must be Anasazi Bridge, a small campsite. It would do. He was too tired to go any farther.

He climbed out and dragged the craft up the slope. Later he could rig up a mooring device. He hadn't thought to bring the pin from the inflatable.

Walking a little way up the talus slope, he scoped out the site. No lights shone in the camps downriver. As far as they'd know, he'd have been here all night.

He rolled out his bedsheet, stretched the kinks from his muscles, and walked down to the riverbank to piss in the water. He wanted nothing more than sleep, but he would use the cover of darkness to finish the chores he'd left undone at Buck Farm.

Back at the kayak, he quietly unpacked his gear. He was getting low on water. He scooped up his water bottles and returned to the shore, upstream of where he'd stood before. Wading in, he filled the bottles from the surface of the swift current. The water looked clear in his headlamp beam, so he zapped each of the bottles for ninety seconds with the UV purifying pen. Dropped in some iodine tablets, just to be on the safe side. It would taste shitty, but he'd had worse.

Rooting around in the kayak, he found his camp stove and cook pot. In a hollow hidden from the river, he filled the pot with water and put it to boil. He opened two packets of instant oatmeal into a bowl, adding a handful of dried fruit, instant milk, and walnuts. He set the bowl on a rock. The water wasn't yet lukewarm. He had time to find out what was in the rear hatch of the hardshell.

Removing the lid to the cargo hold, he pulled out the heavy reinforced bag. The padlock was solid. He could slice through the sack itself, but he might not need to. He found the key ring he'd taken from Chuck's overnight bag. The smallest of four keys fit the padlock.

He unrolled the thick-walled sack, opened it. *What the fuck?*

Gingerly, he reached in and pulled out a cream-colored brick of what looked like modeling clay. C-4. Labeled M-118. Military grade.

Jacob felt beads of sweat gather on his forehead. He would have preferred a bag of rattlesnakes. C-4 was stable, but add blasting caps and some wire, and. . . . He'd seen the effects often enough in his years in the army. But what were the bricks doing here, in a kayaker's hold, forty-four miles into the Grand Canyon?

He gently and carefully removed the bricks from the bag. Searched the bottom for blasting caps or wire. Nothing. Did the same to the hold. Found a small dry bag. In it were Edward Abbey's *The Monkey Wrench Gang* and a notebook with penciled drawings of the Kaibab and Bright Angel suspension bridges—the only connections within the canyon between north and south trails. Bright red Xs marked where C-4 would be planted. And there was a note: *In honor of the 50th anniversary of Rachel Carson's* Silent Spring. *George Hayduke lives!*

It was unsigned. But there were initials on the cover of the notebook: *C. R.*

Chuck Rennie. Good old Chuck, now very much dead.

Shit. Jacob had stolen a kayak from an ecoterrorist. What if Chuck hadn't been working alone? What if he was meeting someone at Phantom Ranch? C-4 was no good without blasting caps and wire. Was someone else bringing those to the clambake?

The water was boiling—had no doubt been boiling happily for minutes. Jacob carefully re-stowed the cargo, splashed water onto his oatmeal, then dumped instant coffee and dry milk into the rest of the boiled water. He'd drink directly from the pot.

He remembered the small notebook he'd found in the dead man's pocket. Chuck had been writing in it when Jacob hailed the camp. If Chuck's friends were coming, Jacob had to assume they'd recognize Chuck's kayak. And they'd want its cargo back.

He needed to cook up a story that would satisfy them, would explain why Chuck wasn't here with the C-4, and he was. . . . And if they didn't rendezvous with Jacob, he needed to figure out what he was going to do with ten bricks of C-4.

A faint gray was seeping into the eastern sky as he dug out the notebook and settled back with his coffee. It was oh-four-fifteen.

Thirty minutes later he turned off his headlamp, washed and put away his dishes, peed in the river again, and lay down, eyes closed to the brightening heavens. He'd learned five things from that notebook. Charles Rennie was a lifelong defender of the planet. He and several friends were planning to meet up today. Blowing up the bridges at Phantom Ranch wasn't a pipe dream, but an action plan. Chuck, a lawyer, was going to take responsibility for the destruction. And Chuck was dying of cancer.

How do you define irony? Murdering a man who would have been dead in short order. And killing him in the canyon where he wanted to die.

The knowledge that he'd inadvertently fulfilled a dying man's last wishes filled Jacob with sadness and anger, not satisfaction.

It was too much to take in. He needed rest. Maybe his subconscious could come up with a plausible cover story if he slept for an hour or two. . . .

26

**Mile 37.9, Tatahatso Campsite,
Marble Canyon**
4:30 a.m.

I woke from the nightmare as I was about to smash into the rocks. I'd been climbing the cliffs near the Bridge of Sighs. No rope. No help. And a man with a gun below me. He'd winged me, and I'd fallen toward him. He smiled as the ground rushed up. Jacob smiled.

Rubbing sleep from my eyes with one hand, I used the other to unwrap the swaddling bedsheet. My whole body ached, inside and out. And I was hungry as a Gila monster just out of hibernation.

I shook sand from my shoes. Checked them for scorpions. Standard operating procedure in the field. Even half-asleep, I went through the motions before heading for the privy. The seat-cushion signal wasn't leaning against the hand-washing station. Someone was there ahead of me.

I sat on a boulder, watching the canyon walls detach themselves from the shadows as if they were being built anew, ledge by finger by butte. Two dimensions becoming three. What had been nothing but a dark presence blotting out the stars the night before resolved itself into rigid rock and mother-of-pearl sky.

I smelled smoke. Nico emerged from the willows and reeds puffing on a cigarette. "You feeling okay?" He handed me the cushion.

"Stiff, sore, and starving, but no reaction to drinking river water. Yet."

"Well, keep an eye on it. If you come down with something, we'll have to separate you from the others in case it's contagious. And remember to wash your hands a lot."

Quarantine. Just what I needed. "Will do," I said, and trundled on down to the john. The can was for number two. Campers had to pee in the river. The water felt colder than last night.

Returning a few minutes later, I dutifully washed my hands and rinsed them twice before climbing back up to my tent. My swimsuit hadn't dried overnight, but I wriggled into it anyway. Grabbing my large coffee can, ecofriendly soap, and a small towel, I trotted down to a sandy-bottomed spot upstream of the rafts. Wading in up to my waist, I poured cans of water over my hair, soaped up, and dunked myself in the river, coming up with a gasp. The soap and water stung my back, shoulder, and upper arms, places I couldn't see. My body felt bruised and battered, but I didn't seem to be running a temperature. I'd come through the first skirmish well, considering I hadn't been expecting trouble. But I was under no illusions. For Jacob, this was war, winner take all. But would the next battleground be here or in Tucson?

The wind didn't answer. My mind came up empty. Above me, the cliffs began to take on color, as if an invisible artist were stroking their surface with watercolors. Faint gold, with here and there a pink blush, reflected off the clouds, remnants of yesterday's storm. Swallows flitted across the surface of the river. I brushed and braided my hair, feeling hugely better, and went over to beg coffee from Nico. Or Roxy. Or Doug. They all were busy, cutting fruit for breakfast and setting out juice and cereal.

"Got your mug?" Nico said.

"It's up there someplace," I waved in the general direction of my tent.

He filled the lid of his thermos and handed me the creamer. I swear, nothing ever tasted as good as that coffee. I took a sip, found it wasn't prohibitively hot, and downed it in three gulps. He poured me a chaser. When that went the way of the first dose of caffeine, I set the cup on the table, saying, "I'll wash it when the water's hot."

"You're pretty banged up," Roxy said, as I turned to go. "You put anything on those cuts?" A rhetorical question, as I couldn't reach most of the raw spots. She squirted hand purifier into her palm. A first-aid kit lay open at the end of the table.

"Now's a good time," she said when I hesitated. "It'll take ten minutes for the griddle to finish heating so I can start cooking."

I presented my back for her ministrations. She clucked and tut-tutted like a mother quail.

"Think I'll live?"

"Looks like road rash and deep bruising, but you took it on the muscle, for the most part." Her fingers were light and deft as they probed and examined. "You have full use of your arms?"

I showed her, wincing only once.

"Did you hit your head?"

I thought back. Shook my head. A little too vigorously. Another wince. "I tried to protect it as well as I could."

"What about your knee?"

"It hurts."

More probing.

"You're damn lucky. No broken bones."

She stuck a thermometer into my mouth, then wrapped an elastic bandage around my knee and pinned it closed. The raft crews were required to have wilderness first-aid training. Some were nurses or EMTs. It was the first time I'd been the recipient. I realized, belatedly, that Roxy had been designated to determine whether I was fit to continue with the trip.

She removed the thermometer. "Ninety-seven point eight."

"I'm always a little low."

"So am I." Checking my eyes, she said, "Headache?"

"No."

"Vision problems?"

"Nada. Am I fit for duty, doc?"

"Far as I can tell." She slathered my upper back and shoulder with antibiotic ointment. "But I'll check on you later, just to be sure nothing festers." She was silent for a moment, finishing up with a little pat. "I'm not going to try to bandage this. The ointment has an analgesic. Should help with the pain."

"It'll heal better in the air anyway."

"Yup. But the PFD might chafe. So wear a shirt today."

"I will. Thanks, Roxy."

A helicopter flew low up the canyon, following the river. NPS. Help was on the way.

I hurried up to my tent, changed into dry swim shorts and bikini top, donned a soft T-shirt, and buttoned a field shirt over that. It didn't take long. Molly arrived as I was zipping the bag. She was lugging my sleeping gear, which she deposited next to her own.

"Thanks," I said. "I'll put them away if you want to head to the john."

"That's kind of you," she said with a shy smile. Turning, she trotted off.

Another five minutes and the waterproof orange sacks we'd rented from the outfitters were stuffed, closed, and locked. I slipped the straps of my day and night bags over my battered shoulders, then lugged the sacks down to the beach. I was first in line for breakfast. This time I remembered my mug.

Direct sunlight hadn't reached the bottom of the canyon, but the morning already was warm and humid. The heat didn't dampen my appetite. I filled my plate with a large pancake capped by eggs-over-medium, a rasher of bacon, and a side of sliced melon, then sank into a canvas chair to demolish my breakfast. I refused to worry about clogged arteries this morning. I was celebrating my survival and savoring what might be my last meal on the river.

Whether the crew would allow me to stay with the trip was now in the hands of the river gods. And the rangers.

Harvey took the seat next to me. I bobbed my head in greeting, my mouth full of pancake. He inserted his coffee mug into the slot in the armrest, set his plate on his lap, and harrumphed a couple of times. But he didn't pick up his fork.

I swallowed. Took a sip of coffee. "Something on your mind, Harvey?"

Another harrumph. "When you went missing, I felt, well, terrible. I'd been in your face. Dora's, too," he said. "Roy—you know Roy?"

I nodded, chewed, swallowed, not sure what was coming next.

"Roy called me on it. Told me I didn't have the right to disrupt the lessons you and Dora were sharing with your students. Just wanted you to know I was sorry. Won't happen again."

"I appreciate that, Harvey."

"I figure we're all after the same thing—the experience of this canyon, and what it can teach us." He tilted his head back to gaze at the towering cliffs, then smiled at me. "What we take away is up to us."

27

After stowing their camping equipment in the truck, Ben Gruber had walked back to the rim at a spot across from Tatahatso Point, farther south than where he'd tossed Eldon's remains over the edge. Ben had spent the night in prayer and contemplation. He'd seen the stars blink out and the faint shimmer in the east that spoke of dawn. He'd had no more revelations. He trusted they would come after he accomplished the next task.

The sun had risen over the lip of the plateau at five-twenty. A short time later a helicopter had passed low overhead, traveling upriver. Ben had hidden under a ledge. Only when it had flown by again had he crawled out and resumed his post.

He'd watched golden light steal slowly down the cliffs that marked the edge of the Navajo Reservation. Only now were the rays reaching the camp where Eldon claimed to have seen his sons. Ben again lifted the binoculars and trained them on the site. Two large rafts. And two search-and-rescue Zodiacs moored beside them. But Ben couldn't see any rangers. Curious.

In a relaxed, unhurried way, people were finishing breakfast, washing dishes, collapsing chairs and tents, piling gear on the beach. Not the regimented hustle and bustle Ben was used to when the Family broke camp. Perhaps the rafters were planning to take a hike before they continued downriver.

He counted twenty-six people. Tatahatso was small for a two-raft party. It made no sense that they'd chosen it when there were larger sites only a little way downriver.

He searched the short stretch of green water winding below him. Empty. Checked the camp again. Three people were looking upstream. What were they waiting for?

And then he saw another Zodiac round a bend in the river. NPS law enforcement. A shiver touched his spine. No, they couldn't be after him, couldn't know what he'd done up here on the rim. They were at Tatahatso for a different reason. But maybe Ben could use it to his advantage.

So far, he'd positively identified only two of Eldon's sons. Everyone wore hats, which made it difficult. But when those two clustered with three other young people, he saw what Eldon had seen—the similarity in build and posture of four of the boys. Definitely Sprague's sons. And the fifth boy was Ethan, the son he'd sent away two months ago. Where those boys were, their sister might also be.

Ben examined the other members of the rafting party. None looked familiar. Just to be thorough, he checked the crew again. He'd identified them earlier, when they were preparing breakfast. The raft group should have a crew of three, but a fourth person had helped with the cooking and cleanup. Another boy. Maybe he was a novice swamper, just learning the ropes. He wore long sleeves and pants. His hat had a flap that covered his neck. His face was in shadow. But he was scrawnier than the others. Almost delicate.

As Ben watched, the boy lifted his hat and drew his

arm across his forehead. Very short black hair. Tattoos on his arms. Pierced ears with small silver studs that glinted in the morning light. And a nose ring . . .

Ben closed his eyes for a moment, then squinted through the glasses. The boy turned his head toward one of the crew and smiled.

Naomi's smile.

28

**Mile 37.9, Tatahatso Camp,
Marble Canyon**
7:05 a.m.

I took my last swallow of coffee and headed for the dishwashing line. Paused at the thrumming of engines. The rangers must have run flat out to have reached Tatahatso this early.

A Zodiac swung toward shore and cut its motor. Six people on board. I recognized four of the men as searchers from the previous day.

A woman ranger tossed the mooring line to Nico. The searchers hopped out and made for the rescued Zodiacs. Nico escorted the remaining two to where I stood by the tables, rinsing my dishes.

Both law enforcement rangers wore dark green pants and gray shirts, NPS arrowheads on left sleeves, sidearms on hips. Badges reflected the early-morning sun from the left front of their vests. Nametags were pinned to the right. Boyd Cheski and Bess Wentworth. Cheski, the ranger in charge, was a tall, spare man on the far side of fifty. Wentworth was in her mid-forties, with curly, graying black hair, cut close to her head.

Cheski looked at Luke, who was standing just behind me.

"How ya been, Boyd?" Luke held out his hand.

Boyd took off his sunglasses, letting them dangle from their safety cord. His eyes were hazel, flecked with brown, faded from years in the sun. He took my brother's hand. "Matt?"

"Luke."

"Never could keep you two straight."

Luke grinned. "Matt's the handsome one. . . . How's Connie?"

"Who's Connie?" I said.

"My daughter," Cheski said.

"She worked summers for the park service," said Luke. "Compliance officer. Did surprise ride-alongs on the rafts to make sure we minded our Ps and Qs. She was sweet on Matt." His eyes smiled, as if they were pleasant memories. "Ranger Boyd Cheski, this is my sister, Frankie."

Cheski introduced his partner, and we all shook hands. Ranger Wentworth said, "We heard you had a rough day yesterday."

Masterful understatement. I smiled, shrugged. "I've had better."

From his left breast pocket Cheski removed a small notebook and a mechanical pencil. "I'd like the other rangers to hear. Would save time."

I nodded, and Cheski waved the rangers up from the beach. Glancing at the ring of people that had slipped in behind me, he said, "Maybe we could find a more private place to talk."

As Nico and Roxy put the rafters to work breaking down camp and loading the rafts, I led Cheski, Wentworth, and the search team to the hollow at the base of the cliff where Molly and I had spent the night. I checked the crevices for snakes before sitting down.

"You're welcome to join me." I gestured to the ledge beside me.

Cheski looked at the red ants scouring the sand for breakfast, then accepted my invitation. The other rangers stood or hunkered down, some facing me, some facing the river and the cliffs opposite. Cheski led me through the sequence of events. Even to my ears, the tale sounded farfetched. A stranger had known my name, followed me down the river, and threatened to kill me. He'd had a knife and a rifle. Yet somehow I'd escaped.

"You're sure about the rifle?" Cheski glanced up from his notes.

"Positive. I can't tell you what kind, but it looked like an assault rifle." I told Cheski about the kayaker following me from Nautiloid Canyon, hiding his boat, and climbing to a better vantage point. "From up there on the cliff he could sink a raft with a couple of shots. That's why I stayed hidden and didn't flag down my group—or your searchers. Even though they were wearing life vests, there would have been casualties."

Cheski's eyes narrowed, as if he were picturing the scene in his head. Jacob could have taken out the searchers before they knew where the shots were coming from. They weren't expecting trouble—not that kind of trouble.

The ranger looked over at Luke, who was standing next to Dora, holding a hand-drawn columnar section of the rocks we'd see along the next stretch of river. The rafts were loaded, and Dora was making good use of the extra time.

Ranger Wentworth broke the silence. "But your choice meant you were going up against an armed man alone."

"Better than having anyone else's blood on my hands. Even if Jacob had let me get on a raft, we'd never have left the area alive."

"Why you?" Cheski said.

I spread my hands. "I've wracked my brain for an answer. He didn't give me any clues except his name—and that might be false. . . . But he was definitely hunting me. I watched him for hours."

Cheski jotted down more notes, then said, "Okay, what happened after you landed here?"

I recounted the scene on the beach, right up to when Jacob retrieved his kayak. Cheski looked at Bess Wentworth. Someone who moved like a ghost had stolen two SAR Zodiacs—without waking or harming the sleeping men. The boats had been recovered here, undamaged, except for cut lines.

Dora finished her geotalk and released the students. Below us, the rafters milled about, laughing and talking, sneaking quick peeks in our direction. A few of them had witnessed the events here last night. They could corroborate my story.

Cheski stood, nodded to the rangers, said, "You know what to do."

The SAR teams headed for the Zodiacs. The boats backed up and took off, cruising slowly down the sides of the river, looking for Jacob's kayak. Or his body. Déjà vu. Instant replay of yesterday's search—only this time I wasn't watching helplessly from a cave.

Cheski and Wentworth split up to interview the crew and rafters, starting with Luke and Doug. I joined the uninvolved rafters sitting in a patch of shade down the beach. I thanked them for their patience, answered questions, and gave them a preview of the archaeological sites we'd visit at our next stop.

Dora joined us as I rolled up my visual aids—enlarged photos of the Nankoweap granary, pit houses on the delta, a mano and metate. She took the rafters on a tour of the boulder-strewn beach to describe the sedimentary textures and structures of the Muav Limestone, which underlay the Undivided Dolomites and the Redwall Limestone. I tagged along at the rear, listening as she brought to life the shallow marine environment in which the Muav sediments had been deposited more than 500 million years ago.

When Cheski and Wentworth finished, they came over to the group. Wentworth sat on a boulder to finish her notes. Cheski's satellite phone rang before he could say anything. He stepped aside, knelt down, jotted more notes in the tablet pinned against his thigh.

Luke sauntered over, put a reassuring hand on my shoulder.

"Ouch."

"Sorry, I forgot."

We turned our back on Dora's group, squatted to check out lenses of blood-red jasper and black chert in a Redwall boulder, then wandered down to where the guides waited at the river's edge. Cheski and Wentworth, after a quick consultation, joined us.

"Well?" I said.

"Searchers think they've found the kayak, his rifle still in it, at Buck Farm Canyon."

"That close?" Buck Farm was only two miles downriver.

"The idiot stole two police boats," Luke said. "Would you stay on the river with rangers hunting your hide?"

Cheski grinned. "You're right. Looks like he took the first trail to the rim after he recovered his kayak."

"Can't have been easy to do by moonlight," Luke said. "All that slippery red mud and boulder hopping."

"Unless he waited till first light," I said.

"So, what's next?" Dora stood behind me. The noise of the river had covered her approach.

"We'd like to take Frankie and Luke down to Buck Farm to identify the kayak," Cheski said. "Could you meet us there?"

"No problem," Nico said. "It's a decent beach. Plenty of parking this time of day."

"What about afterwards?" I couldn't stay with the trip if it would endanger the group—and Nico couldn't let me.

"Let's see what they've turned up at Buck Farm," he said.

Cheski walked ten paces away to call his searchers. I collected my day pack and gave my other gear to Roxy and Doug to stow on the raft.

Luke dropped his pack beside mine. "Another hour,

and you can be sure this nightmare is over—at least for now."

"I'll believe that when I see the kayak." And even then, I'd still be watching over my shoulder.

Ranger Cheski holstered his phone and walked back to us. "Air searches will be scanning the rim and Buck Farm Canyon within the hour. We'll deploy people on the ground at the trailhead, and send some up from the bottom. If he's still in the canyon, we'll flush him out. But if he had a vehicle waiting up on top, he may have gotten away."

"To try again somewhere else," I said.

"Even if he eludes our people and hikes back down to the river, the earliest he'll be able to intercept you will be at Phantom Ranch."

He was right. Nankoweap Trail was too long and difficult for Jacob to reach the delta before we left. Time was on our side. I said, "If necessary, we can skip Phantom."

"Shouldn't be necessary. If we don't catch him today, we'll have people watching the trailheads, north and south, that lead to Phantom. And the rangers at Phantom will be on alert. When do you plan to get there?" he asked Nico.

"Tomorrow, mid-afternoon. We'll camp at Carbon Canyon tonight. Hike the Butte Fault loop in the morning."

Cheski made a note, then looked up at me. "Once you leave the canyon, you'll have to take precautions."

"It would help if I knew who I was guarding against," I said. "A last name, maybe a history."

"We'll do what we can," Cheski said, and leafed back through his notes to check my contact information.

"All set?" Nico said. "Then let's get this show on the road."

29

Mile 43.5, Anasazi Bridge Camp, Marble Canyon

8:30 a.m.

Something nudged Jacob's foot. He woke with a start.

"Whoa there, stranger. We come in peace. You can put the knife down."

A woman's voice. She stood to his right, helmet under her arm, face in shadow. Medium height. Sleeveless arms with well-defined muscles—like a soldier just out of boot camp, or a world-class athlete. Her hair, backlit by the morning light, was an unlikely shade of red.

Jacob sheathed the knife and rolled to his feet. He yawned, stretched, rubbed sleep from his eyes as he assessed the situation. . . . Empty kayak, beached next to Jacob's on the shore. Two men in kayaks holding their position in the water. Five more kayaks and two supply rafts downstream, scouting President Harding Rapid.

"Peaceful people don't generally kick a sleeping camper."

"Sorry," the woman said. She didn't sound sorry. "That your kayak?"

"Chuck loaned it to me. He couldn't make it." Jacob figured that if these were Chuck's compadres, this would raise all kinds of questions. He was right.

"And you are?" she said.

A name popped into his mind. "Walt Perry."

Perry had been Jacob's roommate the first year of med school. They were built along the same lines and had the same coloring. But Perry, from the hills of Virginia, spoke with a regional twang. They still kept in touch. Perry was, at this moment, hiking in the backcountry of New England and blessedly out of cell phone range. What Walt didn't know wouldn't hurt him, Jacob hoped.

"Should we have heard of you?"

"Maybe, maybe not. I've been out of commission for a few years."

She thought about that for a minute, her face transparent. She was trying to fit the random bits of information she knew about Chuck together with what "Walt" was giving her, to make a picture that explained everything. At last she said, "You got caught?"

"Yup. Got out last week." He stretched again, the picture of nonchalance, and moved so that he could get a better look at her face. "Chuck was the first person I called. Wanted to pay my respects before . . . well, you know."

The tension lines around her mouth softened. Apparently she knew about Chuck's cancer. She said, "What were you in for?"

"Arson. Housing development on sacred ground. But we hadn't factored in a night watchman taking a snooze in the model home. Heard him screaming, so I went back to pull him out. By the time the ambulance arrived, it was too late to get away."

"How long did you get?"

"Fifteen to twenty. But I was out in eight."

"Funny that Chuck never mentioned a mission that went bad."

A *"mission"? Who did these guys think they were?*

Jacob shrugged. "I didn't give him up. It would have been pointless and stupid for him to let on to anyone that he was there that night. I went to jail so he could stay active. That was our code. He would have done the same for me."

"He called to tell me he was leaving," she said. "But he didn't call back to tell me there'd been a change in plans."

"Probably 'cause he only made it as far as the back door before he collapsed, right there in the kitchen. I called an ambulance, and before he passed out, he begged me to fill in for him—act as courier. We'd talked about doing this years ago, before I . . . went away. He didn't give me names, just said you'd find the kayak."

"Which we did. It's a one-off, a custom job. Easy to spot."

Jacob sensed she still wasn't buying the story. "What you want's in the rear cargo hold." He nodded toward the kayak, giving them permission to retrieve the parcel. Truth be told, he was grateful to offload the C-4. Made him damned uncomfortable.

The men didn't move.

"If you want to abort, just say so and I'll sink the C-4 and just enjoy my trip down the canyon. Up to you."

"Did he give you the password?" said the man in the closest kayak.

"Password? Jesus fucking Christ, the guy was barely *breathing*." Jacob pretended to think back. "Okay—before they put the oxygen mask on him he was muttering something like 'Hayduke lives.' Or maybe it was 'Abbey lives.'"

"Abbzug lives?" said the second man.

"Could have been. I wasn't really concentrating. Thought he was rambling. Apparently not." Jacob turned back to the woman. She was the leader. "Look, whoever you are, it was important to Chuck that I do this one last thing for him."

"Risky for you. You could end up back inside."

He grinned. "They'll have to catch me first."

The woman nodded to the men.

"His diagram's in there, too," Jacob said. "Under the stuff. Key's in the padlock."

One of the men paddled over to the kayak. Opening the rear hatch, he lifted out the Jack Daniel's, which had been nestled on top. He held it up. Chuck had made quite a dent in it before he'd ever offered a swig to Jacob.

"Looks like you didn't wait for us to start the party," Deanna said. "Explains why we found you asleep on the beach at eight-thirty in the morning."

"I was celebrating being free and on the river. I'm good with saving the rest till our business is wrapped up."

"Don't go all noble on me. Doesn't suit you."

How do you know what suits me? But he didn't let his thoughts show in his face.

"Besides," she said, "we brought our own supplies."

The man at Chuck's kayak took out the dry bag with the C-4. Checked it. Gave a thumbs-up. The woman pulled off her sunglasses, letting them dangle from a Croakie.

"Deanna," she said, holding out her hand. "Deanna Birdsall. That's Butch." She pointed to the man holding the C-4 in one hand, the Jack Daniel's in the other. "And Kent." She nodded to the guy in the other kayak. "We thought Chuck would be a day ahead of us."

Jacob shook her hand. "Chuck probably would have stuck to the schedule. I took my time. Had a little fun at the expense of a couple of Search and Rescue boats last night—liberated them, shall we say."

The skin of her face seemed to tighten. *Nice skin,* Jacob thought. *Looks like she just had dermabrasion. Must be the canyon sand.*

Her voice hardened. "They didn't see you?"

"This isn't my first dance, Deanna Birdsall. I waited till they were bedded down. Left 'em stranded till this morning."

She nodded. "We saw them out searching a couple of miles back. Around Buck Farm. Probably a lost hiker."

"Good. They got their boats back."

"We'd better get going," said Butch, "or the others will start wondering what we're up to."

"They're not in on it?" Jacob said.

"No. Just the three of us."

"Mind if I tag along? I'm not Chuck, but I'd like to be able to tell him I saw it through."

The bomber's plan could be a boon. If Jacob could time their arrival at Phantom Ranch to overlap with Frankie's group, he could dispatch his targets and escape in the mayhem following the bridge explosions. But the big, motorized rafts traveled faster than the kayaks. Somehow he had to find a way to slow down Frankie's group.

Deanna had been weighing his offer. She came to a decision. "We could use an experienced fourth."

"Great," Jacob said. "By the way, what day is this?"

"You really ought to stay away from the hard stuff," she said. "It's Tuesday, July 12. Why?"

Because I'm officially AWOL on Friday night.

Jacob could still finish the mission, report as scheduled, and board transport for Afghanistan. Once overseas, he'd be safe. He could disappear from there when he finished this tour.

"Some place you gotta be, pal?" Butch said.

"Just remembered—I'm supposed to check in with my parole officer in three days."

"You can call him—"

"Her," Jacob said, just to get under Deanna's skin.

She took a breath, enunciated each word, "You can call *her* from Phantom Ranch."

"Okeydokey." Jacob turned away, stowed his kit in the empty hold, fastened his vest, and slipped on his helmet. *Now the fun starts.*

He climbed into the kayak and snapped the splash skirt. He hadn't realized what a talented liar he was. Even he'd bought the story.

One by one, whooping and hollering, they surfed the tongue at President Harding, then caught the wave train till it deposited them in quieter water. He followed the same line as the other kayaks. Paused, breathless, on the other side, before turning to watch the support rafts shoot through. Much more ungainly. But they made it without flipping.

Deanna maneuvered her kayak next to his, facing him. "We'll stop at Nankoweap," she said. "We want to hike up to the granary."

Nankoweap. Where Frankie's party was sure to arrive sometime this morning. He had to come up with a good reason for staying by the kayaks and out of sight.

"I'm not much for heights," Jacob lied. "Chuck always took those jobs. I worked below."

She laughed. "Then you're gonna *love* Deer Creek."

"Maybe you'll get me over my phobia."

"Slow down, pardner," said Butch.

Jacob tilted his head, studying Deanna. "You don't look like you're wearing a brand."

"He's dreaming. Nobody owns me." But she glanced at Jacob in a different way than she had two minutes ago.

"I don't want trouble with Butch."

"Leave Butch to me."

"One last thing," he said, as she dipped her paddle in the water.

"What?"

"Chuck wants to be the one to take credit for the bridges. There's nothing the law can do to him now, and it would leave you guys free to keep working after he's gone. But the authorities will only swallow his story if he's out of the hospital in time to hike down to the bottom of the canyon. He said he'd move hell and heaven combined to get released today, even if he has to sign himself out."

She had tears in her eyes. "That sounds just like Chuck. We'll make it happen for him, don't worry."

"Just pay it forward, Deanna. That's all he asks." *God, I'm getting good at this.*

Deanna set off downriver. Jacob followed, grateful for the cover provided by the group.

Safety in numbers. Just have to hang in there and escape detection till Phantom Ranch.

30

Kaibab Plateau, North Rim,
above Marble Canyon
9:33 a.m.

On his return hike from the overlook, Ben Gruber had worked out the next steps in his plan to recover Naomi.

He headed west, navigating a zigzag route through a network of forest service dirt roads. Turning north on Buffalo Ranch Road, he drove for a few miles before cutting west again on FS 220, the East Side Game Road. It looped through low hills and ridges, climbing steadily but gradually. The perfume of grasses and shrubs scented air heavy with evaporating moisture from the previous night's storm. But soon the stiffening wind would turn the damp road to dust. And dust churned up by his tires could be seen from a distance. He stepped on the gas.

Shrubland gave way to scattered piñon-juniper woodland, and higher still, to ponderosa pine. Around Tater Tank, he knew, the trees were thick enough and the area deserted enough that a fire had a good chance of spreading before anyone discovered and reported it.

The road made a right-angle bend among the trees. He pulled off on a secondary road just past the tank and parked among the trees. Grabbing a tarp from the back, he set off into the woods. He collected as much deadwood and pine duff as he could fit on the tarp, then pulled the corners of the tarp together and hoisted it to his back. His shadow looked like Santa Claus, but without the belly roll.

He carried the tinder to the draw below a lightning-struck pine he remembered from hunting season a few years back. A third of the blackened tree had blown down into the ravine. Sap had oozed from the injured wood, hardening in rivulets. He heaped dead wood around the tree to form a pyre.

He always carried a compass in his pocket, one with a small geologist's hand lens attached. It had been his father's, the only thing his father had left him. Ben suspected that his father had been sending him a message with the gift—that he hoped Ben would somehow find true north again before it was too late. He'd never understood that Ben's true north was the Family. He'd never leave it.

Words came to him out of the air and earth, light and trees, resounding in their power: *"There is in my heart as it were a burning fire shut up in my bones, and I am weary with holding it in, and I cannot."*

Holding the tiny magnifying lens up to the sun, Ben directed the light onto a handful of dry needles. Half a minute later a flame shot up. Ben blew on it, tucked it into the pile of tinder, and fanned the pyre until the wood flared up. When flames were running along the trunk, he took a burning branch from the pile and moved from tree to tree in a circle. Soon the whole copse was ablaze. From above it would look like a flaming eye.

The thickly wooded draw served as a chimney. He watched long enough to see the wind carry sparks to fresh trees, pulling the fire east to the piñon-juniper woodlands and the grassy plateau beyond.

"He makes his messengers winds, his ministers a flaming fire."

The closest ranches were thirty or forty miles away.

They weren't owned by the Family. God would decide if the ranchers were just and would escape the flames.

Ben ran back up the ridge to the truck. Scanned the surrounding area to see if anyone had noticed and was responding to the smoke. All clear.

Hopping in his truck he drove north as fast as he dared on FS 220. It was a long way to Highway 89A, the paved road bisecting this part of the Arizona Strip. But as long as he got to Fredonia and finished his business by dusk, he was okay.

And once on the blacktop, heading northwest, there would be nothing to connect him with a fire down on the rim. Or the remains of a body.

31

Leaving Tatahatso Camp, Colorado River, Marble Canyon
9:50 a.m.

"I have seen almost more beauty than I can bear," Everett Ruess wrote before he disappeared into Davis Gulch more than eighty years ago. November 1934. The artist and writer was twenty, the same age as the eldest of Dora's students.

I thought of Ruess as Luke and I set off with Rangers Cheski and Wentworth. Everett had come to the Southwest in search of the poet's concept of beauty, one that "exceeds all imagining." He found it in the canyons of the Colorado Plateau—in the wedding-cake tiers of intensely colored sandstone and limestone, in the immense swath of time, in the dark, contorted heart of the Vishnu Schist. He discovered a land where cloud-thrown shadows chased each other across the landscape, where thunderstorms swirled above and sometimes reached river level with fingers of wind and drenching rain, exiting just as swiftly under a rainbow bridge. He found beauty and magic here, and he was never heard from again.

Canyon country casts a spell akin to an addiction. The element of surprise lurks around every bend. The energy and drama of the wonderland below the rim stem from the tension between the coursing river and the slow, steady mass-wasting of the canyon walls—between erosion and stasis. The walls of "Marble Canyon" aren't marble, despite geologist John Wesley Powell's naming. They weren't subjected to the immense pressure and temperature required to turn limestone or dolomite into a metamorphic rock. But where water has polished them, or after a storm, the sheer cliffs gleam like the columns and tombs in Westminster Cathedral.

As the Zodiac picked up speed, I saw Luke smile, staring at the cliffs as if seeing them for the first time. I relegated the lingering sense of unease about what we'd find at Buck Farm Canyon to a temporary file in my mind, and opened my eyes and heart to the landscape speeding by. I slid into the geologist's trance, let the gross features fade, zeroed in on the remarkable.

In this place, only a day's drive from Tucson, the earth lay exposed, each vein and bone, vesicle and lens, muscle and ligament and cell. Here the earth spoke in images my synapses linked to form a four-dimensional story. We were traveling through rocks deposited during the early Paleozoic, the era when complex, multicellular life forms with hard exoskeletons exploded in the marine environment. Around me, the earth bled color, saturating the world.

At river's edge the Muav Limestone was a fragmenting, green and tan apron. I spotted the cross section of an ancient channel deposit, the Devonian Temple Butte Formation, cut into the upper beds of the Muav. Above soared the bulwark of the Redwall, stained by the weathering of the iron-rich Supai Group. The more easily eroded Supai beds drew the eye upward toward the loose scree obscuring the Hermit Shale, and then to the white cliffs of Coconino Sandstone. Higher still, the gray Toroweap and Kaibab limestones served as caprock and protector. And between each of those units lay gaps in time.

Time gaps aren't problematical to geologists. What isn't there is as important as what is. Being a geologist means becoming comfortable not only with the vast span of earth time but with the fragmentary nature of the rock record. On his exploratory trips down the Colorado, Powell was struck by the angular discordance between the highly deformed Precambrian Vishnu Complex and the overlying rocks. He called the time gap "the Great Unconformity." At Blacktail Canyon, Mile 120, the students and I would put our hands on an undulating plane representing 1.2 billion years of missing earth history. Rock shock.

Ranger Cheski pointed to a cliff face, breaking the spell. A family of desert bighorn sheep, two ewes and two lambs, tugged at grass and green branches on the steep slope. Petroglyphs come alive. A blue heron glided down from its perch in a tamarisk to snatch lunch from the water. Ahead, ravens circled a camp, beaks open, looking for unguarded snacks and packs, waiting for an opportunity to strike. They reminded me of Jacob, the opportunist. For no reason I could fathom, he had tried to kill me. And would likely try again.

I took out my notebook with the list I'd jotted down in the cave. Read through them again.

Who is Jacob?

Jacob wore a scruffy military shirt. Is he someone from Philo's past who wants to hurt him by hurting me?

How did Jacob know my name?

Identify my intruder.

Did I—or Philo, Killeen, or one of my family members—provoke someone enough that he hired a killer to follow me into the Grand Canyon?

I possessed more information now than I'd had yesterday. Molly McKuen was really Naomi Sprague. She'd run away from a polygamist group. Her father wanted her back so that he could marry her to someone she detested. Her father had the resources to mount a search, and the determination and authority to persist in the search. And Jacob, I'd noted yesterday, *was* persistent.

Molly said none of the men in the Family had served

in the military. But that didn't mean her father couldn't have hired outside help. Either way, the tracker wouldn't know me. He—and it would have to be a male, given what I'd learned of Family dynamics—might be hesitant. He might want me to take off my hat so that he could confirm the identification. But why attack me instead of Molly?

That was the stumbling block. I couldn't connect the dots to form any kind of picture. If Jacob was working for the Family, and killing me was part of his plan, I'd foiled it by surviving. He'd have to climb out of the canyon to make a report to whomever hired him. Hence the abandoned kayak and rifle at Buck Farm Canyon.

That part made sense. But what would happen next? The easiest plan would be for them to nab Molly when the group left the canyon at Whitmore Wash. Only five more days now. Time for them to reorganize.

But surprise, surprise, Molly wouldn't be there. She'd have hiked out to the South Rim.

I put away my notebook and grinned at Luke, who'd been watching me. He laughed. An altocumulus cloud passed in front of the sun for a moment, then drifted away. We basked in the sun, the shadows rippling over burned cliffs, the spray of water, the essence of a timeless landscape, beckoning to be explored.

"Nothing stands between me and the wild," Everett Ruess wrote before he disappeared into the canyonlands. I would always seek out the wild places, knowing I might not survive them. Because only in the wild places can I touch the infinite, and find "almost more beauty than I can bear."

Ahead on river right Buck Farm Canyon cut back into the cliffs. An outwash cone of detritus spread like a fan into the river. The search boats were moored on the near shore. Their occupants clustered ten feet above, among the boulders, dune patches, and brush. The group parted. I saw a flash of reddish-orange.

Jacob's kayak.

My gut knew it instantly. My mind filled in what I couldn't see, identifying the ridges and handholds as if they'd been etched into my skin.

Ranger Wentworth throttled down. Cheski turned his head and raised an eyebrow.

I nodded.

32

Jacob had left us his clothes, food, cooking gear, the container for his inflatable craft, a foot pump, and a field-stripped rifle in a dry bag. But whatever tracks he'd made were lost among others that had churned up the site.

Ranger Wentworth, wearing latex gloves, used tweezers to pluck a few long black hairs from the kayak's webbing. She held them up. "Yours?" she said to me.

"I imagine. You want a comparative sample?"

"Please." She tucked the hairs in a small plastic envelope, then handed me a clean disposable comb.

I took off my hat, unbraided my hair, and tugged the comb through it. Wanted to make sure I got those follicles.

She placed comb and hair in another envelope and labeled both bags. Behind us, Nico nosed the lead raft into shore. Roxy, at the helm of the second raft, eased back on the motor and held her position against the current.

Cheski donned gloves and opened Jacob's dry bag. He took out a rifle's lower receiver group stamped with the symbol of a rearing horse. Beside the logo was the designation COLT, AR-15. Below, it said, "CAL .223, Model SP1."

"Must be nearly forty years old," Cheski said. "My dad had one just like it. Bought it the year they came out."

Luke peered over his shoulder. "What happened to the serial number?"

"Looks like he filed it off."

"Well, at least you know I didn't imagine the gun," I said.

"Crossed my mind a time or two, Dr. MacFarlane. I've never come across a situation like this in the canyon."

"A stalking?"

"One where the intent was murder, yes." Cheski took off his sunglasses, letting them dangle from their cord. His eyes searched mine, looking for answers that weren't there. "But what's Jacob's motive?"

"He might be trying to get to someone else through me," I said. I told him about Dain Investigations, Philo and Killeen's business. That Philo got back from Afghanistan a couple of months ago, and Killeen was retired military intelligence. I told him about my brother, Kit, who practiced international law. I did not mention Molly McKuen's problem. It would come out soon enough if Cheski turned up a link between Jacob and the Family.

Cheski put the glasses back on, saying, "Don't worry, we'll find him. Bess is looking for fingerprints, and we'll try to trace the boat. Might even be able to raise part of that serial number on the rifle."

"Do me a favor?"

"Depends," Cheski said.

"Philo's in D.C., but can you get a message to Killeen?"

"What message?"

"What you said about stalking . . . Someone broke into my house last Thursday. Killeen and Philo found a bug." Nico was signaling from the raft, urging me to hurry. I rushed to get the words out. "A family photo was stolen. Ask Killeen for anything he's turned up on the prints he collected."

"I'll handle it," Wentworth said.

I wrote *E. J. Killeen, Dain Investigations, Tucson* and Killeen's cell number in her notebook. A smile softened the contours of her face. "Tell him Frankie sent me?"

"That should do it. And if you run into problems getting Jacob's prints ID'd, Killeen might be able to help."

I knew Killeen would talk to Philo. Using their connections, Cheski and Wentworth might get answers by the time we reached Phantom Ranch the next day. It was worth a shot.

Wentworth held up an electronic gizmo. "I'll need your prints for comparison."

A minute later, my prints were in their database. Wentworth put her gizmo away and said, "Thanks for not getting our guys killed yesterday."

"Anytime." I looked over my shoulder once, as Luke and I walked down to the raft. All six rangers were in a circle. Cheski was on one knee, drawing in the sand.

Nico gave me a hand boarding the raft. "I guess you made a decision," I said.

He grinned. "It was unanimous. You good to go?"

"And then some." The rangers and my brother had my back. Jacob seemed to have abandoned the chase, at least for today. And the breeze tasted sweet as mesquite honey.

Settling myself in the "bathtub" at the front of the raft, I stretched out my legs. The day was heating up nicely. I looked forward to a good drenching.

President Harding Rapid jolted me out of a trance. I gripped the closest lines as we surfed an emerald wave train. Water slapped me from all sides, like a Disneyland ride, only better. And wetter. Coming out of the last trough, Nico steered toward the quiet water of the downstream eddy to wait for Roxy's raft to shoot the rapid.

I wiped spray from my sunglasses. Nico was looking down at the eddy. "What's up?" I said. The roar of the rapids and whipping wind snatched at my words.

"Just checking," he shouted. "This is where the bodies fetch up—the ones that go in upstream."

I couldn't see his eyes behind his dark glasses. He couldn't see mine. But I knew what he was thinking. This is where *I* might have fetched up, if I hadn't survived yesterday.

"Rafters found a body here not long ago," he said. "Teenage girl. She'd thrown herself off Navajo Bridge."

Navajo Bridge. Mile 4. This was mile 44.

"She'd been on the bottom for three weeks, they think. No ID. But dressed like one of the fundamentalist groups up north. She'd broken every bone in her body. Nobody reported her missing. Nobody claimed her."

I heard Molly's voice in my head describing her sister's suicide. This is where Carrie had surfaced. "What happens to a body when no one claims it?"

He shook his head. The corners of his mouth turned down, acknowledging the pathos of extinguished life, anonymous death. Upstream, Roxy's passengers whooped and hollered as she guided her raft through the churning waves.

I collected the students and moved to the back of the boat, claiming the tearoom so that I could stand and describe the next few miles of riverside geology. Nico revved the motor and we were back in the main current, traveling a little faster than we had before, trying to make up the time we'd lost this morning. But the river was relatively placid here, and I didn't have to yell to make myself heard.

The Bright Angel Shale appeared at river level around Mile 47. The sediments had been deposited not far offshore during the early to middle Cambrian Period, just over half a billion years ago. The area was at the western margin of what was then the coastline of North America —a passive continental margin, the trailing edge, just as the Atlantic coastline is today. But during the Cambrian Period, the continent lay closer to the equator. Trilobites, those extinct cousins of horseshoe crabs, crawled, fed, and shed their carapaces among brachiopods and worms on the muddy seabed.

As the continents were driven onward, the margin flexed. The shoreline continued to advance across the land. The overlying Muav sediments had been deposited farther offshore. Less mud. Fewer fossils. Mostly trilobites and brachiopods, pseudo-doppelgangers of modern bivalves. A gap of roughly 135 million years separates the Cambrian Muav from the Mississippian Redwall. When we pick up the thread of the story again, the sea has transgressed far onto the land. The deepwater rocks contain an abundance of life forms, both swimming and sedentary.

As I answered questions from the students, I was filled with a sense of gratefulness. I'd been given another chance to share the mysteries of this stone book—a book everyone can own and no one can censor, a book written in a language anyone can read. That is its magic. What we own and become intimately familiar with, we're less likely to destroy.

33

The longest rapid in the Marble and Grand Canyons rumbled and churned as we rounded the Little Nankoweap debris fan and approached the point where Nankoweap Creek entered the river. My archaeologist father had told me, long ago, that Nankoweap is a Piute word meaning "the singing canyon" or "echo canyon," or "a place where Indians had a fight." I prefer the first.

Nico and Roxy put in at the foot of the rapid. Luke and I had returned to a place where we'd played with our siblings. The ghost of summers past embraced me, welcoming me home.

I pointed to the small black openings, high above, entrances to an Ancestral Puebloan granary built around AD 1100. The Anasazi had walled in a natural alcove near the base of a massive cliff of Supai, Redwall, and Muav. They'd used it for less than a century before abandoning it to the elements.

An apron of rubble 150 feet high obscured the Bright Angel and lower Muav below the granary. The rubble contained massive angular boulders of cherty Kaibab. The rocks had fallen from the eastern escarpment across the river, perhaps when softer rocks at the base were undercut. Looking at the 3,200-foot distance from rim to river, the greatest in the canyon, I could easily imagine the scene.

Over the last three thousand to four thousand years, debris flows surging down Nankoweap Creek had reached and crossed the main river channel. The debris flows formed a fan, its toe now truncated by the Colorado's constant onslaught.

Luke leaped from Roxy's raft to the gravelly beach. I took off my life jacket, grabbed my backpack, and eased my body down until I stood next to him. A trail led from where we stood to the rubbly slope at the base of the cliffs. Twenty or thirty people trudged up the steep trail to the granary, six hundred feet above. The swelling in my knee had subsided a bit, but I wasn't looking forward to the climb.

The Ancestral Puebloans, forerunners of the Hopi, had farmed the river terraces and deltaic deposits, leaving abundant traces of their occupation. Nico and I agreed to have the lunch break before we explored the delta and ruins. Roxy and Doug would put away the food and then move the rafts to another trailhead, farther downstream, making our trek back to the rafts much shorter.

While the guides set up for lunch, I turned my back on the lure of the ruins to watch the river, mesmerized by its undulations, its disappearing and reappearing whitecaps, its thrumming, pounding, sediment-shifting power. Looking southeast down the river, the canyon widened for the first time. Some geologists considered this point the end of Marble Canyon and the beginning of the Grand Canyon. Not John Wesley Powell. He'd given that prize to the confluence of the Little Colorado and the Colorado, about ten miles downstream. But as far as I was concerned, it was a toss-up.

I waded into the river and leaned on the side of the raft. The cold pressure felt wonderful on my knee. Luke followed a moment later. For a while we didn't speak, content with our own thoughts. The water swirled around our thighs, carrying away the fine particles kicked up by our entrance, burying our feet in sand and gravel. Above us in the raft, Dora was rummaging around in her daypack.

"Coming in?" I said.

"In a minute." She held up her blood glucose meter. I forgot sometimes that she was diabetic.

Luke studied the cliffs behind us. "Remember when we camped in Nankoweap Valley? Mom was helping Dad, so they let us hike up to Mystic Falls by ourselves?"

"Just you, me, Matt, and Kit. We left Jamie behind."

Jamie was our younger brother, the baby of the family. A pediatrician. Two months ago, he'd married Theresa, the daughter of my Apache godfather, Charley Black.

"Jamie'd fallen and banged up his knee." I looked down. "How's that for déjà vu?"

Luke grinned. "That's not how I remember it. We dared him to jump off the wall of a ruin."

"*I* remember you left me at the falls," I said.

"Seemed like a good idea at the time. We were tired of you tagging along."

I'd been six that summer, and tall for my age. The twins were nine, Kit eleven.

"But we hadn't counted on Mom. Boy, was she pissed. She sent us back out and told us not to come back without you."

"We were playing hide-and-seek, and I was It," I said. "I looked everywhere, then sat for what seemed like hours, watching rainbows in the spray. And then I started walking to camp. You met me when I was almost home."

"You didn't cry," Luke said, "or scream or yell. You just stood there in the middle of the trail, hands on your hips, and said, 'I sure hope you've got water.'"

I'd learned early to fend for myself.

"And after all that," he said, "Mom didn't even make a fuss—"

"Dad did. He gave me three licorice buttons from his private stash."

"While Mom made us memorize all seven parts of 'The Rime of the Ancient Mariner.' "

" 'Water, water, every where, And all the boards did shrink—' "

" 'Water, water, every where, Nor any drop to drink,' " Luke finished.

Dora stowed away the glucose meter, jumped to shore, and waded in beside us. Luke put an arm around her shoulders, adding, " 'He prayeth best, who loveth best All things both great and small.' "

Dora's cheeks turned pink.

I laughed. "Clearly, there was method in Mom's madness. She didn't want you to forget the important things."

Luke shook his head. "Took us weeks to recite it perfectly. I was practicing in my sleep. . . . I pictured you as the albatross, of course."

"Of course."

"I'm sorry," he said.

"For what?"

"Leaving you. I knew better."

"You were just trying to fit in with the clan." I kissed his cheek.

He pretended to scrub the cooties off, taking me back a quarter century. But he looked pleased.

34

Mile 53.5, Nankoweap Delta
1 p.m.

Jacob and the rest of Deanna Birdsall's group moored their kayaks and supply rafts on the downstream edge of Nankoweap Delta. The other kayakers and rafters, five men and two women, just nodded hello to Jacob when introductions were made, ate a quick lunch, and set off for the granary. Butch and Kent hung around till Deanna finished filling her CamelBak. All three turned to Jacob.

"You're sure you don't want to come?" Deanna said.

"Don't like heights any more now than I did a couple of hours ago." Jacob rustled around in his overnight kit until he found Chuck Rennie's razor and a pair of scissors. He held them up. "Thought I'd cut my hair. I'd planned to do it while I was staying at Chuck's, but. . . ." He shrugged. "This is as good a time as any. And I can keep an eye on the kayaks and rafts while I work."

Butch and Kent nodded. Their shoulders relaxed.

"You'll miss one hell of a view," Deanna said.

"There's always next time."

She held his gaze. "You're already planning a next time then."

"What can I say? I'm hooked on the place." Jacob gave her a look.

Color flooded Deanna's face. She turned and led her henchmen up the trail.

Jacob fingered his hair, ignored since his return stateside. In case anyone had met and talked with Chuck during his first two days on the river, Jacob wanted to obscure the obvious differences between them. Chuck had been about the same height. He also had light eyes. That was a good start. And Jacob was wearing Chuck's clothes. But the hair . . . Chemo had left Chuck nearly bald. Jacob hoped the little wind-up razor was up to the job.

One benefit of shedding his mane was that Frankie would have described Jacob's hair and clothes to the police—if she'd noticed anything at all during their brief meeting. Eyewitness descriptions are notoriously flawed, he'd discovered while listening to debriefings of his patients in war zones. But Frankie was a scientist. She probably had a good memory for details. So Jacob wanted his appearance to be as different as possible from the one he'd presented at Nautiloid Canyon.

He took off his hat, stripped off his shirt, and placed them on the side of one of the supply rafts, next to his shaving kit, towel, and a clean T-shirt. The bank on this part of the delta was a frigging jungle of willow and tamarisk, with muddy trails meandering through the undergrowth. They'd pulled the kayaks on shore in the breaks between bushes and tied the two rafts to sturdy trunks. From above, no one could see into this inlet. And he wasn't able to see the trail up to the granary without wading well out into the river. He couldn't have chosen a more ideal location to transform himself.

In the privacy of the thicket he did a rough cut with the scissors, finished off with the razor, and buried the hair in a shallow hole. Now for the tough part.

He took off his heavy ring and zipped it into a pocket in his shorts. Soap in hand he stepped into the water next to the raft. He wore his Tevas. No telling what bits of debris might be on the bottom. He waded out into the current till the streambed started to fall away. The water froze his balls. Better make this quick.

He waited a minute until the mud he'd kicked up had been carried away and the water again ran clear. He bobbed under, surfaced sputtering, soaped his head and body, and ducked under again. *Enough.*

Jacob scrambled for shore and was toweling off beside the raft when he heard a woman laugh. He turned, thinking it was Deanna, back sooner than expected. But the willow thickets were empty.

He lowered the towel. Found the source. The noise of the rapids and the bulk of the supply rafts had kept him from noticing the approach of two rafts—the rafts of the MacFarlane group. *Shit.*

The pilot of the far raft went ashore and tied up first, then moored the woman's raft. He gave her a little wave, saying, "I'll help guide the group down." He gave Jacob only a passing glance.

"Cold enough for you?" the woman said to Jacob.

Jacob grinned. "A little bit of Christmas in July." He pulled on the clean shirt and settled the hat over his pale scalp. Tossing the towel over his shoulder, he stepped onto the bank. Stowed his gear in the kayak, except for a bottle of suntan lotion.

She looked at the rafts and the sharp ends of kayaks protruding from the dense shrubbery. "Your group at the granary, too?"

"Yeah." He looked up from slathering lotion on his arms, legs, and face. "I turned my ankle on a hike yesterday. Figured I'd rest it."

"Always smart to listen to your body. A lot of my rafters don't, and then pay for it later."

She climbed over the divider separating a passenger area from the pilot's area, and held up a metal mug. "Want some lemonade or Gatorade? There's plenty."

He couldn't think of a way to refuse politely. Then again, he might not get another chance to sabotage the raft, slow them down. "Sure," he said. "That'd be nice."

He tossed the sunscreen lotion in the kayak, rinsed his hands in the river, and grabbed a water bottle from the supply raft. Pulling himself aboard the big raft, he limped carefully along a pontoon to the five-gallon coolers at the back. His left hand fingered the projectile point in his pocket.

She transferred her cup to her left hand and held out her right. "Roxy Berneer."

"Walt Perry." He set down his bottle and gave her hand a quick shake.

"So, what's your flavor, Walt?"

"Lemonade, please. At least the first round."

"It's the cooler in the middle. Help yourself."

Jacob filled his bottle and sat on the bench seat across from her, glancing up at the cliff face and the trail leading to it. Only the top was visible above the thicket. He thought he saw Frankie MacFarlane's long shape. But not Deanna's. Were they still climbing, or on their way back? Neither party could find him here. But how long did he have?

Assuming a new identity was a tense business. One false step, one slip when his new name was called . . . He shivered.

"Too much sun?" she said.

"No, but that water's mighty chilly." He drained the bottle and refilled it, this time with Gatorade. "My first time in the canyon," he said. "Was plannin' on hikin' another leg of the Appalachian Trail, but this kayakin' spot opened up. Pure dumb luck that one of my buddies had to back out. It's next to impossible to get a permit that fits with my vacation schedule."

"Or any permit," she said. "Which leg of the Appalachian?"

"Hundred Mile Wilderness, up in Maine. Aim to do it while my knees are still good. But, hey, there's always next summer."

"I've done the Arizona Trail and parts of the Pacific Crest, but I've never tried the Appalachian," Roxy said. "I'd like to do it in one shot. But I just can't get the time off."

"What do you do when you're not doing this?"

"Just graduated from NAU. I'm heading to grad school at George Washington this fall. English lit and creative writing."

"Really? We'll be neighbors. I'm a firefighter/EMT. Fairfax County. Stationed in Reston, Virginia."

As long as he was borrowing his friend's identity, Jacob decided to stick close to the facts. Walt Perry had become an EMT and firefighter after washing out of med school.

"Nice part of the country," she said.

"Then you've been to Northern Virginia?"

Her lips lifted in a half-smile. "Once, last fall. Flew into Dulles."

"That's a hop, skip, and a jump from where I live. But it's changed a lot in the last twenty years. They chopped down most of the trees for housing developments. Wish you'd seen it before all that. . . . Did you visit Front Royal, few miles west, up in the limestone belt?"

Roxy shook her head. "Just the campus and downtown D.C. The regular tourist stuff."

"Nothin' prettier than the Shenandoah Valley, especially in the fall."

"So I've heard."

"Where's your group heading next?" he said, as if angling for a little more time with her.

"We'll give the folks a couple of hours at the Little Colorado, then camp at Carbon, if nobody's taken it. Our geologists want to make the loop around Chuar Lava Hill tomorrow morning. Then we'll head for Phantom, with maybe a stop or two for geology along the way. What about you?"

"We're keepin' it loose." He downed half the liquid in the bottle. Took a breath. "It's all about the white water—with a side hike, here and there, to exercise the legs."

"Bet you can't wait for the big rapids—Nevills, Hance, Sockdolager—"

"Grapevine and 83-Mile." He let excitement color his tone. "Jesus, that's gonna be fun."

He finished off the Gatorade and stood. "Well, better get back. I'm way behind on my journal. There's so much goin' on every day—well, you know." He held out his hand. "Thanks for the hospitality, Roxy. If you have a pen and paper, I'll give you my e-mail address. Only fair I should show you around D.C. once you get there."

She found a pencil and her logbook. He recited Walt Perry's e-mail address minus a crucial character. Any emails would be lost in the ether.

"See you in a couple of months, Roxy."

"I look forward to it."

He limped back to the bow, eased himself onto the bank, tossed the bottle onto the supply raft, and followed a narrow path into the jungle. He'd have to hide out till Roxy's party departed. But he wouldn't go far. If she left the rafts for a bathroom break, he might have a chance to sabotage one.

Could he loosen a line to the motor? No, they'd just swap motors. They must carry spares. . . . Cut or fray one of the cords holding the gear on board? Too much chance of it being discovered and replaced . . . A puncture? It would take them time to find it, patch it, let the patch cure, and then pump it up.

That just might work.

Screened by the bushes, Jacob watched and waited for opportunity to strike. He looked down. Hands were rock steady. As he dug out his ring and slipped it back on his finger, he realized the tremor had been gone since he killed Chuck Rennie. It was as if he'd shed the old, damaged carapace of Jacob Presley, like a molting crab. This new Jacob Presley was healthier, stronger. He could cope with whatever life threw at him.

Two minutes later Roxy jumped ashore and followed a path close to the water. How much time did he have?

Enough . . . No, wait.

The little voice in his head stopped him cold, just as he stepped out of the bushes.

It's too soon. You can't do anything that will reveal you're still in the canyon. Not when they've just stopped searching for you on the river. You have to wait until the targets are complacent, confident the danger's past. Otherwise, Chuck's death and the Buck Farm Canyon diversion will be for naught—and you'll jeopardize your end game.

They'll lose tomorrow morning to a hike from Carbon Canyon to Lava Canyon. Tomorrow is soon enough to strike.

But some of the rafters might not make the hike. And he couldn't trust that another opportunity would present itself. Maybe just a small slit . . .

The voice retreated, the river's thunder filled the void, and Jacob melted into the shadowy undergrowth by the water's edge.

35

Molly reached the blessed shade of the cliff face before her brothers. From six hundred feet below, the granary openings had looked like tiny black squares. Up close, they were large enough to climb through, but not to enter standing up. Each room would have slept maybe three or four of her younger sisters, no more.

She studied the ledges in front of the openings. Pictured her brothers playing tag and tumbling off. It was a long way down. She shuddered. Frankie and Dora were right. These weren't rooms of a house, but storage spaces built nine hundred years ago. Yet the walls still stood. Molly was awed by the possibility of creating something that would last forty-five generations.

She took off her hat and fanned her face. In only a few days on the river, she'd grown into the girl with cropped hair. She'd blossomed into someone who questioned the world around her, who spoke up if she had something to say. That the adults seemed interested in her thoughts continued to surprise her.

Molly didn't know if she was cut out to be a geologist or paleontologist. But Frankie, Dora, Roxy, and Luke encouraged her to find out what she *was* good at, what Dora called her *aptitudes*, and then to study whatever excited her imagination and fit her talents.

Her dream of escaping had led her to this place of

mystery. On their first night in the canyon, Frankie had talked to them about the people who once lived here. She'd told them about the vision quests that the young men of many Indian cultures took when they were younger than she was now. How they went off alone into the wilderness and waited for the Great Spirit to speak to them through their dreams. How this trip down the river could be a vision quest for anyone who was open to it—even though they weren't alone, even though they had plenty of good food and water.

Frankie's words had been too much to take in that night. Everything was still so new, and she was terrified of being caught by the Prophet or Brother Ben. But as the days passed, Molly had thought more about those words. And now she was here, among the ruins left by one of those cultures. She wondered what the Anasazi boys had dreamed about when they went on their vision quests. Honor? Courage? What Frankie called a totem animal guide, one that would help them all their lives and give them a name?

Tonight and for as many nights as it took, Molly would pay attention to her dreams. This trip was *her* vision quest, a window into the new life that stretched ahead. Before this trip, she hadn't had a future. Now she did—one she could fashion for herself. In the time she had left on the river, she would learn all she could about her aptitudes and what she might enjoy doing.

On the trail below, Dora, Frankie, Luke, and Molly's brothers were helping people up the steep, rocky cone of boulders and brush. All the rafters were making the climb—good knees or bad—drawn by the magic of the Anasazi site. The ruins below on the delta had required a lot of imagination to picture as they'd once been, although Molly found it easy. She was good at envisioning how a pattern would look and fit when cut and sewn into clothes. And vice versa. She could deconstruct a piece of clothing just by studying it.

Molly had never thought that her sewing skills might be training her mind for science. She hadn't been allowed to study science. And although she'd been better than all the boys at math, especially geometry, her formal education had ended last spring. She'd resented it, but she'd accepted it. Till now. Frankie and Dora had been quick to praise Molly and her brothers for the practical things they already knew and to show them how they could be helpful in the field. It was a heady experience, having strengths.

Ethan pushed past Molly and aimed for the granary.

"Hold up there, Ethan," Frankie called, as breathless as Molly had been. Frankie was leaning on a walking stick Roxy had found for her. "You're not allowed to touch the walls or go inside."

"We climbed all this way, and we can't go inside?"

"Nope. Just take a peek."

Ethan plopped down beside Molly in a patch of shade. Took out a tortilla wrapped around meat, lettuce, and tomatoes. Ethan was always hungry, so the crew let him pack an extra lunch to see him through the afternoon.

He ate his wrap carefully, brushing crumbs off his shorts. "You doing a wash tonight?" he said in Molly's general direction.

"I do one every night."

"Can I add mine to the pile?"

Molly was about to agree when she stopped. Molly wasn't with the Family anymore. The old rules didn't apply.

"Who does your wash in Austin?" she said to him.

"We each do our own."

"That seems fair."

His mouth opened, closed, opened again, like a trout mouthing a worm. "But *you're* here now."

"And I've enough to do just taking care of myself and helping out in camp."

He lapsed into silence as the stragglers joined them. Molly stood to give a middle-aged woman her spot. Her face was red from exertion. Harvey was right behind her, looking not much better, but Ethan didn't move. He was studying a tear in his shorts.

"Did you pack a needle and thread?" he said.

"I bet Roxy has some. She's got everything."

"Would you—"

"Dora," Molly said in a voice that carried, "do you sew for the guys?"

"I showed them how to use the sewing machine," she said.

"It's kinda fun," Adam said.

"Did she show you how to sew on buttons by hand?"

"Yup. Easy peasy."

Molly nudged Ethan. "If you can sew on a button, you can sew two pieces of cloth together. I'll show you how, if you've forgotten, but I won't do it for you."

He glared at Adam for a minute, then switched his focus to the river. Molly guessed he wasn't seeing the vista. He was thinking of the order in the Family's canyon up north. Women and girls did for the menfolk. That was the way God set it up back there in the Garden. No reason to change a system that had worked since the beginning of time.

Molly turned away to listen to Dora's lecture about the rocks. She snapped photos of the people listening, some taking notes. Molly had found she loved taking photographs. When she left this canyon, they'd be visual reminders of the first days of her new life.

"Time to go, guys," Nico said. "We want to be able to spend time swimming at the Little Colorado." He took off down the trail.

Frankie followed Nico, Molly on her heels. Luke brought up the rear. Molly's brothers surged ahead, weaving a twisted path between visitors ascending the trail.

"Don't go too fast, or you won't be able to stop without falling," Frankie called after them.

Molly slowed a bit. The sun, directly overhead, heated the rocks around her. The boulders acted as both supports and guardrails, but they burned like a hot griddle. She took off her neckerchief and wound it around her right hand. Molly had admired the fossil brachiopods and sea lilies on the way up. Now there was time only to carom from one boulder to another.

She lost track of Ethan. Didn't know whether he'd taken the right path at the bottom of the hill. And then she saw his hat. He was poking among the ruins of a pit house on the delta.

"I'll get him," Frankie said, when they reached Molly's brothers, who'd paused at a fork in the trail. "Wait here for Dora and Luke. Ethan and I will meet you at the rafts, if not before."

Molly turned and looked up the slope, amazed at how fast she'd climbed down. Dora was high above them still. Molly took a drink of water and offered some to the others.

"Got some, thanks," Adam said, sitting beside her in crescent of shade thrown by a massive boulder.

The other boys had each found their own bit of shade. *We're the mushroom family*, Molly thought, *trying hard to blend in to a new landscape.* She smiled. They weren't doing too bad a job, either.

"You climbed that trail like an antelope," Adam said. His blue eyes looked even lighter against the tan he'd picked up on the river. "Only five days away, and you seem to have found your feet. Any regrets?"

"None." She picked up a limestone cobble, rubbed her thumb over a lacey bryozoan fossil. "How did you do it, Adam? Ethan can't seem to break away."

Adam fished a coin from his pocket. It was large and bronze and held the words "Dare to Dream" on it. He turned it over to reveal more words: "They who succeed believe they will." Beside the words was a fir tree on a rocky slope.

"Dora gave us each one of these. The man who helped her find the house in Austin gave her ten of them. Said he got them at Alcoholics Anonymous, but they seemed to fit our situation, too. Dora asked us to pass our coin along to someone else when the time was right." He hunched his shoulders, as if loosening some hidden tension. "I'm giving mine to you."

"Really?" She looked down at the coin, warm in her palm. Her eyes filled.

"Really. And some day, when you're feeling more confident, you can pass it along to the next in line."

She hugged him, impulsively, shyly. The Family frowned on displays of affection between brothers and sisters. "Thank you, Adam." She had a thought. "Did Ethan get one, too?"

"He threw his in the river from Navajo Bridge on the way to Cliff Dwellers Lodge."

Navajo Bridge. Where Carrie died.

"He doesn't believe in himself," said Molly. "He's too fearful of the world and what it holds."

Adam nodded. They were silent for a minute, and then he said, "The other sisters, they couldn't have done what you did. Except Carrie."

Carrie was Adam's full sister. When he'd been sent away, there was no one to protect her. Neither Carrie nor Molly had been big enough, strong enough, or powerful enough to counter their father's wishes. Losing her still hurt.

"Carrie and I knew we might have to run for it," Molly said. "We were going to try to find you. Every day we volunteered to take the little ones out to play before supper, after their chores were done. They'd be tired and cranky and hungry, so our mothers would happily send us outside. We played tag. We knotted a rope to a boulder and practiced climbing. We climbed every tree and every large rock in the compound. We taught them how to rescue each other from water, from a rock crevasse, or a hole in the sand. We practiced working together, using whatever was lying around. But mostly we ran races. I rewarded them with crabapples from the orchard and bits of cheese from the dairy. While the other girls were growing softer, Carrie and I were growing stronger."

"And then you lost Carrie."

Adam's words were so soft the breeze almost drowned them. Molly nodded. The raw ache was still there, just below the surface.

Frankie was heading up the slope with Ethan. He sprinted in front of her, as if he didn't feel the heat. Dora was maybe fifty feet up on the granary trail. Twenty-four years ago, she would have looked a lot like Molly. Molly wondered if Dora had ever peeked under the sheets covering the mirrors in the house, wanting to see what she looked like, who she was. She was a scientist now. She must always have been curious, the way Molly was curious about the world. She ached to see it all. To touch it, smell it, taste it, hear its music.

"I won't let them take me back, Adam."

He stood and gave her a hand up. "You're not alone anymore, Naomi."

"Molly. Naomi was another girl in another place."

"Right. I'm sorry. I'll work on that."

"It's important. I don't know why, but it is."

"Sometimes we don't have to know why, Molly. We just have to trust it."

Molly walked behind the others on a trail that wound through blackbrush, cacti, and boulders. She stepped carefully, not wanting to turn an ankle or knee as Harvey had done on the way down. Roy had one arm around Harvey's waist, supporting half his weight. Dora had loaned Harvey her hiking stick, a collapsible affair with a camera mount on top. Harvey's face, brick red at the top of the hill, now bore a purplish hue. But he didn't complain. Just made weak jokes to try to ease the tension.

When they entered the thicket of tamarisk and willow, the path became sandy. Much easier. But the narrow track didn't allow two to walk abreast. Molly heard Nico's voice before she saw him.

"Gals to the right, guys to the left," he said.

The trail had come to a T-intersection, and Nico was directing traffic for pit stops.

"Anyone behind you?" he said to her.

"No."

"Gals to the right," he repeated. "Rafts are over there." He pointed in the opposite direction. "We leave in five minutes."

Molly followed in the footsteps of the other women as Nico went left. She couldn't see anyone, but she could hear quiet voices and laughter in the bushes. She moved silently, lightly, watching for snakes. So she didn't see the man step into the path in front of her until she ran into his back. He cursed and jumped to the side. Turning quickly, his hand dropped from the knife at his belt. He wasn't one of their rafting party.

"Oh, I'm so sorry." Her words came out in a stammer. "I wasn't looking where I was going."

"All my fault." He glanced quickly up the path. Voices were coming toward them. "Are you okay?"

"I'm fine," she said.

A quick smile. "Sorry if I scared you."

He took off his hat, ran a hand over his shaved head, then resettled the hat. He wore reflective sunglasses. She couldn't see his eyes. It unnerved her. But he made no move toward her.

"I—"

"Take care now." He melted into the undergrowth.

Molly listened for the sound of his passing, but he moved as silently as a whipsnake.

Frankie and Dora rounded a bend in the trail. "Would one of you mind coming with me?" She tilted her head toward the privy station.

They stopped, asking in unison, "Did something happen?"

Molly described the man with the knife. His clothes, sandals, hat, hair, sunglasses. The ring on his right hand. His quiet movements. "He's not from the Family," Molly said. "He's nobody I've ever seen before."

"Probably one of the kayakers that parked near our rafts," Frankie said. "I saw them from up on the hill."

"He meant me no harm," Molly said, "but he seemed to be watching for something. Or someone."

"We'll ask the others tonight," Dora said, "see if anyone else ran into him. For all we know he's a friend of Roxy's who was waiting to say good-bye before heading down the river."

"Come on," Frankie said. "We'd better hurry, or they'll leave without us."

36

Ben had made good time on the forest routes, from East Game Drive to Burma Road. Hadn't passed a soul on the gravel and dirt roads. Hadn't spotted dust lingering in the air. Now he waited in the trees to make sure Highway 89A was empty. He didn't want anyone to see him coming from this part of the plateau.

He looked in his rearview mirror. No rising column of smoke. The low following last night's storm brought whipping winds that surged across the plateau, fanning the flames but slicing the crown off the plume. *Perfect.*

But despite the area's isolation, he was surprised no one had reported the fire. Someone traveling the highway or flying from the Box 10 Ranch to Marble Canyon should have seen smoke in the far distance.

He shrugged. They would soon enough. And then fire trucks, firefighters, planes carrying retardant, and helicopters ferrying water would converge on the area. If all went as planned, the crisis would draw attention and some of the personnel away from the North Rim visitor areas tonight and tomorrow. If God continued to walk beside him, the fire would be out of control long after he brought Naomi out of the canyon.

He shifted into first and started to leave the shelter

of the forest. Slammed on the brakes. Flashing lights in the distance. The wail of sirens. All coming from the direction of Jacob Lake. Ben couldn't be seen on this side of the road. He looked across the highway. This dirt road continued, slightly offset, on the other side. He waited for the lights to dip into a swale, then gunned the motor, flew up a slight incline, and angled across the road. Bumped down the far side. Faster, faster. He'd never make the safety of the trees. . . .

Shadows walled him in. He didn't slow. The road widened into a clearing. What now?

He spun the wheel to the left, putting the heaviest thicket between his truck and the highway. Just in time. Two fire trucks slowed and turned onto the Burma Road. Good. Their tracks and dust would cover signs of his passage.

Ben circled the clearing, wanting to get onto the highway before more fire trucks arrived. He was just about to exit the grove when an SUV pulled up and parked across the road.

Hell and damnation. They were setting up a command center to direct other equipment and personnel to the site.

The officer got out and glanced in his direction. Ben's beating heart seemed to fill his chest and thunder in his ears. His hunter's instincts were fully engaged.

Ben left the grove and drove to the edge of the asphalt. Leaving the engine running, he stepped out and called to the officer. "What's up?"

"Fire over near the rim. Probably a lightning strike. Gonna have to shut the road down."

"Hope it don't spread. It's been a bad season already."

"Ain't that the truth."

The deputy nodded and said good-day. Ben got back in the truck and turned sedately onto the highway, heading toward Jacob Lake and Fredonia. He wanted to stomp on the gas pedal, but he held back, kept to within five miles of the speed limit. He didn't want to be stopped by the police. Not yet. A few hours from now it wouldn't matter.

37

Ben Gruber's brother, Vernon, lived two blocks off the highway in their parents' old home. Ben hadn't called ahead. They hadn't spoken in years, and Vern was likely to leave if he knew Ben was coming.

Vern was in the garage tinkering with the engine on his Jeep Wrangler when Ben pulled into the dirt driveway. Vern looked up, then straightened. He wouldn't recognize the truck, Ben realized.

Ben climbed out and waited for an invitation to approach. Watched Vern wipe his hands on a red cloth dangling from his belt. His tow truck was parked on a cement pad beside the garage. He worked all day as a mechanic at a garage down the road, but at night he repaired the most recent junker he'd picked up for a song. Fixing cars and flipping them for a profit—or for parts, if they couldn't be fixed—allowed him to make ends meet.

"Ben," Vern said, nodding hello. "What brings you here?"

"I'd like to borrow Dad's Yamaha for a couple of days."

Vern turned his head toward one of two covered mounds in the second bay of the garage. Howard Gruber had loved motorcycles. In his youth he'd ridden with a club, and later had used a bike to commute to the mines. When he'd died, his two favorite bikes, a Harley and the Yamaha RD 350, had been in the garage.

Vern didn't ride—not since he tore up his arm when he was sixteen. But he'd held onto the bikes. He was more sentimental, and had loved their father more, than Ben. And Howard Gruber had doted on his second son. Ben had noticed almost from the day their mother had brought Vern home from the hospital. He hadn't understood it then, and he didn't now.

Ben watched Vern run the tip of a small screwdriver under his nails. A nervous habit left over from childhood. He cleaned his nails whenever he was troubled or had decisions to make. Sometimes he used his keys. Sometimes a penknife. Whatever was handy. For a grease monkey, Ben thought, Vern had the cleanest nails around.

"I tuned her up last week," Vern said at last, fitting the screwdriver into its slot in his tool chest.

Everything in its place, and a place for everything. Ben sometimes wondered if they were related at all. They certainly didn't look alike. Ben, their mother always said, was the reincarnation of Ishmael, "a wild donkey of a man, his hand against everyone and everyone's hand against him." He was ox-strong and barrel-chested, dark as pitchblende, with a temper to match. But Vern, now . . . Vern was six inches taller, lean and fair-haired, with a dry wit and an easy way with people. Like their father.

Growing up, Ben had felt protective of his little brother. When Vern had been at loose ends after leaving the service, Ben had invited him to live with the Family, hoping he'd see how important Ben had become to the Prophet and the group. The Family had welcomed Vern. The girls had blushed when he was around, followed him with their eyes. They never blushed around Ben. They avoided him. And they never blushed around the other adult men either, especially Eldon Sprague.

The Prophet had noticed. Competition wasn't tolerated, so Sprague sent Vern away. He'd found a job and cared for their parents. And he alone had inherited the house and all it contained. Their parents had shunned Ben even when they knew they were dying. For this, Ben blamed Vern.

Yet Ben needed his brother, too. Especially now. Vern might avoid him, but he never turned him away.

Vern walked over and twitched the canvas covering off the motorcycle. From a drawer in the workbench he pulled a ring with two keys, holding it out to Ben.

"Thanks," Ben said, pocketing the keys. "Want me to pull the truck around back, out of the way?"

"Sure. Is that Eldon's truck?" The words held more than one question.

"Yeah. He decided he needed to be alone in the desert—to fast and pray. I'll pick him up Friday morning. But in the meantime I have to go rescue one of his daughters. She ran off, and now wants to come home."

"Which one?"

"Naomi. You probably don't remember her. She wasn't more than four or five when you stayed with us."

"I remember. A sweet little thing. She loved to climb trees."

"They're all sweet." Ben's voice was harder than he intended. He forced himself to backpedal. "The Prophet chose her to be my third wife."

A shadow touched Vern's eyes. Ben felt the hairs on his neck rise, his hands tingle. "Our mother wasn't much older when she ran off with Dad."

"And look how well that turned out."

Ben felt the black tide rising in him. But he was Prophet now. He must act from reason, not emotion. And his actions must be guided by the Holy Spirit.

"I'll just move the truck," he said, fighting down the anger. "Then I'll get out of your hair." He turned away.

"Supposed to rain again tomorrow night. Anything you want to stash in the garage?"

Ben stopped. "A few things. Thank you, Brother Vern. That'd be nice."

Vern cocked his head to the side, as if perplexed by the formal language. But he smiled, acknowledging that it was the closest they'd come to civility in years.

Ben backed up the truck and drove it around Vern's tow truck to the cleared space behind the garage, parking by the old oil drum they used for burning trash. Smoke rose in thin wisps from the barrel. The apple trees had been pruned, he noticed, and the yard cleared of weeds. The redwood picnic table had a checkered cloth, weighted down at the corners and center by chunks of sandstone. But the wind sent the edges flapping.

"That's going to blow away in a minute," Ben said, climbing out of the truck.

Vern had followed him to the backyard. He collected the cloth, folded it neatly, and tucked it back under the five sandstone weights.

"Expecting company?" Ben said.

"A woman I've been seeing."

"Is it serious?"

"Too soon to tell."

Ben had always wondered why Vern hadn't gotten married. He'd come close a couple of times, but he seemed to shy away at the last minute. When their parents were alive, he'd used that as the excuse. But they'd been gone five years. It must be lonely for him without someone to come home to at night.

"Well, I hope it works out." Ben rolled up the window on the driver's side. He pulled a small plastic bag from under the seat and closed the door. From the bed he collected his pack, shoved the plastic bag inside, and handed the pack to Vern.

"Anything else?" Vern said.

"I can handle the rest."

"See you in the house then. You'll want a meal before you head out."

Ben nodded but didn't bother answering. He was focused on the remaining gear. Sprague's pack was on the passenger seat. He didn't dare leave it in the truck, in case someone stole it.

He lifted out the pack and set it next to the front tire. He'd already taken Sprague's fake passports and drivers' licenses, his Bible, wallet, and watch. They were with Ben's own IDs in his backpack.

He moved his sleeping bag, cooking gear, tarp, and dried food to the cab. Drained the ice chest under a tree, then took out the perishables—a slab of home-cured bacon, a dozen eggs, a gallon of milk. He hadn't had breakfast this morning. He hadn't eaten at all. Suddenly he felt ravenous.

He locked the truck. Food clutched tight to his chest with one arm, he hefted Eldon's pack with the other. Vern was still in the garage. Ben's pack lay on its side at his feet. The top flap was open. Head bent, Vern was examining something in his hands.

"What are you doing, Vern?"

Vern jerked around, holding out the plastic bag. "What am *I* doing?"

Vern looked and sounded like their father. Same frown. Same judgmental tone.

Ben shrugged. "Eldon's dead. So what?"

"How? When?" Vern stopped, held up his hand, forestalling more information. "No, wait. It's none of my business."

It came to Ben in a flash—this was God's second test. The first was killing Eldon Sprague. The third would be recovering Naomi. But now—if Ben could convince Vern of the righteousness of Ben's actions, then he would be able to convince the elders of the Family.

"Of course it's your business," Ben said. "I'm the new Prophet, chosen by God. He spoke to me, acted through me. Do you not see the glow of his might and grace shining like a cloak around me?" Ben threw out his arms. Food landed with thuds, splats, and splashes. It barely registered. "There will be a place for you—"

"Stop it, Ben."

Ben stopped, focused on his brother, saw the sympathy in his eyes.

"I see our mother," Vern said. "You know as well as I do her engine didn't fire on all cylinders. You sound just like her."

Now Ben could see her, standing between her sons, screaming at Ben, accusing him of being the cause of all the pain in her life, the disappointments. He could see his father running into the garage from the kitchen door, yelling for her to stop, catching her arm in the air, gently prying the hatchet from her fingers. Ben had been ten, Vern five.

"And you sound just like Father," Ben said.

"Ben, you don't want to go there."

"Where? Where don't I want to go?"

The sympathy Ben had noticed before had turned to pity. Vern sighed, turned his head toward the towering pine in the front yard, the one with the frayed rope swing. "Guess it's as good a time as any, since you'll be heading up the Family." Vern met Ben's eyes. "Howard Gruber wasn't your father."

Ben blinked, rocked back on his heels, shocked, but not surprised. Some part of him must always have known. It explained everything.

"Who was my father?" Ben said. "Did Mom ever say?"

"No." Vern sighed, as if he'd been holding a breath for a long time. "But Dad, he . . ."

Ben waited. There was no past, no future. His whole life hinged on this moment.

"Your father was just a drifter, Ben, passing through town on his way to nowhere. Stopped by the grocery store where she was bagging. They met up that night. He was gone by the time she figured out she was pregnant. Dad was just the sucker who happened along. Thought he was responsible. Did the right thing."

"That's it? A drifter with no name?"

"For all I know it could have been Eldon Sprague. You favored him, you know—head shape, cheekbones, mouth—and that mane of hair." Vern ran a hand over his own thinning hair. "Hell, Ben, I'll be bald at fifty, just like Dad."

Ben took a step back, out of the shadows, into the sunlight, chilled to his core. Had Eldon been his father? If so, then Ben felt no remorse for ending the life of the man who'd left him to be raised by that crazy bitch of a woman.

What goes around, comes around.

From somewhere far away, Ben heard Vern say, "I'll just get something to clean up this mess."

Ben looked at the garage floor, noticing the eggs and milk. Only the wrapped bacon had survived the crash. He wanted to offer to help, but he couldn't find the words.

Vern picked up a clean red rag from the workbench and rubbed the surface of Eldon's wallet before dropping it back in the plastic bag. He set the bag on the workbench, cleaned both sides of the plastic, then tucked the bag back into Ben's pack.

"I'm still your brother, Ben. Nothing can change that."

Ben nodded, only half listening. Problems loomed. Big ones. If Eldon had fathered him, then Ben had raped his half-sister, Esther.

He wanted to vomit. *Incest.* The most loathsome crime—worse than murder, in Ben's book. Would God have allowed that to happen to Ben, His chosen one? Perhaps, as a test. If so, Ben had failed.

But God had protected him from the repercussions of his act. Esther was dead. The evil fruit of their union had died with her. Ben could still repent and do penance, trust in God's mercy.

Had Carrie sensed a blood link? Was that the real reason she'd thrown herself off the bridge?

Her reasons didn't matter now. If they were siblings, God had saved Ben through her actions. Ben would find a way to celebrate her sacrifice. At the very least, he'd allow her name to be spoken again.

Ben heard Vern's voice in the kitchen. *The bastard's calling the sheriff on me. He's gonna turn me in.*

The black tide was back now, thicker than before, blotting out light and reason. Ben no longer tried to fight it. He picked up a hammer from the toolbox as he ran by. Reached the kitchen door in time to hear Vern say, "Kathy? Could we reschedule? Something's come up. . . . Sure. Saturday would be good. See you then."

Ben said, "Don't you know it's blasphemy to turn your back on the Prophet?"

Ben toted Vern's body to the basement door, opened it, hesitating on the stoop. His mother used to take out the single bulb in the center of the ceiling and leave him down here in the dark. What had he done to deserve those black time-outs?

The voice that had been with him since last night answered him, plain as day. *You forgot to keep a close eye on Vern while she was sleeping off one of her binges. . . . You talked back to her. . . . You put too much milk on Vern's cereal. . . . You took my name in vain. I could go on. . . .*

"No need," Ben said, to the voice in his mind. "I get the picture."

Ben turned on the basement light and started down the stairs. He often took the rod to his children, but he never confined them in dark places. And he never touched alcohol.

The room at the bottom of the stairs surprised him. Vern must have moved down here after he left the compound. A lot more private than being upstairs near the parents. He'd finished the walls and ceilings and painted them a pale blue, the color of the midday sky. He'd put in a half-bath. Books lined the wall-mounted shelves. A double bed stood against the wall, made up as if for a guest. A bedside table held a lamp. Everything was as clean and neat as the upstairs. Ben wouldn't have minded being confined down here if it had looked like this. He wondered if Vern had been erasing his own memories when he'd transformed the space.

He dumped Vern's body on the bed, arranging him as if he were in a casket, hands folded on chest. He knelt by the bed and prayed for Vern's soul. It was the least he could do, considering there'd be nothing left to bury after Ben burned the place down.

But that will have to wait till I get back from the canyon with Naomi. Can't risk having to explain Eldon's truck parked out back.

And then what? Naomi might be his half-sister. Like Carrie.

Get the girl back. Then wait before you seal with her. Take a paternity test. Quietly. If it's positive, you can put her away later.

God had protected him time and again. Even Naomi's flight might turn out to have been a blessing, if it saved Ben from consummating an incestuous marriage. Any doubts Ben had harbored that he was indeed God's chosen Prophet evaporated in the crisp, dry air of the plateau.

38

North Rim
4:52 p.m.

Thirty miles south of Jacob Lake, the junction
of Highways 89A and 67, Ben paid his entrance fee to
the national park. "Fee's good for seven days," the ranger said. "But the campground's full up,"
The only people heading south would have reservations at the lodge or campground, or a backcountry permit. Ben had none of these things.
"No worries." Ben tucked the receipt in his pocket.
"You may have to show that when you leave the
park, so don't lose it."
"Don't plan on it." Ben smiled nicely for the ranger.
Eldon had taught him that people, especially officers, remember the ones who scowl or act belligerent, but rarely those who are pleasant and polite. Add the helmet for
disguise, and this ranger wouldn't be able to pick Ben
out of a lineup, should it ever come to that. The ranger
would be more apt to remember the vintage Yamaha.
But with all the traffic on the road, that was unlikely.
The rim was another fourteen miles down Highway
67. The Colorado River at Phantom Ranch a little over
fourteen miles by foot beyond that. The guidebooks all
warned hikers not to try to hike down to the river and
back in one day, unless they were running a rim-to-rim.
But it wasn't as if Ben was venturing down to see the
sights. He had one goal, and little time to accomplish

it. So he was going to descend at night, aided only by starlight and a nearly full moon. He could always take a nap at the bottom while he was waiting for the rafts to arrive.

Ben planned to head straight back up after delivering his ultimatum to Naomi: She could come with him willingly or know that he'd marry two of her sisters. And those sisters, once his, would be punished every day until Naomi came home. If that was forever, so be it. The choice was Naomi's.

He drove past a beefalo herd in a meadow splashed with lupine, daisies, and Indian paintbrush, through forests of Ponderosa pine, fir, and aspen, and through acres of burned forest that reminded him of what he'd started that morning. It looked ugly and barren, and for a moment he wondered if he'd gone too far. *No regrets*, the voice whispered. *No regrets.*

Thirty minutes later he found a parking space near the Grand Canyon Lodge. He smelled chicken and prime rib. Did he have time?

He looked at Eldon's watch. Not for the formal dining room, but he could get a to-go order from the deli. Might as well start off with a full belly.

Ben strolled through the cabins to the lodge. The line was short at Deli in the Pines. He ordered three slices of pizza, then carried them across a narrow neck of land to Bright Angel Point. Eighty-two hundred feet above sea level. The wind smelled of pine and fir, still drying after last night's rain. To the east, a smoke smudge drifted over the rim and into the canyon. *Still burning. Good.*

He stood, munching his pizza, as a dozen languages stirred the air around him. The light-drenched canyons and mesas were temples in stone. *The glory of God's handiwork*, his father once said. Ben had been fifteen that summer, Vern ten. Their mother was in a treatment center, sobering up. Freed from the pressure of dealing with her moods, Ben had suggested this trip. He'd been amazed when Howard Gruber said yes. They'd explored the upper part of the canyon for a couple of days and nights, camped at Roaring Springs. It was the happiest weekend of Ben's early life.

Now, even Vern was gone.

The sun was heading fast toward day's end. The midsummer light would linger late, but Ben wanted to make the most of it. He retraced his steps, threw the remnants of his meal in a bear-proof bin, and straddled the old Yamaha. Staying within the speed limit, he drove the two miles back to the North Kaibab trailhead and parked in the lot. Day hikers were coming up. Groups of two and three and six. And one pack of Boy Scouts in dust-streaked, sweat-stained uniforms, red-faced from the sun and heat, moving slowly after the long climb, not talking much. He grinned. They'd been run ragged and would sleep well tonight.

He tightened the straps of his pack, walked down to the trailhead, and entered the stillness of the forest.

39

Mile 72.7, Unkar Delta, Colorado River
5:55 p.m.

Jacob finished laying out his tarp and sheet on a wide sandy spot amid the boulders. After a day surrounded by people, albeit in separate kayaks and rafts, he needed space and privacy. This was the most human contact he'd had in months. He wasn't used to it. It jarred after the solitude of his first days on the river.

His sleeping site was well away from the others. Dry brush grew between the rocks. He'd hear if anyone approached in the night. Old habits die hard.

For a moment he was back in Afghanistan, in the dust and heat and harsh sighs of a desert evening, the surrounding mountains reducing the sky to a narrow swath of indigo. He'd volunteered to go on that mission. Unless they were luckier than a Powerball winner, a doctor would be needed. He was. Despite his work, five men had returned in body bags. . . .

He shook himself, unsure how long he'd been lost in reverie. It would be night soon at this old Anasazi dwelling place. He felt their presence, watchful, protective. This had been a peaceful place, a place of farming and fishing, knapping points and preparing hides, stringing and testing new bows, fashioning clay pots and reed figurines, weaving cotton into cloth. But this stranger, Jacob Presley, didn't bring peace. He understood he wasn't welcome here. His thoughts reeked of violence.

Wanting to cleanse his spirit as much as his body, he grabbed a towel, soap, and clean clothes and headed for the beach. Despite spending all day on the river, he felt grimy and sweaty, his pores clogged with dust. The intense heat of day was only now beginning to lift, but the wind coursed up the river like a furnace.

"Walt," Deanna called from a spot ten yards away. Her campsite. Close enough to slip over to his in the middle of the night if she wanted, far enough away for a modicum of privacy if she didn't. "We need to talk."

What now?

"Okay." He paused, waiting for her to cover the distance between them. He let a small smile touch his lips, trying to stay in character. A guy who'd just gotten out of prison wouldn't push away a young female who crossed his path. "About tomorrow?" he said in a quieter tone when she reached him.

"What else?"

He started walking again, not bothering to answer. He was tired right down to his corpuscles. The group had elected not to take a side trip up the Little Colorado. The other kayakers had been there, done that. They'd wanted to get through the lazy bends of the stretch of river between the Nankoweap and Unkar Deltas so that they had only a few miles to cover in the morning. Big whitewater lay ahead. Nevills Rapid was a Cat 6. It would be followed in short order by Hance, Sockdolager, and Grapevine—an 8 and two 7s—as the river funneled into the constricting embrace of Granite Gorge.

Deanna waited to speak till they were at the river's edge. The noise of the water would prevent their conversation from being overheard either by members of their own group or by any of the other parties sharing the delta. It was a popular site, with access to Unkar Creek and the wealth of Anasazi ruins in the area.

Setting his towel and clean clothes on a sandstone

boulder, Jacob stripped off his swim shorts and T-shirt and carried them into the river. The water was a few degrees warmer than it had been at Nankoweap, but it was still cold enough to shrivel his balls. He kept his back to Deanna as he soaped his hair and body, not caring whether she watched. She'd infringed on *his* personal time, not the other way around.

He used some of the soap on his dirty clothes. Dunking body and clothes for a final rinse, he waded quickly to shore. Deanna sat on the boulder, studying the light on the Palisade cliffs across the river. Her face was flushed under its tan. His towel and dry clothes dangled from her outstretched fingers. Only after he'd toweled off and dressed did she turn around.

"Serves me right," she said.

He nodded, liking her for that. He draped the wet clothes and towel over the front of Chuck's kayak, which stood a few feet away. She followed. When he turned, she was standing close enough to kiss him. Apparently she didn't care about personal space, hers or anyone else's.

"You've got scars on your ass," she said.

"Shrapnel."

"You didn't mention you'd been in the military."

"Didn't seem relevant. And it's none of your business."

She was staring at the ring on his right hand. He doubted she'd recognize the symbol, except, perhaps, the caduceus in the center, a universal symbol.

She stared hard at his eyes. Hers, he noted, were somewhere between green and hazel. "I like to know something about the people I work with," she said, "especially on a job like this."

He let the silence grow between them, wanting her to believe that sharing his backstory was difficult for him. Only when he saw her eyes soften did he say, "I was in the army. For about ten minutes. My vehicle hit an

IED—hence the shrapnel wounds. End of story. It was long ago, in another life."

The half-lie slipped out as easily as the truth. He couldn't tell from her expression whether she believed him or not.

"And the ring?" Her eyes narrowed, as if it were more than a casual question. A small scar on her chin turned white.

He pulled a joint and a slim lighter from a waterproof box he'd tucked in the pocket of his swim shorts. Turning his back to the wind, he cupped his hands close to his face to protect the flame. Still took three tries till the joint was going strong.

He held it out. She hesitated, then accepted. The wind dispersed the smoke before it could rise. Would the old gods of this place feel rejected?

"Well?" she prompted, passing the joint.

"The ring was my father's. Desert Storm. He didn't make it back."

His father had been a pilot, not a flight surgeon. But the last part was true. Jacob had started to lose track of all the lies he'd told her. After tomorrow night, it wouldn't matter.

"I'm sorry," Deanna said. "The guys and I talked. If you want to help out tomorrow, we could use you. Two bridges, four people. The math makes sense."

He didn't want to commit himself, so he answered her indirectly. "Where are you planning to camp tomorrow night?"

"Pipe Creek. The rafts and anyone who doesn't want to go into Phantom Ranch will continue downriver, play in the rapid, and set up camp. Some of the guys want to hike up Bright Angel or Pipe Creek and take pictures. The rest of us will park our kayaks on the beach downstream of Silver Bridge. We can use the bridge to access Phantom Ranch. When we're done, we'll paddle down to the camp."

"Leaving chaos in your wake."

"That's the idea. Butch, Kent, and I—and you, if you sign on—will join the others well after dark. They won't discover what happened till we finish the trip next week."

"Won't your friends be suspicious when you lag behind to scout the bridges?"

"No. We tend to break up into small groups and go our own way on land. Some don't hike. Some have been here several times and skip the crowded places like Phantom. Others are newbies and want to see everything. The trip rules—the kayaking club rules, anyway—just say that we have to use the buddy system when we go off on a side trip, and make sure we're at the rendezvous point at the agreed time."

"The rendezvous point being Pipe Creek?"

"Yup."

He offered her the joint again, watched as she inhaled. If he were going to take care of the targets, he had to stay on the Phantom Ranch side of the river until their rafts arrived. He said, "I still need to go into Phantom to call my parole officer."

"I forgot about that." She handed back the nub and thought for a moment. "You're kind of along for the ride, so our rules don't apply. . . . Tell you what, why don't you spend a little time scouting the Kaibab Bridge. See if Chuck's diagram is right, including where he suggested placing the C-4."

"Want me to check out the Phantom side of Silver Bridge as well? Just to have a second opinion?" It would give him an excuse for wandering all over the delta.

"Couldn't hurt." She tucked a strand of hair behind her ear. "You said Chuck would try and meet us at Phantom. Did he say where or when?"

"There wasn't time. I figure if he makes it down, he'll have all afternoon to find us."

He sucked on the nub, then rubbed the end between

his palms, shredding the remains. He raised his hands to the wind, watched the bits whip away.

"I know you brought your own supplies," she said, "but you're welcome to eat with us tonight. There's plenty."

"Don't mind if I do." He picked up his towel and clothes from the kayak. They were almost dry.

The exhaustion he'd felt earlier had been washed away in the river. A calm certainty descended as he started back up the debris fan to his campsite. Tomorrow, all would go right.

If he had to kill one or more of Deanna's crew to get away from Phantom Ranch, he'd deal with it then. But he hoped it wouldn't be Deanna. She reminded him of a woman he'd known long ago, before Iraq and Afghanistan. Before the deaths of Jenny and Sean and his mother.

Deanna walked close enough that her arm brushed his. He smiled. He'd avoided committing to participating in the bridge bombing. And tonight, for the first time in ages, he might not be sleeping alone.

40

Mile 65.1, Carbon Camp
6:33 p.m.

The camp at the mouth of Carbon Canyon was a large, sandy site rimmed by the more than billion-year-old red shale and siltstone beds of the Dox Sandstone. The Cambrian Tapeats Sandstone formed the cliffs above and contributed boulders to the beach. The undulatory plane between the two units represented around 600 million years.

But tomorrow's journey would reveal an even greater time gap. Only sixteen miles downriver, the Tapeats sat directly on the oldest rocks in the canyon, the Vishnu Schist Complex, more than 1.7 billion years old.

I watched the students—and half of Harvey's rafters, who were listening in—do the math in their heads. The Great Unconformity represented more than 1.1 billion years of missing earth history. An awe-inspiring concept.

The revelation marked the end of my lecture. We'd discussed what they'd seen from the rafts since leaving the milky turquoise waters of the Little Colorado River, where we'd ridden the river currents for hours, PFDs fastened over our swimsuits like bulky diapers, bodies forming human chains. They'd been exhausted after the swim and the hike back to the raft, and most had only half-heard what Dora and I had told them to watch for along the riverbanks Crash Canyon, where two airliners collided in 1956 while dipping below the rim to give their passengers a better view of the canyon. One hundred and twenty-eight dead. The wreckage still dotted the slopes, winking in the sunlight. . . . The salt mines, sacred ground of the Navajo and Hopi, to which young men hiked, carrying a feather, and returned with salt and a feather left by a previous seeker. . . . The first appearance of the Tapeats Sandstone, the oldest Cambrian unit in the canyon, which contained trilobite tracks and sitzmarks, evidence of large, complex life forms with exoskeletons, a huge leap from the primitive life forms found in Precambrian rocks. . . .

The dinner gong sounded. Thai tonight. I stretched sore muscles and rewrapped my knee, looking forward to sitting in a beach chair eating a hot dinner, drinking a glass of wine. Last night at this time I'd been in a cave, wondering if I'd survive another few hours.

Nico came up from the water's edge wiping his hands on a cloth. When we'd returned to the rafts after playing in the Little Colorado, he'd discovered that the main part of his raft was low on air. We'd limped into camp and he'd set about finding and patching the leak.

A ranger accompanied our head guide. Nan Lomax had hitched a ride at Nankoweap, so she could report on how well Nico, Roxy, and Doug enforced the safety rules of the river. Ranger Lomax would leave us tomorrow at Phantom Ranch, then hike up Bright Angel Trail to the summit.

"Find the leak?" I asked Nico.

He took something from his breast pocket and held it out to me. A fluted projectile point, perhaps two and a half inches long.

I picked it up from his palm, turning it to catch the light. Obsidian. Lanceolate shape. Weathered, reworked tip. Bifacial percussion flaking. Faintly concave base, finely ground to fit on a haft. Channel flakes removed from both sides, near the base. Deep patina of age.

"No way," I said.

"Way."

"Clovis?" I said to Luke, who had come up beside me. I handed him the point.

He did his own examination. Nodded. "Extraordinary workmanship."

"You know where it was made?" Nico said.

"Not around here," we said together. Then laughed.

"You go," I said to Luke. He'd majored in southwestern archaeology at UA.

"Well, our dad's the expert, but we can say this much," he said. "There's no obsidian source in the canyon. The closest would be the San Francisco Volcanic Field down near Flagstaff. But further south, Cow Canyon was mined back in Clovis time, thirteen thousand to thirteen-and-a-half thousand years ago. So was Valles Caldera over in New Mexico. And there are quite a few other possible source areas."

"But the tribes that inhabited this region traded raw materials," I said, "and perhaps finished points as well."

Nan took the point from my brother. "Someone found part of a Clovis point on the North Rim a few years ago. It proved they were using the cross-canyon route long before the Anasazi."

"So it could have been something Doug picked up when he landed at Nankoweap?" Nico said.

"How much of the point was embedded in the raft?" I said.

Nico placed the tip of his index finger halfway down the artifact.

"He'd have had to ram the bank full throttle to drive it in that far," Luke said. "He's too good a pilot for that."

"And Roxy would have reported it," I said.

"Then how'd it get there?" Nico was pissed and confused. He wanted answers.

"Did you look at the hole before you plugged and sealed it?" I said.

"Yeah. Just a simple slit. Clean edges." Light dawned. "You mean someone used a knife and then plugged the slit with the arrowhead?"

"That'd be my guess," I said.

Luke nodded. "You've got yourself a little case of sabotage."

Nan untied her neckerchief and opened it out. Nico set the point in the center. She folded the cloth into a tidy bundle and buttoned it into her pocket. The provenance might not be known, but the artifact had been recovered in the canyon. "Any problems with other rafting companies?" she asked him.

He lifted one shoulder. "Not this season."

I hesitated, scanning their faces. "Not to sound paranoid or anything, but what about Jacob?"

"How'd he get from Buck Farm to Nankoweap?" Nico said. "And how would anyone have done it? One of us has stayed with the rafts ever since Tatahatso."

When no one answered, Nico shook his head and turned toward the kitchen area. "I'm starving. Let's eat."

We filled our plates. Nan slipped into the chair next to mine. At the Little Colorado River, during a lull in the activities, I'd filled her in on my adventures the night before. She'd heard the other half of the story from Boyd Cheski. One reason she'd hooked up with us, she told me, was because Cheski had radioed down and asked her to keep an eye on things.

As we ate dessert, fudge brownies, Dora gave a talk about the following morning's hike up Carbon Canyon to the Butte Fault. We'd follow the fault south around Chuar Lava Hill until the fault crossed Lava Canyon, our route back to the rafts. The fault showed two episodes of major movement during the late Precambrian, before the Tapeats Sandstone and overlying rocks had been laid down. The first episode of faulting had moved one side of the fault down six thousand feet relative to the other side. The second episode had reversed the movement by about three thousand feet. Needless to say, the rocks along the fault plane had been brutalized and deformed.

Doug would hike with us, while Nico and Roxy guided the rafts over to Lava Canyon to pick us up. Because we'd be moving fast, Harvey and most of his group opted to skip the side trip. Many had stressed ankles and knees from boulder scrambling at Nankoweap and the Little Colorado. But Harvey had recovered enough to lead a short walk up Lava Canyon to see the volcanic rocks. The Cardenas Basalt, which overlay the Dox Sandstone, formed steep, iron-stained hillsides. Quite a change from the sedimentary landscape through which we'd been traveling. But he also offered to show them salt casts, desiccation cracks, and ripple marks in the Dox. And, if they were lucky, they'd find an algal stromatolite—a fossilized mound of cyanobacteria interlayered with fine sediment. When Harvey asked for a show of hands to see who was interested in joining him, seven shot up.

I washed my dishes, then joined the students to watch the sunset, reflected in the water. Luke sat down next to me. "Now?" I asked him.

"Now," he said.

I told Dora, Molly, and the boys about Carrie's body being recovered at President Harding Rapid. Luke was staring out at the bats and swallows swooping over the darkening water. The haunted look was back, deepening the lines and furrows of his face.

Molly, tears sliding from her eyes, reached out for her brothers' hands. The circle extended as Luke, Dora, and I joined her. Adam said a simple prayer. And then we were silent for a minute or two.

"Don't worry, we'll take care of Carrie," Dora said, breaking the circle. Bobby, Craig, and David rubbed their eyes on their sleeves. Ethan moved a little apart, shoulders hunched, face turned away.

"Thank you," Molly said, wiping her cheeks. She took out her notebook and pencil. They seemed to be her constant companions. But she wasn't making notes. She was drawing something that looked like bird wings surrounding a shield with a snake on it. Above the shield she drew a star.

Nan came up from her inspection of the cooking area. "You have a good eye," she said, looking over Molly's shoulder.

Molly described her meeting with the man at Nankoweap, ending with, "I told Frankie and Dora he was wearing a ring. I just wanted to draw it while it's still fresh in my mind—so they'll recognize him if they run into him."

What Molly didn't say was that she was scared that the Family had hired someone to take her back—someone like the man in the bushes.

It was almost too dark to make out the lines of her drawing. Nan turned on her headlamp and pointed it at the notebook. "My uncle has a patch with the same insignia. He was a senior flight surgeon in Vietnam."

"Molly's mystery man's a doctor?" Dora said.

"That's my guess," Nan said.

"A doctor." Molly smiled. The lines of worry faded from around her eyes.

Nico called to Nan, asking if she wanted to share a drink on the raft. "Be right there," she called back.

Molly watched the ranger walk down to the water. "The man's not one of the Family," she said, when Nan was out of earshot. "None of our men have been trained as doctors—unless you count Elder Hargrove," she said. "He's a chiropractor. He delivers babies, too, with the help of the sister wives."

"At least you have midwives," I said.

"Not officially," Dora said. "Few of the women are educated after age sixteen. Occasionally, a woman's allowed to take a college course, with the permission of the Prophet and her husband or father. But she attends online."

I shook my head. The red light from my headlamp danced back and forth. "I wouldn't last two minutes in that environment."

Luke grinned and nudged me with his shoulder. "I want no more complaints, ever, about the sins of your brothers and cousins."

"Deal."

But I was only half-listening. I was picturing Jacob's hands. Like the man at Nankoweap, Jacob had worn a gold ring on his right hand. A narrow band, thinner at the center. Had it been a signet ring like the one Molly described, but with the heavy side turned toward his palm?

It couldn't be. He'd abandoned his kayak at Buck Farm. He hadn't had time to hike to Nankoweap.

I was at my campsite, laying out my sleeping gear when Nico and Roxy came running up the beach. Doug and Nan were a few steps behind. We all waited for Nico to catch his breath.

"Damn, I have to quit smoking," he said, still breathing hard. "Roxy may have met Molly's mystery man at Nankoweap."

"I told them," Nan said to me. "Sorry if I stepped on any toes."

Neither Dora nor I had thought to mention Molly's incident to the crew. In the hubbub at the Little Colorado, it had slipped our minds.

Roxy described her meeting with Walt Perry, the firefighter from Virginia. He resembled the man who'd scared Molly. "Walt wasn't wearing a ring," Roxy said. "But he was wearing a Reston Fire Department T-shirt. He seemed legit."

I said, "Why don't you ask Molly if she noticed anything about the shirt her mystery man was wearing?"

Before I even finished the thought, Roxy was off

through the sand to where Molly was washing in the river.

"A kayaking party left Nankoweap before we did," Doug said. "We passed them a couple of miles downstream."

"I didn't notice," I said. I'd been telling Bobby and Adam about the rocks.

Roxy came huffing back over the dunes. "Same T-shirt," she said.

I looked at Luke. Molly's mystery man had a name.

Nico touched Roxy's shoulder. "Did you leave the rafts untended at Nankoweap?"

"Only long enough for a pit stop. But Walt had already gone back to his kayak."

"Then Perry, or any of his party, could have sabotaged the raft at Nankoweap," Nan said.

"But why?" said Nico.

I said, "Jacob might have an accomplice in the canyon."

Nan did an about-face. "I'm going to call Boyd and have him do a search on Walt Perry of Reston, Virginia. With any luck, he'll have something by the time we reach Phantom tomorrow."

41

Ranger Boyd Cheski sat with his feet up on his scarred metal desk, a sheaf of reports in his hand. He stared out the window to where the last rays of the sun painted the buildings a warm ocher. Grand Canyon Village was a hive of activity. Laggards among the visitors were heading for a spot on the rim. The sun would officially set in half an hour, but twilight would linger for thirty minutes after that.

It was the same every night. A free light show, always different, always dazzling. He normally joined the flow, gave directions to good photography spots, answered questions he'd answered thousands of times before. He waited until the purple shadows had coalesced in the canyon and risen to the rim, waited for the round of applause that always accompanied this event. It was the grandest show on earth, in one of the Seven Wonders of the Natural World. He did not take it for granted.

But his nightly jaunts among the sightseers weren't just a way of confirming that he was doing what he was born to do. They also were a delaying tactic, a way of avoiding going home to an empty house and dinner alone. Connie was working in Great Smoky Mountains National Park. Sheila had died two years ago. Inside him was a fissure so deep he had yet to see the bottom. Work kept him sane.

Tonight, though, he was still at his desk, waiting for a call from the searchers. Teams had started from the bottom and the top of Buck Farm Canyon, meeting roughly in the middle. No trace of Jacob.

Other teams, joined by county searchers, had fanned out along the North Rim to see if they could pick up Jacob's trail. If that was even his real name. Boyd doubted it. The man's words had been nonspecific. "Call me Jacob," he'd said. Boyd hadn't missed the echo of the opening line of *Moby Dick*. He wasn't sure what it meant, if anything.

Cheski twisted his neck to ease the stiffness, heard the crackle of vertebrae rubbing against each other. He was getting old. Maybe it was time to retire. He was only fifty-six, but he hadn't yet seen all six of the other natural wonders of the world—or the man-made ones either. The modern ones, anyway. What was left of the Alexandria Lighthouse was under water, and the remains of the Colossus of Rhodes had been sold for scrap metal by the Arabs long ago.

The phone rang. "Cheski."

"Got a hit," said a voice. Kentucky accent. "But you ain't gonna like it."

"Bernie?"

"You got another lab tech on speed dial?"

"What did you find?"

"The only fingerprints I could identify from the inflatable kayak, besides the ones Dr. MacFarlane gave you for comparison, were found on a plastic guitar pick and a button. They were in a jacket pocket. Belong to a Charles Augustus Rennie, age sixty-six, of Tempe, Arizona. A lawyer with a history of ecoterrorism."

"An Abbey acolyte?"

"Whatever that means."

"Hold a minute, Bernie." Cheski set down the phone and tapped a few keys on his computer. Picked up the phone again. "Right. Thought I recognized the name. Solo kayaker. He checked in three days ago. . . . White male. Age sixty-six. Which means Rennie can't be the guy my witness described. What about the rifle?"

"I was able to acid-etch the site and raise most of a serial number. Since the weapon's old and has probably had lots of owners—"

"Who don't have to register it in Arizona," Cheski said.

"Or a few other states. Anyway, I doubt if I'll get a hit, but I requested ballistics test-fire the weapon and enter the partial serial number and particulars into the database. They said it would take a week or two."

"We don't have a week or two."

"I know. Sorry. Best I could do."

"My witness gave Bess the name of a friend who might help." Cheski brought up the incident report on his screen. "E. J. Killeen. Partner in Dain Investigations down in Tucson. If you give me the partial serial, I'll see if he can expedite a search."

Bernie read the first five digits of the serial number. "I think the sixth number is a three or five. Couldn't do jack with the seventh."

"You did great. And thank you—for everything. The Chivas will be in the mail. Friend to friend, mind you. No bribery intended."

"Just bring it the next time you come to town. I don't drink alone anymore. You know how it is."

Bernie was a veteran of three tours in Iraq. He'd been hit by shrapnel a couple of times, but he kept going back till he lost the lower half of his left leg to an IED. For a while, Cheski knew, Bernie had used alcohol to dull the emotional pain.

Cheski had been down that road. "It's a deal, Bernie," he said.

He hung up, feeling grateful for the friends who'd seen him through his own rough patch. He pulled open the lower right desk drawer, looked at the half-empty bottle of scotch. *Half-empty, not half-full.* It was time he changed the way he looked at the world. Bernie was smart not to drink alone.

Cheski picked up the bottle, walked down the hall to the break room, and poured the rest of the amber liquid down the drain. Rinsing the bottle, he added it to the pile of glass in the recycling bin. They were trying to save the world, one jar, can, paper, and box at a time. He refused to think about the futility of it, knowing how much recyclable material was tossed in trashcans throughout the park.

Back at his desk, he called Tucson. Killeen answered on the second ring. Cheski introduced himself and outlined the problem. When Killeen offered to help, Cheski gave him the partial serial number. Killeen said he'd get right on it. When Cheski asked if Killeen had received an ID from the fingerprint on the bug, he said no, not yet, but he'd see if he could speed up the process.

Boyd wandered back to the break room to make a fresh pot of coffee. It would be a long night. While the coffee brewed, he stared at two large maps hanging over the counter that held coffeemaker, hotpot, and microwave. The maps showed the eastern and western halves of Grand Canyon National Park. They had contour lines and extended beyond the park boundaries.

Where are you, Jacob? And why were Charles Rennie's prints in your kayak?

His index finger found Lee's Ferry, Mile Zero for all rafting trips through the canyon. The MacFarlane party and Rennie had launched there. Presumably Jacob had, too, though his name hadn't popped up on Cheski's permit search. Rennie's permit listed him as traveling alone. Frankie said Jacob also appeared to be traveling solo. Did that mean anything?

Jacob and Rennie could have launched at the same time, or met up later and traveled part of the way together. Either meeting could explain how Rennie's prints got into Jacob's kayak. Cheski would ask Frankie and

Luke tomorrow, when he saw them at Phantom Ranch, if they'd noticed Rennie on the river. If they remembered seeing Rennie and Jacob together on the first or second day, then Rennie might be a threat. Cheski would have no choice but to evacuate Frankie from Phantom Ranch.

He traced the blue line of the Colorado River to Nautiloid Canyon, site of Jacob's first act of aggression against Frankie. His finger moved again, following the route Jacob had taken as he tracked Frankie to Tatahatso Camp. He'd reclaimed his kayak and paddled in the dark to Buck Farm Canyon. And there the trail went cold.

Cheski needed to start over. He'd been thinking too small. He looked again at Lee's Ferry. If Frankie's kayaker behaved like other boaters, he'd have left a vehicle in the vicinity of the launch site. And if he were planning to hike out, he'd have stashed some mode of transportation at a North Rim trailhead so that he could get back to his vehicle at Mile Zero.

Cheski called the rangers at Lee's Ferry. Asked them to copy down the license numbers of all the vehicles parked in their lot or stored at Marble Canyon, then do a computer search to match them with names. If they found Rennie's car, and vehicles that didn't correspond to names on the wilderness permits or commercial raft lists, they were to sit on them and call Cheski.

The phone rang as he replaced the receiver. Killeen. "That was fast," Cheski said.

"I got a match for the fingerprint on the bug at Frankie's house. Jacob Anderson Presley, army flight surgeon, home on compassionate leave. Reason he's stateside—" Killeen paused. Papers rustled, as if he'd set aside his notes. "Here's the thing, Cheski—Presley buried his whole family a few months back. In Prescott."

That could unhinge anyone. But what was Presley's connection to Frankie MacFarlane?

"What happened to his family?" Cheski said. "Car accident?"

"No, the sister and brother died at Denali. Matt and Luke MacFarlane, Frankie's brothers—"

"I know them," Cheski said.

"Good. Saves time. They guided the wilderness trip. You should be able to get the NPS report. And I called Matt. He said that the mother died shortly after they brought the remains home. Heart attack."

Boyd silently digested the information, rearranging the pieces on his chessboard.

"Cheski?"

"Yeah, sorry. I was figuring out where to go next. . . . Luke said he didn't know anyone named Jacob."

"They never met. Matt didn't recognize the name at first either. I checked with a neighbor in Prescott. Presley's family called him Trey."

"T-r-e-y?"

"Correct. The neighbor hasn't seen him in days. I checked to see if Presley had reported for duty. Not yet. But his leave is up on Friday."

"Great work, Killeen. Can you give me Matt's number?" Boyd jotted it down. "Did you have any luck with the serial number?"

"Still working on it. I'll be in touch."

Cheski felt a surge of energy as he hung up. He had a last name for Jacob. And maybe a motive. But if they were going to catch Presley, they needed to get into his head.

Back in the break room, Cheski topped off his coffee cup. Looked at the map of the eastern Grand Canyon. What was Presley's original plan? Or had his thinking been too disordered to form a coherent plan?

Cheski traced Buck Farm Canyon with his index finger. Presley didn't leave only his kayak there. He left his rifle, clothes, cooking gear, and some food, suggesting that he'd given up. But searchers hadn't found any sign that he'd climbed out of the canyon. Could he still be on the river?

Not on foot, surely. He'd never keep up with the rafting party. He'd have to have found alternate transportation. Or an accomplice. Charles Rennie?

Cheski jumped as the wind blew the back door open, banging it against the wall. A hot wind, but he felt chilled. He closed the door, leaning against it until he heard it latch. His heartbeat slowed.

What did Presley gain by abandoning his kayak, gun, and gear?

Everything. A breathing space. Frankie MacFarlane would let down her guard. She'd be vulnerable.

Cheski had believed Frankie's attacker was gone. He might be right, but he had to act as if Presley was still in pursuit. Where would Presley have gone next if he'd stayed on the river?

Nankoweap.

Cheski found it on the map. Nan Lomax was in the canyon, riding with raft groups. When she'd called in at lunchtime, he'd told her what was behind the search operation she'd noticed at Buck Farm. She'd offered to hitch a ride with the MacFarlane party, just to keep an eye on things. She'd leave them at Phantom Ranch tomorrow afternoon. She said she'd phone in if she had anything to report. She hadn't called back from Nankoweap, so everything must have gone smoothly.

He looked at his watch. Eight-thirty. Where had the MacFarlane group been heading after they left Nankoweap?

He checked his notes. Little Colorado River. Camp at Carbon Canyon. Hike around Chuar Lava Hill tomorrow morning. He checked his watch again. Even if they'd dallied for hours at the Little Colorado, they should have reached Carbon by now. He'd give Nan another half hour to settle in. If he hadn't heard from her by nine, he'd call her. Frankie MacFarlane and the raft crew would want to know the results of the search at Buck Farm Canyon.

Where are you hiding, Jacob Presley?

Boyd shifted his attention to the North Rim map. This time his finger found the locus of a forest fire that had started last night or this morning. Had Jacob climbed out of the canyon, driven to the forested plateau, and started a diversionary fire? Or had it been caused by lightning? If the latter, they wouldn't know for days. The fire was out of control and whipping east. The pall could be seen from both rims. And it would get worse before it got better.

His finger dropped away from the map. All those thought paths led to question marks. Cheski needed to work angles that would provide solid information about Presley. Like the NPS report on the deaths of Presley's siblings at Denali.

He headed back to his office again, thinking he was missing something. Something big. What was it?

His phone rang. Nan's satellite call had been patched through to his office.

"The canyon's pretty tight," she said. "I'll only have a couple of minutes before I'm cut off."

"First, please tell Frankie that her attacker may still be in the canyon. So be alert."

"We already are, after what happened today." Nan told him about Roxy, Walt Perry and his flight surgeon's ring, the nonincident with Molly at Nankoweap, and the sabotage to the raft.

"A Clovis point?"

"The real deal."

"What the hell does *that* mean?"

"That's your department."

"You're right. Ask Luke—"

The line went dead. That was the problem with sat phones. They only worked when a satellite was passing over the canyon. But it was better than a cell phone, which didn't receive at all.

The abrupt end to Nan's call left Cheski with questions about Walt Perry's appearance on the scene, his possible link to Jacob Presley, and that flight surgeon's ring. Too damned many coincidences.

The phone rang. A search party reporting in after working along the rim. They'd found a Honda CRF250X, a lightweight dirt bike, secreted near the head of South Canyon. No license plate. Probably left by a hiker or geologist making a loop—something to transport him back to his truck or van. They gave Cheski the vehicle identification number, in case he wanted to check it out.

Another trip to the map. South Canyon was the next major canyon and trail upriver from Buck Farm. Cheski put an X at the trailhead. If the dirt bike was Presley's, had he originally planned to attack Frankie last night near North Canyon? Escape from the river would be easy enough. He could paddle down to South Canyon, scuttle his kayak, and hike out. But if that was his plan, something had interrupted it. Instead of aborting his mission, Jacob had followed them down the river until he found another opportunity.

Cheski shook his head. He now had multiple angles to chase down. If Jacob, thwarted for perhaps a second time, was still on the river and/or had an accomplice in Walt Perry or Charles Rennie, they probably wouldn't have a chance to do more damage tonight. But it was easy enough for them to guess where the MacFarlanes would stop tomorrow. Phantom Ranch.

He called Bess Wentworth. "I need some help."

"My uniform's in the dryer."

"Come as you are."

A warm chuckle came down the line. "If I did, you'd have to arrest me. Be there in ten."

42

Mile 65.1, Carbon Camp
8:40 p.m.

Molly sorted her gear and repacked it. To-morrow afternoon she would be leaving the group at Phantom Ranch, hiking to the South Rim with Annie's husband, Paul. Four days ago Molly had worried about whether she was fit enough for a nine-mile climb. But the day hikes she'd taken with Frankie and Dora had given her confidence.

She set aside her daypack with two filled water bottles. Dora would collect bottles from the boys after the morning hike. They'd be staying near a water source for the rest of the trip. Molly wouldn't be. Whether Paul chose to hike the longer Bright Angel Trail or the shorter, steeper Kaibab Trail, there would be limited shade during the climb. To avoid dehydration, she needed to carry as much water as she could manage. She refused to be a burden to her rescuer.

The little pile of hiking supplies contained sunscreen, hat, sunglasses, long-sleeved shirt, lip balm, and a tiny first-aid kit with tweezers. She'd pack an extra lunch tomorrow and get energy bars from Roxy. She added her notebook and camera, which recorded her personal transformation—her vision quest.

She looked down at her arms. The henna tattoos that Annie had applied were almost gone. She and Dora had planned to refresh them last night, but they'd both forgotten. The tattooed skin was lighter, like the negative of a black-and-white photograph. The henna had acted as additional sunscreen. She liked the white-on-brown pattern. It made her arms look graceful and exotic, not at all like Naomi's pale limbs.

Frankie called to her from outside the tent. Molly unzipped the flap. "Come in."

"About tomorrow," Frankie said. "Because you have a long hike later in the day, I think it would be better if you skipped the hike in the morning. I don't want to risk having you strain an ankle. There'll be a lot of scrambling in Carbon Canyon."

Molly smiled and pointed to the little pile next to her pack. "I hate to miss the Butte Fault, but I'd already decided not to go. I've been figuring out what to take and what to leave."

"Can I help?"

"I'm pretty well set, thanks. The only thing I don't have is a map of the canyon. I'd like to work on my map skills on the way up."

"I noticed you picked them up more quickly than the boys did—except for Adam. But Dora said he's already had a few geology classes. I brought a topo map of the Bright Angel and Kaibab Trails. You can have that."

"I promise to send it back when I finish."

"No, keep it. Jot notes on it. The park is so much more than you can see from the river or the rims. Maybe you'll come back some day."

"You've been—you've all been so good to me. Even though you didn't know I'd be tagging along. I want you to know I won't forget it." Molly picked up her notebook, turned to the back, and carefully tore out a page. "I was going to give this to you tomorrow, but things might be rushed."

Frankie took the page. Tilting her headlamp down, she studied the drawing of her face, in profile, smiling as she looked at the Clovis point. "It's remarkable," she said. "I'll treasure it always." Putting her arms around Molly, she hugged her tightly.

"I have drawings for Luke and Roxy, too," Molly said when Frankie released her, "though I expect I'll be seeing Luke again soon."

Frankie laughed. "You noticed."

"That he and Dora both light up when they're around each other? It's sweet."

"Sometimes, Molly, I think you're the oldest soul in the group."

She smiled. "Sometimes, I think you're right."

"Well, when you get to Austin, don't be afraid to enjoy what's left of your teens."

"I'm in no hurry to grow up. There's too much to do, too much to learn and experience. I feel like I've missed so much."

"That's how you should feel when you're sixteen. Just enjoy each day and what it brings. And if you need a second refuge, come find me in Tucson."

"Really?"

"Really. You'll like my family."

Molly smiled. "I already do. And if things work out between Dora and Luke, I'll be a part of it. She may be only my half-sister, but I'm claiming full family rights."

Frankie turned to go. Molly put a hand on her arm. Frankie said, "Forget something?"

"Discovered something, I think." Molly hesitated, searching for the right words. Frankie waited. "You told us how the young men used to go on vision quests. Well, I've been paying attention to my dreams, like you suggested. Last night I dreamed I was in a deep canyon, looking up at a red-tailed hawk. And then suddenly I was the hawk, circling in the sky, hunting. . . ." Her voice trailed off.

"What did you see down below?"

"Two groups of people climbing out of the canyon.

There was something wrong, but I didn't know what—only that it scared me so much I woke up."

"My godfather taught me that hawks are the messengers between this world and the next, between the seen and the unseen. Charley would suggest that you be alert for incoming messages—warnings *and* opportunities. But only you can decide what this animal and dream mean to you and your journey."

Frankie put her hand on Molly's head. "Stay safe," she said. "And drop me a note after you get settled. I want to know what happens next in your saga."

"Craig's promised to teach me how to use the computer," Molly said. "You're the first one I'll email."

When Frankie was gone, Molly stood outside the tent staring at the river. Tomorrow they'd enter Granite Gorge, the heart of the canyon. Would Paul travel safely down to the river to fetch her? Would Family members be waiting at the top to snatch her back? Would Annie be safe up top waiting for them?

The journey so far had brought a peace and security Molly had never known. She hated to leave the adventure with Frankie and Dora and her brothers. Hated to leave the protective fortress of rock walls for the unknown, chaotic, scary world above the rim. She felt small, *was* small. What could she do if Ben or her father were waiting for her tomorrow?

A weapon. She needed a weapon. And she knew just where to find one.

A headlamp bobbed up the path. Even in the dim light, she recognized the shape beneath it. Luke. Good. She could give him his picture now.

"Ahoy the camp," he said softly, when he was ten paces out. "Permission to intrude."

"Have a seat." She gestured to her sleeping mat, spread in front of the open tent.

He turned off his lamp and sat down. "Just a minute," she said, ducking into the tent. She turned on her headlamp, found and tore off the correct page, then joined him on the mat. "For you." She handed him the drawing.

He ran a finger over the lines. "You even caught the scar on my jaw."

"You rub it when you're thinking about something."

"Something good or something bad?"

"I don't know yet."

"Well, let me know when you figure it out."

The wind gusted, fluttering the paper. He tucked the edge under his thigh and then took a thin leather cord from around his neck. "Frankie asked me to bring this to you."

Molly took the cord from his outstretched hand, tilting her head so that the light caught the donut-shaped pendant that dangled from one side. The disc served as a counterweight for a long, slender leather sheath. She pulled out the knife, touched the blade. Exquisitely sharp.

"An old woman, a Spanish Gypsy, gave it to Frankie a few years back. It has saved her life a time or two. She wants you to wear it tomorrow."

Molly had seen and admired the pendant. Frankie always wore it on long hikes. She would have worn it the next day on the Carbon Canyon hike.

"How did she know?" Molly said.

"That you were worrying about protecting yourself?"

She nodded. The headlamp flashed.

"Call it a MacFarlane trait. Frankie was showing me the picture you drew of her, and then suddenly she was taking this off—at the same moment I was trying to get the hunting knife off my belt. Didn't you hear us laughing?"

"I didn't think anything of it. You two laugh a lot together."

"Well, we decided that her stiletto would be a lot

lighter than my knife. But you're welcome to both, if it would make you feel better."

"Thanks, Luke, but Frankie's should be enough." She touched the pendant. In sunlight, the surface had flashed like a hummingbird's wing with iridescent hues of green, blue, yellow, and gray. Now the stone was a shimmering smoky gray. "Do you know what the mineral is?"

"Labradorite. A form of plagioclase feldspar. Forms in magma, deep within the earth."

"Please tell her I'll guard the stone and knife and return them to her safely."

"I will. But, Molly?"

She looked up. "Yes?"

"Will you be able to use it if you have to?"

Will I be able to kill a man, he's asking. Or at least hurt him enough so I can get away?

She thought of her father and Ben Gruber, of what they'd done to Dora and Carrie and Molly's brothers. *And to me*, she added, feeling the anger well up. She would tap that anger if she felt scared.

"I think so," she said.

"Good." He stood, right hand on the haft of the knife at his belt, left hand holding her drawing. "Tomorrow, at Phantom Ranch and the river crossing, I'll stay with you till you rendezvous with Paul."

She stood up, too. Kissed his cheek shyly. "Okay."

"Do you want me to hike out with you?"

A tempting offer.

"I don't need to finish out the trip," he said. "The guides are on high alert for anything out of the ordinary."

She smiled. "What about Dora?"

His answering grin was a quick flash of white. "We'll just have to postpone getting better acquainted—if that's what she wants."

"Do you?"

"Absolutely."

"Well, so does she. But if you're offering, then yes, I'd feel much safer if you were with me."

"Good," he said again, and turned to leave.

"Luke?"

He stopped, one eyebrow raised.

"Would you keep an eye on Ethan tomorrow?"

He eyed her for a long moment, then nodded. "Consider it done."

43

"So what have we got?" Boyd Cheski said.

He was standing in the doorway of the office that Bess Wentworth shared with a couple of other law enforcement rangers. At this hour, she had it to herself.

Bess was on the phone. She put a hand over the mouthpiece and pointed toward a space she'd cleared under the window. She'd stacked the work reports in three piles at one end. Bess was always trying to impose order on a disordered system. She refused to give in to entropy, afraid that the chaos would overwhelm her.

Cheski carried printouts of his own reports on the stolen SAR craft, Frankie's attack, and his talk with Nan Lomax. He arranged them in chronological order. His last printout was the NPS report about the deaths of Sean and Jennifer Presley in Denali National Park. After reading it, he'd called the investigator who'd handled the incident. Luckily no one went to bed early in Alaska during midsummer. Boyd had worked Denali for a couple of years. It was hard to maintain a diurnal rhythm in a land where the sun never set.

When Bess had arrived that evening, Cheski had gone over everything he'd learned. Then they'd divvied up the tasks. She'd focused on Walt Perry, a tough assignment because the East Coast was three hours ahead. Boyd had brought her coffee an hour later, which she'd received with a nod before waving him away. That she was still on the phone was a tribute to her Rottweiler nature.

Her physique didn't match her personality. She was slightly built and small-boned. And more fit than most people half her age.

She hung up, typed a few lines, hit the print button, and took a deep breath. "Well, that was fun."

He smiled. "I'll show you mine, if you'll show me yours."

She plucked the papers from the printer and scooted her chair over next to his at the table. She looked at her watch. "Tell me you've already called down to alert Phantom."

"Right after I spoke to Lee's Ferry the first time."

"Good. Here's what I have."

As Cheski anticipated, Bess went first, a pattern established over two years of working together. She confirmed what Nan had told him about Perry being an EMT and firefighter from Reston, Virginia.

"But I wasn't able to talk to him," she said. "According to his chief, Perry's out hiking a stretch of the Appalachian Trail."

"Where?" Cheski said.

"Maine. Unreachable by phone."

"So no way to confirm he really *is* on the trail."

"You expected this to be easy?"

"There's always a first time. When's he due back?"

"Next Wednesday."

"That's no help. Did the chief happen to know if Perry knows Jacob Presley?"

"He didn't, but he passed me on to someone who did. Fritz—" she look down at her notes, "Decker. Another firefighter, and Perry's closest friend. He said Perry and Presley met in med school. U Maryland. Perry dropped out the first year, but they stayed in touch. And Jacob reached out to Walt when he came stateside to deal with the family deaths. Walt Perry was so bummed out he told Fritz the whole story."

"Did you get a description of Perry?"

"I pulled up his driver's license photo." Bess rummaged in one of the piles and came up with a printout of Perry's license. "Thirty-five, five-eleven, light brown hair, blue eyes." She laid it next to Presley's army ID, faxed to her by Killeen.

"Presley's thirty-five, six-three, light brown hair, green eyes. They look enough alike to be brothers."

"Too bad Nan didn't give us an approximate height for Roxy's visitor before the sat line conked out. That'd be a clincher."

"We got enough," Cheski said. "The girl who ran into Perry said he was wearing a ring with a flight surgeon's insignia."

"But Perry washed out of med school."

"Right. So unless Walt Perry was with Jacob Presley at Nankoweap, and they'd both shaved their heads, and they were wearing identical T-shirts—"

Bess held up her hand. "Too much coincidence. I'll vote for the simplest explanation. One bad guy. No accomplices."

"That we've identified. We can't forget that he's traveling with a kayaking group. And Charles Rennie may be with them."

"Did the rangers at Lee's Ferry find his vehicle?"

Cheski nodded. "Parked in their lot. They found a pickup registered to Sean Presley, too. The rangers have staked out both vehicles."

"Is Sean Presley's truck bed big enough to transport a dirt bike?"

"It's a Ram 1500 with tie downs in the back."

"So that'd be a big yes." Bess Wentworth picked up a printout from a second pile. "I ran the VIN of the Honda dirt bike the searchers found near the South Canyon trailhead. It was advertised online. A guy answered the ad, arrived at the seller's house by taxi, left a cash deposit, and took the bike out for a test drive. Didn't return."

"Where and when was it stolen?" Cheski said.

"Tucson. Last Wednesday."

"Around the time Presley broke into Frankie Mac-Farlane's house."

Bess leaned back and looked at the ceiling. "As soon as he heard her plans, he drove to the park. Dropped the dirt bike off at the head of South Canyon, then drove the truck to Lee's Ferry, where he launched, probably in the middle of the night, since he didn't have a permit."

"His original plan must have been to kill Frankie at their first night's stop and hike out South Canyon," Cheski said. "But for some reason Presley failed to act. So he went with Plan B. And failed again."

"And then he had a problem. He knew we'd be looking for his kayak. He had to come up with a diversion—Buck Farm Canyon—in order to stay on the river. Somehow he latched onto a kayaking party. But he still had to slow down the MacFarlane rafts so he could have another go at Frankie. Roxy gave him his opportunity at Nankoweap."

"Presley must want Frankie very badly," Cheski said. "Why didn't he just kill her in Tucson? It would have been easier. No one would have linked him to the crime."

There was silence in the room, except for the institutional gray and white clock on the wall. *Midnight.* The ticking seemed to mock them. *It'll be twilight again in just over four hours.*

Bess sat up straight and looked at Cheski. "Tell me about Denali. Maybe what happened there will shed some light on the situation."

Boyd found the NPS report, but he held it closed on his lap. The story was still fresh in his mind. "Presley's younger sister and brother—Jennifer, twenty-eight, and Sean, thirty—were seasoned climbers and hikers. They'd climbed with Matt and Luke MacFarlane a couple of years ago in the Andes. Aconcagua."

Bess looked impressed. "Almost twenty-three thousand feet. Tallest peak in the Americas. That's hardcore."

"Yup. And the MacFarlane treks were accident-free till this spring. The group summited Denali safely. The problem happened the day after they flew back from base camp. The Presleys were part of a smaller group that followed the climb with a backcountry camping tour of the national park, also led by Matt and Luke. At lunch break on the second day, Jennifer went off to make a pit stop. Sean went with her to stand guard because they'd seen grizzly sign on the trail.

"They must have surprised a mother and her cubs. Fifteen minutes later, when Jenny and Sean hadn't returned, Matt and Luke went to check. They and the other hikers scared off the bears and called for help. But the Presleys were dead, their necks broken, their faces and—"

"I got it." Bess took a deep breath, letting it out slowly. "Luke and Matt escorted the remains back to Prescott?"

"And ran into a firestorm," Cheski said. "I called Matt to get the details. Apparently the mother threatened to sue until the guys showed her the contracts Jennifer and Sean had signed. Ironclad. The MacFarlanes were off the hook. The mother ordered them to stay away from the funeral. A day later, she suffered a fatal heart attack."

Cheski shook his head, overwhelmed by the tragedy of it. *How much sorrow can one person stand?*

The phone in his office rang. "You expecting a call?" Bess said, following him in.

"Just one." He picked up the receiver and identified himself. It was Killeen. Cheski said, "Tell me you turned up something on the serial number."

"You wouldn't think it, but the NRA has the most complete—"

"Stop right there," Cheski said. "I'd rather not know how or where you got your information."

"Understood. Anyway, we generated a list of possible owners from the registered sales, including any resales. Incomplete, but it was enough. The name Jacob Presley shows up on the list. Purchased a Colt AR-15 in 1977, when he was twenty-one. Different driver's license number than the one I got for Frankie's intruder. And this Jacob Presley wasn't a flight surgeon. He was an F-15 pilot. Died January 1991."

"Desert Storm?"

"Yeah. Military records and obit say he was the son of Jacob and Martha Presley, father of Jacob Presley, the third, Sean, and Jennifer."

"Hence our Jacob's nickname," Cheski said.

"That's all I got. Except, well, this army doctor's decorated up the ying-yang. He's saved a hell of a lot of lives—including one of our agents. Cinna Hightower. So treat Presley with respect when you find him, know what I mean?"

"I'll try, Killeen. And thanks—you've done amazing work in a short time."

"I had help. The staff pitched in. Anything else you need, just let me know," Killeen said. "And I speak for Philo and the MacFarlane family, too. We're all pretty worried."

"We're working as fast as we can." Cheski hung up. Turned to Bess Wentworth.

"That's it, then," she said. "Presley's trying to balance things that can't be balanced."

"But two siblings died. If Jacob wants Matt to suffer as he did, he'll be after Luke, too. An eye for an eye."

"And Frankie and Luke will be sitting ducks tomorrow at Phantom Ranch."

Part IV

On the River
Grand Canyon National Park, Arizona
Wednesday, July 13

"August 14, 1869. The gorge is black and narrow below, red and gray and flaring above, with crags and angular projections on the walls. Down in these grand gloomy depths we glide, ever listening, ever watching.

"August 15, 1869. Early in the afternoon we discover a stream entering from the north—a clear beautiful creek, coming down through a gorgeous red canyon. We conclude to name it 'Bright Angel.'"

—John Wesley Powell, *Exploration of the Colorado River of the West and Its Tributaries,* 1875

" 'There is no satisfaction in vengeance unless the offender has time to realize who it is that strikes him, and why retribution has come upon him. I had my plans arranged by which I should have the opportunity of making the man who had wronged me understand that his old sin had found him out.' "

—A. Conan Doyle, *A Study in Scarlet,* 1887

44

Ben Gruber had taken his time on the trail, stopping to refill his water bottles at Supai Tunnel, Roaring Springs, and Cottonwood Camp. There was plenty of light left to guide him through the steep section of rimrock, above where the trail entered Bright Angel Canyon. Sunset and moonrise had happened within minutes of each other. But he'd had to rely on ambient light and a flashlight once he'd entered the shadowy canyon.

He'd moved carefully, easily, despite the heat that grew as he descended. At the deli where he'd bought dinner, he'd overheard a couple just back from the river describe the conditions in Bright Angel Canyon. "A hundred and twelve in the Box," the man said. "Damn near melted the soles of my boots."

Preposterous, Ben had thought. *It* can't *be that hot down below.*

But as he approached the area called the Box on his map, he could feel the warmth emanating from the black rock, giving back what it had absorbed during the day. Moonlight caught distant peaks, but wasn't yet high enough to penetrate walls over a thousand feet high.

As quickly as his pants and shirt became soaked with sweat, the wind dried them, bringing no relief. And he'd run out of water.

But God was with him, as always. Even here in this hell on earth, the trail crisscrossed Bright Angel Creek, burbling in its bed. He hadn't bothered to bring water purification tablets. Had been sure two bottles of water, filled along the way, would be enough to get him to Phantom Ranch. He turned his flashlight beam onto the creek. The water looked clear and was moving swiftly.

He found the easiest route down to the stream. Filled his water bottles once, drained them both, then filled them again. Much better.

Phantom Ranch was only a couple of miles ahead. The Colorado River a half mile beyond that. He had no camping permit, but he'd find a place to wait—a place with a good view of the river and the rafts. Only twelve hours to go, fourteen at the outside, and Naomi would be forced to accept the inevitable.

But how would he get her alone?

He started walking again, worrying about the problem. Then laughed, the sound echoing from the steep cliffs until it sounded as if a whole group of spirits were laughing with him.

She'd been on a raft for four days. What would be the one thing she'd miss more than anything else?

A flush toilet. A woman would hike a mile just for that. There was bound to be one at Phantom Ranch, and a line of people waiting to use it. So simple. All he had to do was stake it out and catch her coming or going. Sidle up to her, grasp her arm, whisper the ultimatum in her ear, and she'd meekly follow him back to the rim.

45

**Mile 88.4, Beach below Bright Angel
Bridge, Granite Gorge**
10:30 a.m.

Jacob raised his paddle to the supply rafts and
two kayakers who'd elected to skip Phantom Ranch and
proceed to Pipe Creek. His kayaking mates already were
putting in to the small, sandy beach downstream, below
the Bright Angel suspension bridge. He'd heard someone
call it the Silver Bridge. They'd referred to the Kaibab
Bridge upstream as the Black Bridge. Jacob didn't much
care what they were called. For today, they provided
routes to and from the west bank and Phantom Ranch.

All night long, after Deanna had left his bedroll and
gone back to her own, he'd lain awake, his mind focused on a single problem: How far would he get after
killing Frankie and Luke MacFarlane?

Not far, if he were seen by anyone other than his intended victims. But that didn't matter as long as Matt
MacFarlane and his parents suffered a loss as great as
Jacob's. Matt would learn what it was like to lose a
brother and sister in the wild.

Jacob didn't doubt he'd locate Luke and Frankie.
Phantom Ranch had only one main trail to and from the
boat beach. And he knew thirty ways to distract a group
and isolate one or two members.

He'd studied group behavior, watched soldiers he

served with after they'd been stationed at a forward operating base for a time and were then reassigned to a base near a town. They had become a family, so they tended to travel in a pack for companionship and support. Only later, when they'd sussed out the situation, would they split up into smaller groups.

He expected the same thing to happen here after the rafts docked. The crew would announce a designated time for the party to return. The passengers would head off together, but they'd be moving at different speeds due to age, relationship dynamics, or infirmity. Over the hike to Phantom, the large group would naturally break down into smaller groups spaced farther apart. Jacob was counting on it.

Some of the crew would stay on the boat beach, leery of leaving their rafts alone. Jacob had triggered that response by damaging the lead raft just enough that they'd have to repair it. They'd probably send only one guide into Phantom to round up any stragglers as the meeting time approached.

Jacob had scoped out the boat beach as he paddled past. He'd expected one ranger to be there. The presence of a second ranger—on a rise, glassing the kayakers—surprised him. Casually, he tacked so that his back was to the ranger. Something was up.

He pulled his kayak on shore in the shadow of Silver Bridge. Heat waves danced in the humid air above the cobble-strewn slope. Behind him, the river was the color of dirt. When had the color changed from green to yellow-brown? Why hadn't he noticed?

He thought back. It had been that way since he'd gotten up this morning. Yesterday's storms must have carried debris down the Unkar River to the delta. Or something. But if his mind was missing details like the color of water, what else was it missing?

"You coming?" Deanna asked.

Four kayakers, daypacks on and water bottles in

hand, were climbing the small beach to the bridge. Deanna stood with Butch in the shade of the span.

Butch, the designated watchdog. Don't want to leave the C-4 unattended.

"Sorry," Jacob said, putting his helmet in the kayak and draping his vest over the bow to dry. "Just have to remember where I put that phone number."

"We'll catch up," Deanna called to Kent. Got a wave in return.

Safety in numbers. Camouflage.

Jacob rummaged around in the hold. Found his kit. Extracted credit card, cash, a pencil, and Chuck's small, black notebook. Into the notebook, he slid two photos.

"Shoes?" Deanna said when he'd donned his hat and tucked everything else into his daypack.

He looked down. "Good idea." *Focus, Presley, focus.*

He knew what was distracting him from the work at hand. How was he going to maneuver around the delta with the rangers on alert? And for what, or for whom, were they watching?

He put on socks and boots, checked that he had the tiny digital camera Deanna had given him the night before, and climbed the slope to where she waited. The dark walls of the gorge were heating up quickly. Must be a hundred degrees out, and it wasn't even noon. But it would be worse when they were away from the river breeze.

The closest hikers were out of earshot on the trail above, but Jacob spoke softly anyway. "I'll head over to the Kaibab Bridge before it gets any hotter. Take pictures of the spots Chuck marked on his map, then walk up to Phantom Ranch. Want to rendezvous by the stream?"

She slipped her hand into his for a moment. "I'll see if I can find some beer to chill in the stream."

"Sounds perfect." He smiled and squeezed her hand gently before disengaging. Butch stiffened and turned his back.

Jacob set off on the sandy trail that paralleled the river, connecting the South Kaibab and Bright Angel Trails and the two bridges. He didn't pass anyone. The hikers were all on the bridges or had crossed to the opposite bank.

Every once in a while he stopped and held his camera up as if he were taking a photo. He was using the lens to zero in on the rangers and see where they were focusing their surveillance. In each case, it was the river. They seemed to be ignoring trail traffic.

Had they somehow discovered Jacob's identity? Had they found Chuck Rennie's body and gotten a description of his kayak? Or were they looking for Walt Perry because he might have sabotaged the raft?

He reviewed the end of his time at Nankoweap. He was alone with the rafts, screened by bushes. Roxy had waited till he was out of sight before she left. She couldn't have seen him prick the raft and shove in the arrowhead.

What about the girl he'd stumbled into on the trail? She'd looked startled, then scared. An unusual reaction along the river. She'd seemed reassured by his apology and his rapid departure from the scene, but she might have been upset enough to tell Roxy, the only person who could connect Jacob to his Walt Perry pseudonym. Could the girl have described anything about him that would sound an alarm with Frankie or Roxy?

He looked down as he trudged along the rocky trail above the river. No visible tattoos or scars . . . Clothes—different from yesterday, and from when he'd threatened Frankie . . . Boots—he'd been wearing Tevas when he bathed in the river and when he ran into the girl. Frankie hadn't seen him in a hat, only with and without his helmet. He'd traded that helmet for Chuck's. . . .

His ring caught the light. Frankie probably hadn't noticed it at Nautiloid. Things had happened too fast, and her eyes had been focused on the knife. He remembered taking off the ring before he'd washed in the river, afraid the cold, rushing water would carry it away. So Roxy wouldn't have seen it. . . . He'd put it back on while he was waiting for Roxy to leave the raft. Before he bumped into the girl in the thicket. So she might have seen it. And if anyone checked, Walt Perry wouldn't be wearing a ring with a flight surgeon's insignia. But had there been time for anyone to check on Perry?

He took off the ring, clipping it to the key hook in a pocket of his daypack. Might be too little, too late, but he'd have to hope for the best.

Shit. If they'd somehow managed to ID him, his photo could be floating around among the rangers, or even posted on a bulletin board. Was there any way to disguise himself more than he already had?

He couldn't morph into a woman or a child or a sixty-six-year-old man. He *could* buy a new hat and an over-large T-shirt at the ranch. Maybe pad his waistline a bit. Walk with a shuffle, leaning on a hiking stick, as if he had blisters. Just might work—except that it would raise questions among the kayakers, especially Deanna. After last night, she knew his body as intimately as he did hers.

The plan was painfully weak. A distraction would help. Something that would send law enforcement barking up a different tree while he was taking care of the MacFarlanes . . .

Standing in the tunnel entrance to the Kaibab bridge, taking photos of potential placement points for C-4, the solution to his problem "smacked him topside the head with a two-by-four," as Sean used to say. Jacob smiled. *It might work. It just might work.*

Thirteen hundred hours. The intense heat sapped Jacob's energy as he hurried over the bridge and along the path on the west side of the river, staying above the boat beach. He didn't see any of the kayakers on the trail. Deanna and Kent would have finished their perusal of

Silver Bridge. They should already be cooling their feet in the stream, having a beer or two while they waited for him. He decided to locate them before he set the rest of his plan in motion. There wouldn't be time later.

Off to the left, a wooden bridge led to Bright Angel campground. If he followed the creekside path, he was bound to run into Deanna. A cold beer, though dehydrating, sounded pretty good.

Cottonwoods and willows rimmed the creek and turned the narrow valley into an oasis. Wild roses grew along the grassy bank amid daisies and penstemon. The shifting shade welcomed and revived him. He wanted to pitch a tent and stay here forever.

A forward operating base in Afghanistan seemed light years away. Jacob couldn't go back to that noisy theater of death. He had to find a way to disappear after he finished his business. If the army thought he was dead, they'd stop looking for him. Maybe he could become Chuck Rennie until a better solution appeared. . . .

Jacob followed a meandering dirt path, nodding to people as he skirted their camps. A garter snake slid through the grass. Drifts of yellow and orange butterflies lifted from flowers as he passed. The wind in the trees and the chuckling water covered human sounds until he felt as if he were alone with the bees, the soporific heat, and the stunning light of afternoon.

"Hey, buddy, can I buy you a Coke?"

Deanna was sitting beside another low bridge, her feet in the creek. Kent reclined against the bank, a hat over his face.

"No beer?" Jacob said, squeezing into their small slice of shade.

Deanna handed him a can. "Figured the caffeine would be more refreshing." She glanced around to make sure they were alone, then said, "Well?"

"You want the good news or the bad news? Scratch that. There is no good news."

"Told you." The hat muffled Kent's voice, but the disheartened tone came through.

Deanna sighed, took another can from the stream, popped the top. "We don't have nearly enough C-4 to take out two bridges?"

"Right. They're beautifully constructed. But you could cause a lot of trouble by closing one end of each of them."

"Which end of Kaibab?"

"The south end of the tunnel, I think. Should be deserted by midnight," he said. "Maybe earlier. But by three or four in the morning, people will be crossing south again, trying to avoid climbing in the heat and full sunlight."

"You check out Silver Bridge yet?"

"Haven't had time. I'm on my way to the ranch. Did you pick an end?"

"South side again. But I'd like another opinion."

"What about Butch?"

"I know he'll side with Kent. They're a team," she said. "Isn't that right, Kent?"

The hat was silent.

"Well, I got a call to make," Jacob said. "See you back here in an hour?"

"I'm not going anyplace. Kent's gonna relieve Butch in a couple of hours. We can't do anything till dark."

Jacob looked at her watch. "Eight hours from now. Okay, I'll take my time." He drained his Coke and smashed the can between his palms. "Want me to take your empties?"

She handed him the remains of a six-pack. Then said, "Wait." From her pocket she took two postcards of Phantom Ranch, addressed and stamped. "Mail these for me?"

"Sure thing."

He headed toward the thicker density of trees in the distance. A mule brayed off to the right, maybe one of the mules that carried the mail up to the rim. Jacob stopped by the fence, read the postcards, jotted down Deanna's return address and the name and address of the people she was sending them to. Relatives. Parents and sister, probably. All named Birdsall. In Ashland, Oregon.

He mailed them at the post office before finding the little store. Decided against using padding as a disguise. Too damn hot.

He bought two collapsible hiking poles; a tank top decorated with a map of the Colorado River; a floppy-brimmed, fisherman's-style green hat; more Coke; and salted trail mix. He changed clothes in the restroom. He looked like a hiker just down from the rim, not someone who'd been on the river for days. They wouldn't glance at him twice.

He filled his water bottles at the spigot near the restrooms. Checking out Silver Bridge could wait, he decided. He started back to Kaibab Bridge. The dark coolness of the entrance was the perfect place to wait for the MacFarlane rafts. He could see the river from the dim interior, but no one could see him.

Twenty minutes later he arrived at the bridge in time to see a raft approaching, about a mile off. A second raft appeared. They were orange and silver, the colors of the MacFarlane group's rafts.

He worked to calm his nerves as he waited for the rafts to get close enough for him to confirm their numbers. Half a minute later, he was sure.

Jacob turned his back on the river. Time to make his phone call.

46

I'd last been to Phantom Ranch five years ago
on a rim-to-rim hike with geology classmates. I felt like
I was coming home.

At the turn of the twentieth century, cartographers
had established a camp here when they were creating
the first topographic map of the canyon. They'd built a
trail up Bright Angel Creek to the North Rim to facili-
tate resupply during long field seasons. There wasn't a
bridge across the river then. But soon after, David Rust
had begun creating a way station for tourists traveling
down to view the Inner Gorge.

Rust had planted fruit trees to help feed the visitors,
and cottonwood trees to shade the main building and
cabins. Rust's Camp had been a going concern when
President Teddy Roosevelt visited in 1913. After Roosevelt wrote about his trip, the public began referring to
the place as Roosevelt Camp.

Nine years later, renowned southwestern architect
Mary Jane Colter designed and built a new lodge on
the site. She renamed the facility Phantom Ranch after a tributary creek that feeds Bright Angel. She also
designed buildings for Fred Harvey on the South Rim,
including Desert View Watchtower. I'd pointed it out

to the students yesterday, as we'd unloaded the rafts at Carbon Canyon.

When Phantom Ranch became part of Grand Canyon National Park in 1933, the park service took over. In the midst of the Great Depression, the Civilian Conservation Corps lived and worked at what became Bright Angel Campground. They improved trails to the rim, constructed new ones to natural attractions up side canyons, dug a swimming pool at the ranch, and added trees to the valley. The cottonwoods and orchard had survived, but the park service had filled in the pool long before I was born.

Nico passed under Kaibab Bridge and throttled down for the approach to the boat beach. I could see hikers on the bridge and zigzagging down the cliff trails from the South Rim. Though the trails were crowded, ours were the only rafts at the boat landing, a pale swath of beach sand and mud on the upstream side of Bright Angel Delta. I welcomed not having to fight rafting crowds as we rendezvoused with Paul and handed Molly into his care—and into Luke's, I'd learned last night. I didn't know Paul, but I knew Luke was more than capable of escorting her safely to the rim.

I'd have to trust my own safety to the crew, park law enforcement, and my own heightened senses. I suspected something would happen during my ninety-minute visit to Phantom Ranch. I didn't know what, but I was glad Luke would be around for the next hour or so.

While Doug moored the rafts, Nico and Nan hopped off and met with the Phantom ranger standing a little way above us. I'd noticed a second ranger higher on the delta, binoculars glued to her eyes. I hooked my mug to the lashings holding the tarp in place. Did the same with a dry bag full of things from my daypack that I wouldn't need on the short hike to Phantom. Was it only two days ago that I'd gone through the same motions at Nautiloid Creek?

I looked down at my knee. The swelling, which had receded overnight, was on the rise again. I'd rested the knee after walking to the swimming area at the Little Colorado River yesterday. I'd soaked my body in the warm turquoise water. But the hike in Carbon and Lava Canyons this morning had stressed the knee again. Too much, too soon. I wished I could stay on the boat beach, but Molly's safe transfer took priority.

I popped four ibuprofen and rewrapped the knee. By the time I finished, the rest of the rafters, led by Dora and Harvey, were on the trail to Phantom Ranch. Nan and Nico were talking to the ranger with the binoculars. Luke was with Roxy and Doug on the shore, filling water bottles and drink coolers. Luke's daypack bulged as he stuffed plastic bags of trail mix down between the bottles.

I made my way to the bow and down onto the sand. "Molly's with Dora and the boys?" I said.

Luke straightened up. "Yup. They'll guard her till Paul arrives. I've decided to wait till evening to start climbing. Follow the shadows up Bright Angel. It's an oven in the late afternoon."

"I remember."

Nico, Nan, and the ranger with the binoculars came down to us. It was Bess Wentworth, the law enforcement officer who'd been with Boyd Cheski the day before. She'd helicoptered down this morning, she said, shaking our hands. And then she filled us in on what they'd learned during the night.

"Trey Presley attacked Frankie?" Luke sank to the sand, a stunned look on his face. "Sean and Jenny talked about him so much, I felt like I knew him. He was their *hero*."

I sat next to my brother and slipped my arm around his waist. He stared out at the river, but his mind was someplace else.

"Trey wasn't back yet when Matt and I brought the

bodies home. We didn't meet him—" He looked up at Wentworth. "You know about Presley's mother?"

She nodded. "Her death must have been the final straw."

Luke shook his head in disbelief. "Why didn't Trey come talk to us? When we heard about it, we sent flowers from the family, but . . . damn, he must have felt so alone."

"We think Presley wants to hurt your family as much as he's been hurt."

"There's a bizarre kind of logic to his thinking." I squeezed Luke's shoulder, stood, and pulled him to his feet. "You think Mom's on his list?"

"Oh, Christ," he said. "Ranger Wentworth—"

"Killeen said to tell you he's got her covered," she said. "Matt, too."

Roxy had been standing a few feet away, listening. "You're saying I offered lemonade to the man who attacked Frankie?"

"Walt Perry's an old friend of Presley's," Wentworth said. "We think he just borrowed the name."

"But he didn't set off any alarm bells. He was . . . charming." Roxy shook her head. "How could he be so charming?"

I had no answer for her. I turned to Wentworth. "You think Presley will show up here today?"

"Yes. He's in a kayak. Once you get farther into Granite Gorge, he'll have a tough time staying with the motorized rafts. Plus, he left his rifle at Buck Farm. He'll have to show himself in order to reach you. That's when we'll pick him up."

"That puts a different spin on things," said Luke. "I can't leave—"

"You were planning to hike out?" Wentworth gave him an assessing glance. She seemed to sense that something was awry.

We were on shaky ground. Luke and Paul had no

legal right to escort Molly anywhere, or to prevent her family from retrieving her. In addition, Molly was traveling under an assumed name. Luke could get into all sorts of trouble if he wasn't careful.

"I was going to help out a friend who hasn't done the climb before," Luke said. "But if Presley's coming, I can't leave Frankie to deal with him alone."

"I won't be alone," I said. "And this time we know who Jacob is and what he wants. We'll be prepared. And it'll be easier if the rangers only have me to protect."

Luke frowned, unconvinced. To Wentworth, he said, "You're sure he's working alone?"

"Not absolutely certain. Roxy said he's traveling with kayakers, but they may not know that they're helping him. And there's one other person who's involved somehow. His name's Charles Rennie. His prints were found in Jacob's kayak. Ever heard of him?"

"No," I said.

"Name rings a bell from way back," Luke said. "When I worked on the river . . . I think he was on an Abbey memorial trip."

"That fits," she said. "But your family hasn't had any dealings with him? He's a lawyer in Tempe."

"My brother Kit's the family lawyer—or my uncle David. You could ask them."

"I will."

"Have any kayak groups stopped by Phantom today?" I said.

"A few. This morning. All of them have left. One group passed by a couple of hours ago. Didn't stop. It's been quiet—or as quiet as this delta ever is. But we'll keep watch until your party leaves."

Nan cleared her throat. She'd been standing quietly in the background, listening to the debate. She joined the little circle. "I think it would solve everyone's problem if Frankie and Luke both left the canyon."

"Cheski and I discussed that. Concluded we'd just be

kicking the rock down the road," Wentworth said. "But I get your point. Removing the targets now will keep everyone safe. And that's our job." She turned to Luke and me. "Luke, you can hike out, as planned. Frankie, you'll leave on the helicopter with me."

And that was that.

"If you're going to Phantom," Nico said, "you'd better get a move on. I'll roust out your night bag, and Doug can carry it to the ranch."

"Will there be room for me to fly with you?" Nan said to Wentworth. "Or should I hike out?"

"We can give you a lift. We'll leave around six. Well before sunset. But you'll have to hump your gear to the ranch."

"No problem," Nan said.

Ranger Wentworth went with Luke and me. I didn't try to make conversation. I was angry at the way the tide had turned. One minute I was continuing downriver, the next I was ejected from the canyon. It didn't help knowing that the two rangers were right.

Away from the river wind, the heat settled in the canyon, sucking moisture from our bodies. The trees along the creek and trail provided occasional shade, but the temperature continued to climb. It must be well into the triple digits. I was wearing swim shorts, a bikini top, camp shirt, and daypack. I slathered more sunscreen on my legs, face, and neck as we walked.

We passed a kiosk with announcements for rafting crews and messages left by hikers. Rangers had posted a flyer warning about Jacob Presley. I stopped. The first picture on the flyer showed a smiling young man, no older than Bobby or Craig, with only a passing resemblance to the man who'd threatened me. Beside it was the picture from Jacob's military ID. Unsmiling. Less hair than the man who'd threatened me at Nautiloid Canyon. But the eyes . . . I shivered, despite the heat. Those eyes haunted my dreams.

I caught up with the others, who waited near the first bridge. Pleading that I needed relief for my knee, I dropped my daypack and shirt on the bank and immersed myself in the cold creek. Luke did the same. Wentworth sat in the shade and called the ranger station on her radio.

I felt my body temperature dropping, but my mood remained at boiling point. I just wasn't ready to leave the canyon.

Luke put his arm around me. "Sorry," he said.

"Not your fault." I tried a smile. Failed miserably.

"You can cry on my shoulder."

"Don't tempt me. Besides, doesn't that shoulder have a reserved sign on it?"

"Yeah." A soft smile erased the tension from his face. "Dora's one good thing that came of this abortive adventure. I owe you big time."

"I'm not sure Matt will feel the same."

"We were weighing our options anyway. We'll figure it out. Maybe I'll open an adventure-tour branch in Austin."

We lapsed into silence. I tried to absorb every nuance of the place, the day, not knowing when I'd be back. The ancient rocks surrounded us, reassuringly sturdy, worn by rain and wind and the grinding action of waterborne sediment that even now tickled my feet. A hot breeze fluttered the cottonwood leaves. Arpeggios of running water underlay the hum of insects in the grass. Someone at a campsite laughed.

The sounds brought back memories of playing in Nankoweap Creek the summer our father worked on the Anasazi sites. I wished I could sit here forever.

"Damn it," I said. "I'll miss Blacktail Canyon."

Luke hugged me. "Next time."

"Promise?"

"Promise."

47

Phantom Ranch, Bright Angel Canyon
2:45 p.m.

Three minutes later Ranger Wentworth finished her call. "Time to go."

Luke and I slipped on our shirts and packs and dripped our way up the dusty trail. It was too hot for conversation.

Wentworth's radio squawked as we passed the mule pasture. She stopped. We continued on. Then she was beside us, face serious. "Somebody called in a bomb threat. Said ecoterrorists were targeting both bridges. The rangers are evacuating the campground and closing the bridges."

I looked at Luke. How would Luke and Paul get Molly across the river and onto the trail? "We need to find Dora," I said.

The three of us broke into a lope—or Luke and Wentworth did. They slowed to a trot when they saw I couldn't manage more than a fast walk.

"Was the caller a man or a woman?" I said.

"A man, I think," Wentworth said.

"Presley's clever and resourceful. Buck Farm Canyon was classic misdirection."

Luke said, "Frankie, you're becoming paranoid."

"If you say so."

But if this wasn't Jacob's doing, had Molly's family discovered her hiding place?

We parted company at the ranger station so that Wentworth could get a status report. "Be careful. Keep your eyes open," she said. "I'll find you in a minute."

Luke and I hurried on to the center of the ranch. A crowd was gathering in front of the office and canteen. Where were all the people coming from?

I climbed onto a boulder to look for our group. Saw Dora standing in the shadow of the little store studying something in her hand. Her meter. She was testing her blood sugar. The boys, except Ethan, stood in a little knot behind her. "I don't see Molly."

"I'll find her." Luke headed toward Dora.

Around me, people were all talking at once, trying to figure out how the bomb threat would affect their plans. The conversations were in half a dozen languages. Above the commotion, I heard a shout. Luke's voice.

I'd lost him in the milling throng. I looked for a UA hat. Found it. But Luke was hunched over at an odd angle, clutching his left side. His shirt was crimson. No one around him seemed to have noticed. Except one man. He was holding a knife.

Jacob.

He wore a hat and different clothing, but I would have recognized him anywhere.

I whistled, then shouted, "Luke, behind you." From the corner of my eye I saw Dora's head come up.

Luke pivoted on his good side, lowered his right shoulder, and plowed into Jacob. Knocked off balance, he took two steps to the side. Recovered. Danced back, swinging the knife in an arc, aiming for Luke's neck.

I jumped off the boulder, landing on my good leg, and forced a path through the crowd. Glimpsed Luke feinting and parrying with his hiking stick. His bulging backpack slowed his movements. One strap slid down as he dropped the stick and grabbed for Jacob's knife arm. Luke's bloody hands slipped off.

A rough circle formed around the men, like students

at a middle-school brawl. People were yelling, screaming for them to stop. I expected Jacob to break off and try to escape through the crowd, but he stayed with my brother. It was as if Luke were his entire reason for being.

"Frankie!"

Dora's voice. I saw her arm waving above the crowd as she slid between taller people. I waved back, then dove through an opening at the edge of the circle. Luke's hand was twisted in Jacob's tank top. Luke tugged and turned, trying to throw Jacob over his hip. Jacob pulled back, stumbled. His knife swung wide.

I reached for my stiletto. Damn. I'd given it to Molly. Where was Luke's knife?

I checked his right hip. The heavy pack had shifted to cover the sheath.

I snatched up Luke's hiking pole. Ran closer. Swung it at Jacob's head. He sensed it coming and twisted away. The pole glanced off his arm. But it gave Luke enough time to slip behind Jacob and catch his shoulders in a wrestler's hold, arms bent, restrained. Luke's knees hit the back of Jacob's, and they both went down, Luke on top.

I grabbed Jacob's knife wrist with both hands. Jesus, the man was strong. He bucked like a man on PCP. His left arm broke free. He groped around, found my hat, and jerked. The string was choking me. Black dots danced before my eyes.

Luke struggled to subdue Jacob. His wrist twisted in my sweaty grip. The tip of a blade nicked my arm. I smelled blood.

"I got it," Dora said.

A foot in a river shoe stepped by my nose to pinion Jacob's right arm, crunching his wrist. He yelped, but didn't drop the knife.

Luke regained control of Jacob's other arm. The pressure on my throat eased a bit. Not enough.

Dora's shadow bent and stretched toward Luke's hip. Something flashed in the sunlight. The hat string parted. I gulped air.

Dragging off my hat, I threw it to the side. Jacob was still trying to buck Luke off. Dora had two feet and her full weight planted on Jacob's knife hand and wrist. This was my chance.

I pushed myself up. Balancing on my bad leg, I swung my left foot back as if kicking a field goal. I had to miss Luke's head and connect with the crown of Jacob's. Any lower and I might kill him.

The clip sounded like a melon dropped on cement. The impact sent a wave of pain up my leg. Jacob lay still.

"Thanks," I croaked to Dora, rubbing my throat.

"Sounded like you broke a couple of toes." Her voice was cool, composed, not even breathing hard.

"It was worth it." I pried the knife from Jacob's hand and tucked it in my waistband.

The crowd noise had reduced to a murmur. Luke's head had dropped onto Jacob's. They both were out cold.

The boys stripped off Luke's heavy daypack. Adam and Bobby rolled him off Jacob, then hunkered down to keep an eye on the MacFarlane nemesis. He wasn't going anywhere.

I knelt and lifted my brother's bloody shirt. Jacob's knife had come in at an angle, slicing along his ribs. I could see white bone. He must have turned at just the right moment. If the knife had entered between the ribs, he'd have bled out by now.

"Adam, get a ranger," I said. Shrugging out of my daypack, I shucked my shirt and pressed it to the wound, trying to staunch the bleeding. I didn't even look at Jacob. I was afraid I'd finish the job my foot had started.

"I'm here." The crowd parted to allow Ranger Wentworth through. "Sorry I'm late. The bomb threat's caused a logistical nightmare."

"Which Jacob took advantage of," I said. "He stabbed Luke but didn't penetrate the ribcage." My voice faltered on the last word. I nodded toward the area covered by my hands.

"How bad?"

"Clean. Shallow. May have nicked the lowest rib. He'll need stitches. But the bleeding seems to have slowed."

"He was lucky." She turned Jacob over to check his eyes, the bruised and swollen head, the battered wrist. "Somebody did a number on him. Looks like he may have a concussion and some broken bones."

Dora smiled. "It was a joint effort." I winced at the pun.

A Phantom ranger ran up as Wentworth tightened a plastic tie around Jacob's wrists. If he'd been conscious, the pain would have put him out. The ranger handed Wentworth a first-aid kit.

"Thanks, John."

Ranger John's face swung from Luke to the handcuffed man lying beside him in the dirt. "Jacob Presley?"

"In the flesh," she said. "I heard a helicopter. Cheski arrive?"

"Yeah. Said he'll be here in ten."

"We have Jacob's knife," I said. "Dora?"

Dora eased the blade from my waistband, passing it hilt-first to Ranger John. As he bagged and labeled the weapon, another couple of rangers arrived with a stretcher.

Jacob groaned. His eyelids fluttered, closed again. Wentworth checked his eyes.

"Presley first?" John said.

She nodded. "That head injury could be serious. But be careful—he's attempted murder twice."

"Got it."

The rangers braced Jacob's neck and loaded him on to the stretcher. Luke was awake and aware. Wentworth checked his eyes. "I just fainted, that's all," he said. "No head injury."

"You thirsty?" I said.

"God, yes."

"Headache?" Wentworth asked.

"Ditto."

"Dehydrated, probably," said Ranger John.

Wentworth pulled a bottle of Gatorade from her backpack. "It's not cold, but—"

"I can't drink lying down." Luke tried to sit up. Didn't make it.

"Let me," Dora said.

She sat cross-legged behind his shoulders. While I kept pressure on Luke's wound, Wentworth helped prop him up against Dora's lap. He emptied the bottle in short order.

"Enough?" Wentworth said.

He nodded.

"I can take over now, if you want," Ranger John said to me.

"Please."

John pulled on gloves, knelt down beside me, and slid his hand under mine. Luke winced.

"Don't croak on me," I said. "Dora and I wouldn't forgive you."

His smile turned to a grimace as John cleaned the area and applied butterfly bandages to hold the cut edges together.

"I should have seen it coming," Luke said.

"Don't be an ass."

Wentworth began cleaning and dressing my arm. Her touch was gentle. She dabbed something greasy on my neck. It stung, then numbed the pain. She moved down to my back and left shoulder, smoothing on antibiotic ointment.

The students had moved back and were keeping the crowd at bay. I met Adam's eyes. "Where's Molly?"

David answered for him. "She went to the restroom a while ago—before the ruckus started."

"Was she with Ethan?"

"Yes," Adam said.

"Find them," said Dora.

"You bet. Come on, guys."

When the students had gone, I said, "Did Paul arrive?"

Dora shook her head.

"Who's Paul?" Wentworth closed the first-aid kit and stretched a kink out of her back.

"My son-in-law," Dora said. "He's hiking down from South Rim to collect one of the students."

"Which one?"

"Molly . . . Molly McKuen." Dora spoke the name she'd used on Naomi's river-trip forms. It was one of the few protections they had against discovery by the Family.

Wentworth checked her watch. "They closed the bridges a good hour ago. If you haven't found him yet, he probably didn't make it across."

Adam ran up, breathless. He and Bobby, the tallest brother, were each holding one of Ethan's arms. His face was flushed, his eyes swollen and red. He'd been crying.

"Molly took off up the canyon trail with, um, Ben," Adam said.

Dora and I exchanged glances. She started to shake her head, then paused, nodded.

"Ranger Wentworth," I said, "we have a problem."

Wentworth looked up from her notes. "Another one?"

"Molly's in trouble. We need your help. I'll explain on the way."

Wentworth jotted a last note, said, "John, you're in charge till Cheski arrives."

"No problem."

I turned to Ethan. "Show us where you left her."

48

I emptied Luke's pack of the water bottles and passed them out to the boys. My toes and knee hurt. My throat burned. My forearm was on fire. I didn't care. Jacob was in custody. Luke would be okay. And I'd be able to stay on the river. But first I had to get Molly back.

Dora wanted to come, but I refused to put her anywhere near Ben Gruber. Besides, one of the two of us had to stay with Luke till he was medevacked out. She reluctantly agreed.

Ranger Wentworth was beside me as the boys and I started up Bright Angel Canyon. She had a sidearm. I had Luke's knife. Dora had slipped it to me when the rangers weren't looking. I'd tucked it in my waistband, hidden by my bloody camp shirt.

The boys were aware of the stakes. They knew Ben Gruber. And the older boys were furious with Ethan, and with themselves, for letting their sister be taken from under their noses. I didn't even try to calm them down. I wanted them alert and fired up for the coming confrontation.

We moved through Phantom Ranch at a fast walk, passing groups of hikers arriving from the rim. I spent the first ten minutes giving Wentworth some background on Ben Gruber, Carrie, Eldon Sprague, and Molly. I didn't mention Ben's connection with Dora and Annie. That was their secret.

Ethan stopped abruptly, saying, "Here."

Bright Angel Canyon narrowed ahead where the creek trail traversed more than three miles of dark Vishnu Schist, shot through with dikes and fat intrusions of pink Zoroaster Granite. The black V of the Box held the heat of day like an iron kettle over a slow fire.

"This is where you left Molly and Gruber?" I said.

He nodded.

"How long ago?"

He looked at his watch. "Forty minutes or so, I guess."

"Were they moving quickly?" Wentworth said.

Another nod.

"Then they may be a couple of miles ahead of us," I said. "Let's go."

I increased my pace. Everyone followed suit. The Box was a maze of twists and turns, the trail crisscrossing Bright Angel Creek over low footbridges.

"What did Gruber say to make Molly go with him?" Wentworth asked Ethan.

He studied the dusty trail with great intensity. "I only heard part of it. He was whispering in her ear."

"And?"

"He said, er, if she didn't come willingly he'd take two of her sisters instead. And he'd make their lives a living hell until she came home."

Craig cleared his throat. "The Prophet wouldn't allow that."

"Your father's dead." Ethan's steps faltered. He looked up, eyes tight with pain. "My father said *he's* the new Prophet."

Dora had introduced the boys by their first names. I'd assumed they were all Eldon Sprague's sons, as she and Naomi were his daughters. Dora had organized the trip, so she kept the paperwork. I hadn't thought it was important. Now I mentally kicked myself for not asking to see the list of names.

"Your father's Ben Gruber?" I said to Ethan.

"Of course." He gave me the look. Clearly, I was an idiot.

Adam got in Ethan's face. "When did the Prophet die? How?"

"God came to my father in a dream. He told him what to do. Something about fire and coyotes and ants—I didn't really follow it."

"But your father killed Sprague?" Wentworth said.

"That's what he said."

Wentworth looked at me. This changed things. We weren't just dealing with a kidnapped girl. We'd be facing a murderer.

"I'm calling in," Wentworth said. "Locate Gruber, but don't engage him. I'll catch up with you in a minute."

We left her behind, radio to her ear. I doubted she'd get reception in the Box. She might have to run back to where the valley widened out.

"Did you really think Ben would take you home with him?" Adam said.

Ethan stopped again. He looked from face to face, as if searching for a friend in a sea of strangers.

"We've got to keep moving." David took his elbow, urging him forward.

Ethan jerked his arm away. "He lied—my father *lied* to me. He just wanted Naomi." His lower lip trembled, and he caught it between his teeth. He'd been abandoned twice.

"Don't you get it?" Bobby said. "They've been lying to us forever."

"It's the Family way," Adam said. "It won't stop just because they choose a new prophet. You have to accept the fact that you can't go back. None of us can."

I put my hand on Ethan's shoulder. "Adam's right—

you can't go back. But you can make a new home with Dora, Molly, and the boys."

Craig harrumphed and swallowed. "Yeah, but first we have to find her."

"Go," I told the other boys. "When you locate Ben and Molly, stay out of sight." They loped off. "And stay hydrated," I yelled after them. Bobby waved back.

A group of hikers passed us, giving me and my bloody shirt a wide berth. I dropped my daypack, stripped off the shirt, and quickly rinsed it in the stream. The stain turned from dark red-brown to pinky-beige. Better. I'd blend in with the Zoroaster Granite.

"I couldn't talk in front of them," Ethan said, looking away as I buttoned my shirt and slipped on my pack. "Father knows about Dora."

"Knows what about Dora?" I started walking. He matched my pace.

"Everything. I'm sorry. I didn't think."

"You'll have to be a little more specific, Ethan."

"Father found me first. I told him Molly—only I said, Naomi—was planning to hike out with Paul. Father asked who Paul was, and I said, 'Annie's husband, Dora's son-in-law.' So he asked about Dora. I said she was the woman who'd taken us in—that she'd been raised in the Family, but her name was Esther then. Esther Sprague."

"How did you find out?"

"I overheard Dora and Annie talking one night. About Annie's father. About how bad it would be if he or the Prophet ever found out Dora was alive. What Dora said, and the way she said it—well, I figured out that *my* father was Annie's father, and Dora had refused to stay with him. . . ."

His whole body was shaking, as if he were in shock. I put my arm around him, saying, "I'm so sorry, Ethan. You must have been devastated."

He took a deep breath, nodded. "I didn't want to believe it. Dora had to be lying. I went through her things when she was in class and my brothers were out. I found a little notebook with the name 'Esther Sprague' on it, and a newspaper clipping about the death of her mother. There was a picture of them together. On the back someone had written 'Esther and Linda Sprague,' and the year. That's how I knew for sure that Dora was Esther. She's older, of course, but she hasn't changed that much."

"And you chose not to tell the other boys?"

"Yeah." He stepped away from me and blew his nose on a large red handkerchief. "I thought maybe, somehow, I could use the information to get back to the Family. That's why I begged to be allowed to come on this trip, even though I'd only been with Dora for a couple of months. I studied harder than I ever had before, harder than any of my brothers. I thought that if I could just get back to Arizona, I could find my way home. I never thought—I didn't want anyone to get hurt—"

The tears streamed in earnest again. He mopped his cheeks and eyes, but nothing staunched the flow.

I handed him my neckerchief. "So somehow Ben asked the right questions, then put two and two together."

Ethan nodded, mopped some more. "He asked if Dora was married, and I said no, she'd raised Annie on her own. Then he got real quiet and asked how old Annie was. I said a couple of years older than Adam."

"What did your father say? Exactly. It's important."

Ethan blew his nose again and screwed up his face, wanting to do this one thing right, as if it would make up for everything else. "He said Annie was an *abomination*—that Esther and Annie both were abominations in the eyes of the Lord. He asked me if I would be his right hand, his hammer, as *he* used to be for Prophet Sprague. But I couldn't. . . . I *won't* do the things he did. I just can't."

"What things?"

"He visits people at night. They repent and change their ways. . . . Sometimes they disappear."

"And becoming like him was the price you'd have to pay to be taken back into the Family?"

He nodded. "When I refused, he took out a knife and said that if I didn't run, he'd do to me what God had told him to do to the Prophet. He said if I ever showed my face again, or ever told anyone about him taking Naomi, he'd know. . . . He was so *angry*, Frankie. He started talking to God, saying, 'Why do I have to do everything myself?' I didn't wait around. I ran as fast as I could for Phantom. I was afraid I'd missed the boat."

An *abomination*. To a man like Ben Gruber, that designation would be a call to action. But what would he do?

Fueled by anger, he'd probably continue up the trail as he puzzled over the news. Eventually he'd realize that Esther was close, *so* close, after all these years. Maybe he could reclaim her *and* Naomi at the same time. And then he'd go after Annie.

Was Gruber even now heading back to Phantom, coming up with a plan as he walked? If so, Molly would slow him down. Unless he stashed her somewhere. Either way, if Gruber decided to go back for Dora, we'd encounter him any moment. That two-mile lead he'd gained would have evaporated. The boys might already have intercepted him.

"Can you run and warn Officer Wentworth?" I asked Ethan.

"No problem."

"Tell her everything you told me. And ask her to have Ranger Cheski keep an eye on Dora."

He handed me back the sodden neckerchief and took off like a startled lizard.

I began to run, ignoring the pain in my knee and foot. I'd gone no more than a hundred yards when I rounded a curve and saw the next footbridge. A man was just starting back across it. Molly was a pace behind. And in the water below, concealed by the bridge, were the four boys. The canyon walls were steep and close here. They'd had nowhere else to hide.

I slowed to a walk. Took deep, steadying breaths as I prepared to meet the man who'd been given a license to brutalize others in the name of a self-proclaimed prophet. I'd never liked bullies. I had to stop him.

The boys saw me at the same time Molly did. Bobby started to leave the shelter. I bent my right arm as if I were working kinks out, then straightened it, palm down, signaling the boys to stay hidden. Adam got it, and pulled his brother back.

Molly wasn't crying. I could see by the determined look on her face that she was planning, searching for a way out. I saw her hand go to her neck, under her hat, and finger the leather thong that held my stiletto.

Gruber turned and grabbed her upper arm. "Walk faster. You can rest at the ranch."

"Brother Ben, I'm very thirsty. I haven't had anything to drink since lunch."

He stopped in the middle of the bridge. It wasn't very wide. If he looked over the edge, he'd see the boys. Adam and Craig seemed to be taking things from around their waists. Bobby and David had sticks.

"Then go down and drink from the creek," Ben said.

"But the raft crew said we mustn't—that all the creeks have parasites."

I was almost to the near end of the bridge. Ben was an imposing man—shorter than I, but massive. He was hatless in the canyon shade. He had a high forehead with a widow's peak, graying black hair, and eyes dark as peat. Hair, face, khaki pants, and plaid shirt were soaked with sweat.

His voice carried. "God created this stream. I drank from it all night, and I'm fine. Just hurry up." Turning, he seemed to notice me for the first time.

"Afternoon," I said, stepping to the right of the trail,

trying to draw his eyes away from the creek. My hand rested on my hip, covering the haft of Luke's knife. "Hot enough for you?"

He nodded curtly. The distraction was all that the boys needed. Adam and Craig popped up on one side of the bridge, Bobby and David on the other. From either side, they grabbed Ben's legs and jerked them back. Ben toppled to the bridge, arms out to break his fall. I felt the shockwaves beneath my feet.

Molly was on him in an instant. She sat on his back, holding my stiletto to his throat. "Don't move. Don't speak," she said. "Don't give me an excuse to use this." Her other hand removed the knife from his belt and tossed it onto the bank. Adam splashed out and picked it up.

As the boys and I swarmed around them, Ben arched his back, shoved against the planks, and dislodged Molly. The stiletto clattered onto the slats. I grabbed it before it slipped over the edge. Blood stained the tip and oozed from a nick under his ear.

Gruber was trapped. Two boys, Molly, and his hunting knife in one direction. Two boys, Luke's knife, my stiletto, and me in the other.

49

Ben Gruber got to his feet. "Who are you?" he said, frowning up at the slim, black-haired woman.

"I'm a friend of Molly's."

Molly? He thought for a moment. His eyes shifted to find and pin the girl. "You mean Naomi."

"Not anymore." The woman's gray eyes matched the color of the hunting knife in her left hand. Her open stare showed curiosity. No fear.

This was new territory. It irritated him that she was so much taller, and that she didn't address him with respect.

The Amazon handed her knife to Bobby and stepped so close to Ben that her nose was almost touching his. He didn't move. Adam held Ben's knife. He didn't think the boy would use it, but why didn't they all just take Naomi and leave?

The woman's right arm moved. He felt the tip of a knife on his Adam's apple—the stiletto Naomi had held to his neck moments before. He tensed, waiting to see what the woman would do.

"If anyone tries to hurt Molly, Dora, or the boys again, my friends and I will know." Her voice grated like sandpaper on wood. "And we won't like it. Understood?"

Anger rose in him, a heat more palpable than the waves flowing from the canyon walls. He felt as if he'd explode.

"Understood?" she repeated, twisting the tip so it bit into his skin.

Ben flinched in spite of himself. He prayed for help, for intervention. But his guiding voice was silent.

"This knife has a memory, Ben Gruber. It reads blood. It knows what you've done, and it would love to bury itself in your neck so you never have the chance to harm anyone again. Ever. If God gives me a sign, I'll let it do just that."

She waited. He gave the slightest of nods.

"Good. We understand each other. Is anyone else hunting Naomi?"

He wanted to lie. This wasn't the time. "I called them back before I started down," he said.

"Hear that, guys?"

A chorus of young voices murmured assent. Clearly, they'd been brainwashed.

The woman stepped back. "But in case he's lying, you'll still have to keep an eye out for trouble on the way home."

They will never make it home. They will be punished for their complicity.

Ben heard the voice as if the very stones had spoken. He smiled. God had not abandoned him.

He took a breath and sank to his knees. Raising his hands and eyes to the sky, he opened his mind and heart to receive God's plan. Above, a red-tailed hawk floated on the rising thermals, describing a vortex of lazy circles that widened and narrowed and shifted with never a flap of wings, just feather tips flexing to catch the faintest currents. From the corner of his eye Ben saw movement on the trail. A ranger, coming around a bend. With Ethan. The ranger was unsnapping the holster at her side.

So that's what they'd been waiting for. Did they think he'd go quietly?

You are the chosen one, Benjamin Gruber. Bullets cannot harm you. Ties cannot bind. Your feet have wings.

Of course.

Ben stood, feinted to one side, pivoted, and leaped toward the woman. She glided right and turned sideways, her back to him. Bobby and David, shoulder to shoulder, blocked his path.

"Stop," yelled a woman's voice. The ranger.

Foolish woman. The Prophet obeyed only one authority.

Ben bent his head and charged the boys. Felt a stabbing pain. His right leg folded. He struggled, tried to stand. The leg wouldn't support his weight. She'd slashed the tendons at the back of his knee. He smelled and felt his own warm blood soaking his pants.

"Had enough?" She pushed him down onto his chest. When he didn't answer, she said, "If you move, I'll do the other one."

Ben felt pressure on the crook of his knee, the vibration of feet on the bridge. "Are you Benjamin Gruber?" the ranger's voice asked. She was breathing hard.

He grunted. He had nothing to say to this woman, or to anyone.

"I'm arresting you for the murder of Eldon Sprague."

My God, my God, why have you forsaken me?

50

Phantom Ranch Ranger Station
6 p.m.

I sat with my foot up on a chair, ice packs on knee and toes, listening to Rangers Cheski and Wentworth interview witnesses in the adjoining rooms at the Phantom Ranger Station. Outside the window, shadows splayed up the Vishnu Schist, black on black. Soon it would be too late, at least for today, to continue down the river.

I felt battered and bruised, physically and emotionally. A few hours before I'd given in to the violence that lives in all of us. I'd threatened a man's life and been prepared, in that moment, to follow through. The mother bear instinct. Like Dora, I'd accepted the responsibility of protecting Molly and her brothers. But more than that, I'd reacted to Ben Gruber and the threat he represented as if I were standing up for all young women across the globe—those with limited access to education, those without the freedom and resources to choose a life path. They were songbirds bereft of song, and the world was a poorer place without their music. But at least I'd helped set one bird free.

I shifted in my chair, turned over the ice bags. The adrenaline rush had seeped away long ago. I felt as desiccated and empty as a cornstalk after harvest, good only for plowing back into the sandy desert soil. Somewhere I'd have to find the energy and enthusiasm to continue the trip down the river. I still had half the course to teach. I owed it to Dora and the boys. But I yearned to navigate the river alone, speaking to no one, letting the rock walls and light and rushing water heal me.

Rangers Cheski and Wentworth met outside the door to review their checklist. Wentworth had interviewed us on the hike back to Phantom. When Ethan and I had told her about Gruber claiming to have killed Eldon Sprague, Wentworth had relayed the info to Cheski. He'd flown up to check out a body discovered by firefighters as they were being ferried to a wildfire. Cheski had taken digital images of the body, flown back to Phantom, and matched the photos with Sprague's driver's license. Dora and Adam had viewed the images and confirmed the ID once we reached the station.

Hikers streamed by on the Phantom Ranch trail, heading toward the river. The campground and bridges had been reopened. Nico had moved our rafts up and across the river to a campsite reserved for craft rendezvousing with hikers. I wondered when he would get the word.

I shrugged and leaned my head against the wall. I couldn't reunite with my group until the rangers had gleaned all the information they could from me. Frustrating. But at least it wasn't a one-way street. I'd overheard updates about the major players. Half an hour ago a call had come in from one of the county investigators Cheski had met at Sprague's crime scene. A woman had discovered the body of her boyfriend in Fredonia. His name was Vernon Gruber. Ben Gruber's and Eldon Sprague's belongings and truck were at the scene.

Ben, it appeared, would be prosecuted in several jurisdictions. He hadn't said a word on the way back from the Box, or while he was waiting to be medevacked out, under heavy guard. But even if he remained silent, prosecutors had enough evidence to put him away for life.

Federal agents had been called in to head up the

bomb investigation. While the ATF and FBI agents were in transit, Cheski and a couple of Phantom Rangers went looking for the kayaks the anonymous caller said were beached by Silver Bridge. They'd found them—along with C-4, plans, and the IDs of three ecoterrorists named by the caller. With the bridges closed and the kayaks impounded, the rangers had little trouble rounding up the trio. One of them had confessed that the fourth kayak belonged to a lawyer named Chuck Rennie.

The rangers who carted Presley to the helicopter found Rennie's notebook in Jacob's pocket. Tomorrow morning, a crew would start combing the area around Buck Farm Canyon for Rennie's remains. In the meantime, Cheski planned to charge Presley with multiple counts of attempted murder.

Jacob Presley had still been unconscious when he arrived at the hospital in Flagstaff. He was in surgery to reduce swelling on his brain, the result of my well-placed kick. When he recovered, the decorated hero would be locked up in a hospital or prison for a long time.

Cheski had found two photographs in Rennie's notebook. One was a family portrait of Presley, in uniform, with his mother, sister, and brother. The other was the photo Philo had taken of my brothers and me at Jamie's wedding—the picture stolen from my home a week ago. Jacob had put Xs over my face and Matt's. Not Luke's. He'd mistaken one identical twin for the other. Or perhaps Presley hadn't cared which one he killed.

I'd expected Cheski and Wentworth to be anxious to get shut of my whole group. Because of us they had three men in the hospital, two bodies recovered, and three ecoterrorists in custody. But they also faced a mountain of paperwork and witnesses who would be disappearing down the river as soon as possible.

And there was the question of what to do with Molly. She was a minor, traveling under an assumed name, who'd been abducted by a double murderer—a man who was also her prospective husband and the leader of her family. She feared retribution if authorities sent her home. No one wanted to see her put into the foster-care system.

"This is going to be a legal and logistical nightmare," Cheski said to Wentworth. Interviews over, they were sitting at computers, typing reports. "Ms. Simpson harbored a fugitive child and lied about her name to the rafting company. We can't ignore that. If we go by the book, we should contact Child Protective Services to meet us at the rim."

"I won't send her back to a family that condoned her sister's rape and attempted murder," Wentworth said. "There's a pattern of violence there that goes back at least two generations."

"Do we have a choice?"

"Her half-brothers and -sister are here right now."

"But they're not her legal guardians. And the girl would have to cross state lines to reach their safe house."

Wentworth tapped a couple of buttons. A printer whirred in the corner. She stood and collected some pages from the printer. "My report states that a sixteen-year-old girl was abducted from a rafting party visiting Phantom Ranch and coerced to hike approximately three miles up the North Kaibab Trail."

Wentworth looked down and read the next part. "Ranger Elizabeth Wentworth recovered the girl from her alleged abductor, Benjamin Gruber, a resident of Coconino County, Arizona. An EMT examined the girl and confirmed that she sustained no physical injuries. She was released to the care of her relatives, who refused to press charges against Gruber. The girl's name is being withheld to protect her identity.

"Benjamin Gruber has been arrested and charged in the murders of Eldon Sprague and Vernon Gruber. Benjamin Gruber also stands accused of setting an arson fire on the North Rim. The abductee was not a witness to the murders or arson. Officer Wentworth ascertained that the girl was on the river with a commercial rafting party when the crimes were committed."

"A bit thin," Cheski said.

"Paper-thin."

"I'll take the heat if anyone complains."

Wentworth grinned. "Thanks, boss. I've requested that Molly call me once she reaches Austin to assure me she's okay. And Dora Simpson gave me a contact number for follow-up questions."

"Good." Cheski smiled. "Print me out a copy of your report."

"Already done." Bess Wentworth handed it to him.

"Good job, by the way."

"I second the motion," I said from my spot in the corner.

Wentworth turned sharply, as if she'd forgotten I was there. "Thanks," she said.

"Okay if I call my parents?" I said. "I'd like to get an update on Luke's status before I head down the river."

Wentworth nodded and pointed to the phone. She was packing notes and evidence into transport cartons, preparing to yield the cramped office to the federal investigators. She and Cheski would be flying out shortly.

I reached my mother on her cell. The surgery had gone smoothly. My parents were already on the road to Flagstaff. As soon as he could travel, probably tomorrow, they'd collect Luke and take him back to Tucson.

My mother asked for the story. I told her Luke would provide it. And Killeen. "I'll call when I pick up my truck on Saturday morning," I said, just before signing off. "And if you want to help Luke heal faster, ask him about Dora Simpson."

"Really?" Cheski said. "Luke and Dora?"

"Looks that way, but it's early days yet," I said. "Am I free to go?"

"Yes. Please call us when you get home. We may have more questions for you."

"Will do. And thanks for everything."

"I think we should be thanking you," Wentworth said.

"Well, if you could see your way to rigging the backcountry permit lottery—"

"Not a chance," Cheski said. But I swear I saw him wink at Wentworth.

I shook hands with them both, returned the icepacks, collected my daypack, and stepped out of the crowded ranger station into the breathlessly hot evening. It took a moment for my eyes to adjust to the light.

"Look who followed me home," Dora said from the porch rail. I could hear the delight in her voice. "Can I keep him?"

At the bottom of the stairs, sitting on a rock, was a tall, fit man in shorts, T-shirt, and dusty hiking boots. He stood.

"You made it!" I said, limping down the steps and throwing my arms around Philo's neck.

"Is this Paul?" Ranger Wentworth said from the doorway.

"Who's Paul?" said Philo.

"You didn't tell him?" I said to Dora.

"Only the Cliff Notes version," she said.

I twined my fingers with Philo's. "Ranger Bess Wentworth, this is my fiancé, Philo Dain."

She came down the stairs to shake his hand. "Please thank Killeen again for the help." When he nodded, she turned to Dora. "Molly's free to hike out with Paul."

Dora blushed.

"I take it they've already gone," Wentworth said.

"Thirty minutes ago."

"So Paul made it through?" I asked Dora.

Dora grinned. "Yup. And Nan Lomax offered to hike

out with them, rather than take the helicopter. Molly should be safe."

"Good plan," Wentworth said. "Cheski or I will meet them at the rim." To me she said, "We'll be in touch," before striding off toward the center of the complex.

"Who's Molly?" Philo said.

"We'll explain on the way," I said. "The other natives must be getting restless."

"How's Luke?" Dora said, falling into step with us.

"All stitched up," I said. "They're keeping him overnight and pumping him full of antibiotics. The cavalry's en route."

She laughed and hurried a few steps ahead to give us privacy. Philo and I started walking toward the river—or, in my case, hobbling. And Philo's limp, I noticed, seemed more pronounced. I said, "God, it's good to see you. How many hours did it take you to hike down?"

"Only three. Would have done it in two and a half, but I stopped for a snooze at Indian Gardens."

"Animal." I noted the dark smudges around his eyes. "Did you get any sleep in the last four days?"

"On the plane. It doesn't matter. We're both finally here, in the canyon."

"And alive."

He grinned the crooked grin I'd fallen in love with as a child. "Sure beats the alternative." He dropped my hand, put his arm around my waist. "Seems like a lot's happened in a few days."

"You don't know the half of it. And tonight I'll give you a primer on the wonders we'll see down the river."

"The Great Unconformity?"

"Yup. And Anasazi handprints at Deer Creek, if my knee is strong enough for the climb. It's a devil of a trail."

He yawned. "Tomorrow you can show me all of that. Tonight I'm going to sleep."

"At least part of the time." I pulled his head down so I could kiss him. "I may be injured, but I'm not dead."

Acknowledgments

My books come to fruition with the help of a small cadre of readers, editors, advisors, and general supporters. I'd like to thank, in particular, Elizabeth Gunn, J. M. "Mike" Hayes, Diana Kamilli, and Wynne Brown, my stalwart first (and in Mike's case, second) readers, and copyeditor Bob Land. Wynne also contributed the illustrations.

Early in the writing process, two writers, guides, and canyon experts, Scott Thybony and Wayne Ranney, offered suggestions on North Rim trails and discussed the geologic history of the Grand Canyon. Craig Little of Summit Hut in Tucson, and Jenny Moore of Manzanita Outdoor in Prescott, Arizona, discussed plot aspects from the river guide's and kayaker's perspectives. Kevin Horstman and Logan Matti provided detailed information about assault rifles. Greg Willitts advised me about dirt bikes. Paul Berkowitz, retired criminal investigator, Department of the Interior; Daniel Wirth, U.S. (Park Service) ranger / senior special agent (Retired); Brian Bloom, river district ranger, Grand Canyon National Park (NP); Johanna Lombard, writer/editor, Center for Creative Media, Grand Canyon NP; Jessica Pope and Erin Riley, National Park Service rangers, Grand Canyon NP; Peggy Kolar, Visitor and Resource Protection, Lee's Ferry, Grand Canyon NP / Glen Canyon NRA; and Helen Ranney, associate director of philanthropy, Grand Canyon Association, answered questions about park service procedures in Grand Canyon NP. I have tried to work within the actual framework of NPS law enforcement and search-and-rescue operations. Where I've deviated for the sake of the story—or indulged in poetic license—the blame is mine, not theirs.

The age assignment of the eras and systems/periods shown on my figure of the Grand Canyon geologic rock units came from *The Concise Geologic Time Scale* by J. G. Ogg, Gabi Ogg, and F. M. Gradstein (Cambridge University Press, 2008). In this book I follow the convention for western big-water rivers by using the 1–10 rating scale for rapids rather than the International Scale of River Difficulty (Class I–VI).

I'm grateful to an array of people for making my summer 2011 raft trip down the Colorado River through Grand and Marble Canyons the best research adventure ever. The cast of characters includes the crew of Hatch River Expeditions—Mark Franke, Rachel Hanson, and Parke Steffensen; geoscientists Alison Jones and Fred Beck, organizers of the trip; geologist Stan Beus; and my raft mates, especially Sean Murphy Stone, who took wonderful notes and photos on the journey. And to Jonathan, Jordan, and Logan Matti: *Muchas gracias* for holding down the fort in my absence.

I would like to thank Joanna Conrad, editor in chief and assistant director; Courtney Burkholder, director; Judith Keeling, editor in chief and assistant director (retired); and the Texas Tech University Press staff for supporting geoscience outreach through fiction. The need to demonstrate the joys of science and the scientific method is as relevant now as it was when we began this series more than a decade ago. Frankie MacFarlane couldn't have reached a broad audience without you. I'm profoundly grateful.

About the Author

Susan Cummins Miller, a former field geologist with the U.S. Geological Survey and college instructor, is a research affiliate and SIROW Scholar with the University of Arizona's Southwest Institute for Research on Women. She is editor of *A Sweet, Separate Intimacy: Women Writers of the American Frontier, 1800-1922* (TTUP). She lives in Tucson. *Chasm*, the sixth Frankie Macfarlane, geologist, mystery, follows *Death Assemblage, Detachment Fault, Quarry, Hoodoo,* and *Fracture.*